WHISPERS

WHISPERS

Pam Rhodes

Hodder & Stoughton

Words by Dan Hill and Barry Mann taken from the song 'Sometimes When We Touch'. By kind permission Sony/ATV Music Publishing

Copyright © 1999 Pam Rhodes

First Published in Great Britain in 1999
by Hodder and Stoughton
A division of Hodder Headline PLC

The right of Pam Rhodes to be identified as the Author of
the Work has been asserted by her in accordance with the Copyright,
Designs and Patents Act 1988.

10 9 8 7 6 5 4 3 2 1

A CIP catalogue record for this title is available
from the British Library

ISBN 0 340 71237 6

Typeset by
Phoenix Typesetting, Ilkley, West Yorkshire
Printed and bound in Great Britain by
Caledonian International Book Manufacturing Ltd, Glasgow.

Hodder and Stoughton
A division of Hodder Headline PLC
338 Euston Road
London NW1 3BH

For Kevin
because his story inspired mine

Chapter One

'Doctors' surgery, hold the line please!'

With deft efficiency, Joan cradled the receiver in one hand while running the tip of her pencil down the appointments list with the other. It was only twenty to nine, yet already the queue of patients stretched out of sight round the corner of the reception desk. Monday mornings, she thought, always the same!

She turned her attention once again to Mrs Donaghue, as she stood on the other side of the desk clutching her grey nylon shopping bag, her anxious face framed by neatly permed hair. The pensioner was staring down at the appointments sheet trying to make sense of it, even though it was upside down from where she stood. 'No, it's got to be Dr Gatward. He always sees me. He'd see me now, if he realised I was here. You ask him! I bake cakes for him. He'll fit me in, I know he will.'

'Sorry, but he's so busy today. Dr Norris could see you . . .'

'Too young. Still wet behind the ears!'

Joan stiffened, then pushed her glasses firmly on to her nose. 'Alistair Norris is a fully qualified doctor. I can give you an appointment for later this afternoon.'

'No.'

'Dr Bryant then? Half past ten tomorrow?'

'No.'

Joan sighed. 'Well, you can see Dr Gatward at quarter to eleven on Wednesday morning. Will that do?'

'I could be dead by then,' huffed the older woman. 'No, I'll just wait. When he knows I'm here, he'll see me this morning.'

'He can't,' was the patient reply. 'He's only in the surgery for an hour, then he's out on his rounds. Just look at the queue!'

But Mrs Donaghue was already heading for the only empty chair in the waiting room. 'You tell him Doris is here,' she called back over her shoulder, 'then we'll see!'

Further along the desk Moira caught Joan's exasperated expression, and grinned. Although the reception team was now six strong, they had been the two original members of front-office staff when the practice first expanded many years before. Since then, they'd gossiped their way through everything, their children, in-laws, husbands, their business – and whenever possible, other people's business too. In the overgrown village community of Berston, the doctors' surgery was the hub of local life. It was the job of the receptionists to be good listeners, to notice when people had problems. And whether those problems were medical or not, very little got past the eagle eyes and ears of Joan and Moira. Their interest was kindly, and generally welcomed by the patients. It gave the practice a family feel, as if every single one of them mattered. And in honesty, to Joan and Moira, they really did.

As Joan began to deal with the next patient in line, a mug of steaming tea was placed in front of her on the counter below the desk. She glanced over her shoulder to thank the youngest member of the reception team.

'That's OK,' acknowledged Christine, 'and I've given you one sugar. You may be watching your waistline, but we all reckon you get grumpy if you don't have your sugar fix.'

With a wry grin, Joan sighed. 'I'm never going to get into that outfit for my daughter's wedding. And her mother-in-law-to-be is like a bean pole. I'm going to look like a beached whale in the photos.'

'Have you got any notes for me?' Jill Dunbar strode through the door into the reception area.

'Coming up,' replied Christine. 'They're on my desk.'

Jill was a popular member of the surgery team, much sought after by the patients for her skill and compassion as the practice nurse, and appreciated by the staff for her quick wit and easy-going, yet totally professional approach to work. Considering they'd all celebrated her fiftieth birthday with a Blue Suede Shoes party a couple of years before, she was still a woman to turn heads, with her stylishly cut short dark hair, trim figure and smooth complexion that probably owed more to sunshine and fresh air than to expensive cosmetics.

'Is Simon in?' she asked, sifting through the pile of papers she'd been handed.

'Since eight o'clock. And he'll be here till eight o'clock tonight if he doesn't get a move on, and keep his appointments to time. He's twenty minutes behind already, and he's only seen three patients.'

Jill smiled to herself. Typical of Simon. He didn't watch the clock. That's why all the patients loved him, especially those who simply wanted someone to talk to. Simon was a good listener.

'Tell him I'd like a word before he goes out on his calls, will you?'

Christine nodded, and turned back to the computer screen.

In fact, along the corridor in Surgery Two, Simon wasn't listening at all. He couldn't listen. He couldn't hear himself think. Young Abigail Williams, two and a half years old and in pain from an ear infection, was screaming like a banshee. She wouldn't let the doctor look inside her ear. She wouldn't let him near her. And she wouldn't stop crying, not for her mother, not for a sweetie, and certainly not for the horrible man who was coming at her with something in his hand that looked as if it might hurt if he put it anywhere near her sore ear.

'She's tired, I think,' her exhausted mother tried to explain.

'She didn't get much sleep last night.'

'Neither did you, by the look of it,' shouted Simon in reply. 'Look, we're not getting far, are we? I don't like taking chances with children, and I'm pretty sure it's just a common-or-garden infection. I'll prescribe some antibiotics, and we'll see how she gets on. If you have any doubts, just give me a ring, and I'll pop in to see her later on home territory.'

'Oh, doctor, would you? Thanks so much.' Relief flooded across the young woman's face.

As he began writing out the prescription, he smiled hopefully at Abigail who replied by unleashing another earsplitting scream. He grimaced. 'See what a winning way I have with women!'

His next few patients were mostly women. There was Mrs Kennelly, who had arthritis and very limited movement in her shoulder. Then there was Miss Barber, who was imprecise about exactly what she'd come for until she reached the door handle on her way out, then burst into tears. She had been looking after her elderly mother with great devotion for years. Now the old lady was suffering from quite severe dementia which made her forgetful and difficult to please. Miss Barber was at the end of her tether, no longer able to cope on her own but torn apart by guilt that she should even think of her own dear mother going into a home. A quarter of an hour later, a quiet reassuring talk with Simon had set the wheels in motion to investigate what would be the best solution for both her mother and her own sanity.

And there was Ms Barbara Gordon ('*but please call me Babs*'), the forty-something divorcee who'd become the talk of the village as she re-established herself as a single woman after her husband ran off with the woman next door. As Simon examined the wrist she said was painful, her eyes never left his face.

'Good job it's not my right arm, or I wouldn't be able to play tennis. I love tennis,' she added softly.

Simon didn't reply.

'Do you play?'

'Not really,' he answered, still looking down as he gently manipulated her wrist.

'Only I wondered if you'd like to come along to the club one day? The exercise would do you good.'

He laughed. 'It probably would. And I expect I'd give all the other players a laugh too, because I'm well past my best for chasing round anything other than a golf ball.'

'I could teach you,' she replied, looking steadily into his eyes.

'Not my scene, I'm afraid. Well, I can't find much wrong with your wrist. You've probably got a slight sprain. Try wearing an elasticated bandage for a couple of days to give it a bit of extra support. That should do the trick.'

'Should I come back to see you if there's no improvement?'

'Of course – but stay off the tennis until it's completely recovered. Goodbye.'

Next came his old friend Bert Davies, who'd done Simon's garden for years. Bert's back problem was hardly helped by the hours of digging and bending he put in every week at dozens of homes around the village. He was way beyond retirement age of course, but he loved his job so much the doctor knew that whatever advice he was given to cut down his workload would be politely ignored.

'You're your own worst enemy, Bert. I can't help you, unless you help yourself.'

'Want to dig your own garden then, do you?'

'I couldn't do it. Not enough time, and definitely not enough energy. But at least I know my limitations. You're pushing yourself too hard. You need to slow down, hang up your wellies. Give that back of yours a chance to recover.'

'I'll slow down when you do.'

'I'm fifty. You're seventy.'

'You'll never slow down because you love your job. So do I.'

'I'd like to send you for another x-ray.'

'I can't be doing with all that. Just give me some more of

those tablets. They worked a treat.'

'OK, I'll stop employing you. I'll get someone else to do the digging, and you can just sort out the flowers.'

'And what about all the other gardens I do? Stop fussing, doc. Give me the prescription, and I'll be round on Thursday morning as usual. By the way, you need a new wheelbarrow – and more petrol for the lawnmower. And you were very short on teabags last week. I hope you've got a new supply in.'

Two hours later Simon finally reached the end of his list for that morning, and even found time to squeeze in Doris Donaghue, who presented Simon with a walnut cream cake, spent five minutes moaning about her husband's snoring, two minutes on her bunion, then left with a triumphant smile in Joan's direction.

Simon looked up from the computer screen at the quiet knock, as Jill popped her head around his door. 'If I make you a cup of coffee, can you spare a moment for us to catch up?'

He grinned gratefully. His friendship with Jill went back a long way, much earlier than twelve years ago when he'd joined the practice, to the days when they'd both been in London, he at the start of his GP training, she as a new staff nurse. They'd been part of a larger group of medical students and newly qualified doctors and nurses then, who'd worked, slept and drunk together in a fog of overwork and exhaustion. Jill had noticed Simon straight away with his sandy hair, warm blue eyes and tall well-built frame. The rapport between them was mutual and instant, except the romance Jill would have welcomed never quite happened. She'd always wondered why. The chemistry seemed to be there, for her at least. For him? Well, he teased and flirted in a way that made her feel special and attractive, but romance between them had never been more than wishful thinking.

She studied him now, as he finished his notes while the coffee cooled. He was still a striking man, the silver strands in his fair hair adding distinction and character to his long, pleasant face. His blue eyes mostly peered through glasses these days, but this was a man whose expression could be compassionate one moment and creased with good humour the next. The years had been kind to him. His frame was still tall and lean, much the same as she remembered him in the days when Saturday afternoons had been filled with bruising, boisterous rugby matches. Once, she had put her best nursing skill into action when his eyebrow was cut open by the studs of a rugby boot. The scar was still visible. Sometimes, she thought of reaching out to stroke it – but she never did.

The next ten minutes were spent discussing patients, paperwork and follow-up needed on cases that concerned them both. Then Simon leaned back in his chair and stretched, putting his hands behind his head.

'You look tired,' she said sternly. 'You're doing too much.'

'Oh, don't you start! I've already had Bert nagging me this morning.'

'You take it all too seriously, Simon. You don't have to jump every time a patient calls. You'll be laid up yourself, if you don't watch it.'

'You sound like a wife.'

'I am a wife – but not yours.'

'Hmm,' said Simon, the smile leaving his face. 'How is Michael? Still raking it in?'

She shrugged. 'You know what he's like. Fingers in lots of pies.'

'You'd think being a GP would be enough.'

'Not for him.'

There was a silence for a moment.

'Are you all set for tonight?'

He upended his cup to gulp down the last mouthful of coffee. 'I can't wait. What a barrel of laughs that should be – our respected leader, Gerald, talking about the Rotary Club all evening; his wife Patricia, our highly efficient practice manager, lecturing us on how we're spending too much; and your beloved husband lording it over the lot of us. Thank God you're going. At least you'll be good company!'

Jill chuckled. 'Oh, come on, it is Patricia's birthday. And Michael's not that bad. You don't know him.'

'He's awful. You're far too good for him.'

'You're probably right – but he proposed when you didn't.'

He grinned. 'Now, isn't that the story of my life? Let it slip through my fingers!'

She got up abruptly to head for the door, laughing as she called back over her shoulder, 'More fool you!'

Then closing the door behind her, she leaned against the frame for just a second as the familiar sense of loss swept over her. More fool her!

No one was at all surprised that Simon should be the last to arrive at the restaurant. The others had already chosen from the menu and were on their second aperitif when he hurried in to join them. He made straight for Patricia, sweeping her into a theatrical hug.

'Happy birthday! Apologies for my tardiness! That home birth – Mrs Westfield – went into labour two weeks early, and I promised I'd be there.'

'What about Wendy? Couldn't she cope? Midwives don't come much more experienced than her.'

'Absolutely right,' agreed Simon, pulling up a chair, and helping himself to an olive from a dish in the middle of the table. 'She could have managed fine. And to be fair, Mrs Westfield probably knows a good deal more about having babies than I do – this is, what, her fourth? But because she was planning a home birth, and I've seen her right through this pregnancy, I did say I'd be there – although I reckon the only useful thing I did this evening was to make a cup of tea when it was all over.'

'Simon, this was supposed to be your night off,' pointed out

Patricia. 'It is a special evening, my birthday. Just for once, it would have been nice if you'd been here on time.'

'Right again!' agreed Simon. 'I'm starving! What's on the specials board?'

Jill stretched over to fill his glass with chablis. 'Was it a boy or girl?'

He smiled at her. 'A boy. Simon. Made it all worthwhile really.'

Much later, Simon cast a subtle eye around the group as they leaned back in their chairs, replete, yet still finding room for paper-thin chocolate mints to help their coffee down.

'The thing is,' said Michael on the opposite side of the table, 'there's quite a lot at stake here. As a company, Roxborough has always worked to nurture good relations with its employees. There are very few places to rival the conditions offered to people who work there. But some of them are just out to milk the system. All that business in the papers recently about working too long at computer terminals? That brought them out in their droves. I've seen three RSI women this week complaining their wrists are aching because of constantly working with them in the same position, and two men talking about headaches caused by staring at their VDU's. And it's not just a cure they're after. It's the sniff of compensation.'

Typical of the man, thought Simon. Always pontificating about something or another. He'd been exactly the same in all the years he'd known him. In those early days, Michael's arrogance had come from the fact that he was two years older than Simon, and therefore two years further down the line in his GP training. It also stemmed from his well-do-do family and public-school upbringing, which led him to believe he had nothing to learn, as he was undoubtedly right about everything. He expected to make a good living as a doctor, and his ambition had brought him position and financial reward. His income as a part-time GP was boosted by a lucrative post as the Occupational Health Consultant at Roxborough's, the largest engineering firm in the area. He added to that healthy bonuses from private clinics for treatments as varied as life insurance medicals to second signatures on abortions. And, of course, his cherished position on the local medical committee, allowing him to oversee the work of all general medical practitioners in the area, gave him added status. Whereas Simon was a doctor because he loved people, Michael saw his medical training as a means to power and position. Simon was appalled at Michael's lack of genuine care for his patients. Michael was amused at Simon's lack of acumen when it came to making his profession pay.

Why Jill had ever married him, Simon could only wonder.

His gaze moved round the table to Gerald, senior partner at the King Street surgery. He liked Gerald. True, he could be a bit stuffy and stuck in his ways, but he was getting on a bit now. As the pace of life quickened, and pressures increased on everyone in the medical profession, Gerald chose to remain stoically unmoved by progress. If it weren't for Patricia as both his wife and practice manager, ten years his junior with her razor-sharp business mind, the partnership might have gone under years ago.

To look at them, they seemed an oddly matched couple. He was shorter than his wife, his thick greying hair and silver-rimmed glasses giving him a slightly boffin-like air. She, on the other hand, was an elegant, handsome woman, strong in both body and character. She ran the practice with painstaking efficiency, so that every patient, every hour, and every penny was accounted for. The only misshapen cog in the wheel was Dr Simon Gatward. The very qualities which made patients adore him and demand his time caused her endless irritation and inconvenience. He was always late, always missing, and always behind with paperwork. His surgeries overran, his list of house calls seemed never-ending, and cost didn't even enter his head as he referred this patient, or prescribed that drug. She recognised he was a good doctor. Infuriatingly, over-generously good.

Jill caught his eye and smiled in his direction. In the soft light of the restaurant, Simon thought how lovely she looked, but then Jill's beauty went far beyond the prettiness of her face, or her neat, eye-catching figure. She had a warmth about her which drew others in for comfort and confidences. It had been that warmth which had fascinated him from the start, and made her stand out from the noisy crowd of nurses of which she'd been part. He remembered how he'd sought her company to walk with him on leisurely meanders along the River Thames. He remembered the ease of their discussion, the daftness of their jokes, the simple pleasure they found in each other. They were intimate, but only in conversation. They hugged, but didn't kiss. They were a pair, never a couple. Friends, not lovers.

He watched her now as she chatted to Gerald, and wondered yet again why he'd never made the move to claim her when the chance was there. Too soon, Michael had come on the scene with his classy car and even classier accent. Too late, he realised the newcomer was out to win her at all costs. While Simon buried himself in work, expecting the romance to blow over, Michael wooed her with his ambitious plans and smooth good looks. She was flattered and overwhelmed until before Simon knew it, they were engaged, married, and living in Berkshire. He lost touch with them then. Years passed, successful for them, with a well-appointed house and two fine children to their credit. And the years passed for Simon too – that dark time, too painful to remember . . .

'Why didn't you go, Simon? Israel would have done you a power of good!' Michael directed the question at him across the table.

'I'm not into freebies. There's always a price to pay.'

'It's a perk, not a freebie. And it's a conference, not a holiday. We had demonstrations and lectures . . .'

'Which probably lasted a whole morning,' interrupted

Simon. 'It was a free week's holiday, provided by a pharmaceutical company, for doctors they hope will prescribe their product. Bribery. A freebie.'

'It's a good product.'

'It's over-hyped, over-priced and there are better, cheaper alternatives already on the market.'

Michael's expression was dangerously calm. 'It works.'

'Come off it, Michael, this drug is nothing new. It's just more of the same, with a glossy marketing package – and you don't believe that rubbish any more than I do! We both know any drug can only do half the job. In the end, a patient with depression needs time as much as they need prescriptions, and I believe that's where the real potential for healing lies – in doctors having time to listen, to counsel . . .'

'Oh Simon, wake up! Time is the one luxury doctors don't have these days! Ask Patricia! Ask anyone in medical practice!'

'If you ask me,' Jill's voice cut in, 'it's getting late. You've got an early start in the morning, Michael. It's been lovely. Thank you so much for inviting us.' She rose to kiss Patricia and Gerald warmly, and with an intense look and the barest wave in Simon's direction, she led the way as she and Michael left the restaurant.

'She insists on seeing you. You know what she's like.'

Simon had been cornered by Lynn Webster, the health visitor, the moment he came in from his house calls the following afternoon.

'That woman is a martyr to her joints,' he said, making his way through to the surgery with Lynn hot on his heels. 'And she expects me to be a martyr to them too!'

'It's Mr Brown who really worries me,' she replied, closing the surgery door behind her. 'She has him running round after her like a little dog, and his shaking looked worse than ever this morning.'

'Well, I've warned him. I've asked him to pop in to see me here, so we can do some proper tests.'

'And if he came here, he might actually be able to *talk* to you himself. Have you noticed how if you ask him something in the kitchen, she'll answer for him from the living room?'

'How come you went there this morning? I pop in every fortnight, so it must only have been last Monday, Tuesday perhaps, when I was there? Did she have a problem today?'

'She *is* a problem. She decided her knee needed dressing again. You know she took that tumble?'

'Oh, that was fine, just a graze really. I put a very important-looking bandage on it, and that seemed to do the trick!'

'So important, she wanted another just like it today. She's a terror, really she is!'

'And why does she want me to call in this time?'

'Because she's convinced her knee is infected. It isn't, of course, but she thinks she won't last the week unless she sees you, and nobody but you.'

Simon sighed. 'I'll ring her. That'll do until I make my regular call next week.'

'I wouldn't give in to her – but then, that's me,' retorted Lynn, glancing at her watch.

'How's David?'

'Busy. End-of-year accounts. He's been burning the midnight oil all week.'

'When he comes up for air, tell him I'm game for a round of golf.'

'Will do. Look, I must go. Jamie's in a swimming gala after school today, and I promised I'd be there.'

'Rachel going too?'

'Not likely! She's going through her "I hate my brother" stage at the moment. Just thank your lucky stars you haven't got kids. Nothing but trouble!'

And in the flurry of leaving the room, she didn't notice that, just for a second, the smile left Simon's face.

★

His surgery that evening was fairly typical for a Friday – mostly bouts of flu, and minor aches and pains, except for Bob Smith, whose wheezing chest almost drowned out the sound of the television the Patients' Participation Committee had thought-fully provided for the waiting room. The one bright spot of interest was a visit by Sean Williams, the hunky rugby player who was a bit of a local hero since he'd been selected for the England team. It always amused Simon to see the reception staff go into a twitter any time Sean was due to visit. Christine was even wearing a *dress*, and what a nice chance that made from her usual black trousers and serviceable jersey. As a young single mum, money was always tight, and her social life non-existent. Knowing how much she liked the look of Sean, Moira and Joan made sure she was on the desk to check him in. Being a man more of action than words, beyond giving his name, Sean said nothing – not that Christine noticed, judging from the starry-eyed look on her face.

'I look just like him in shorts.'

Christine spun round to see Alistair Norris standing at her elbow. The young doctor, with his mop of light brown hair, round face and boyish good looks, had only just joined the prac-tice where Simon was his special tutor for his third year of GP training.

She grinned back at him. 'Your legs could never be as shapely as his.'

'Oh yes they are – better, in fact! I haven't got a gammy knee!'

She gazed over to where Sean sat totally oblivious to the fact he was the subject of observation. 'I could kiss his knee better . . .'

'Well, I *do* have the odd twinge in my knee every now and then . . .'

'And I'd rub embrocation into all his important little places . . .'

'My places are *very* important – and they're not so little!'

Christine turned to face him, her face alight with laughter. 'Alistair, behave! And you're late for surgery. You've got two patients waiting already.'

Reluctantly, with a wink over his shoulder, Alistair headed off watched by Moira.

'He fancies you, you know,' she commented quietly.

Christine flushed, although her attention appeared to be completely focused on the appointments sheet. 'Of course not. He's just a typical bachelor, looking for someone to wash his socks.'

'You could do worse. He's a nice chap.'

'I'm off men,' Christine replied, looking cheekily out the corner of her eye at Moira, 'except for Sean, of course.'

When Simon finally came to the last patient on his list that evening, he didn't recognise the name. Keith Ryder. There were no notes on him, which was unusual. Obviously a new patient. His address suggested he was quite well-to-do. The houses in Byron Close were large and expensive. Probably an older man then. What was his date of birth?

The twenty-fourth of May, 1971.

The twenty-fourth of May . . . the words swam before his eyes, as he heard Mr Ryder's tentative knock upon the door.

Keith Ryder looked ill at ease as he perched on the edge of the chair beside the desk.

Simon looked up, his face composed. 'How can I help?'

'I need a prescription, some things I've got to have.'

'Uh-huh. Have you got a letter from your usual doctor?'

Keith began to fish in his jacket pocket. 'It's here some-where.'

'We've not met before, have we?'

'No.'

'You live here?'

'I do now.'

'And where were you before that?'

'West Hampstead.'

'London, eh? Been there long?'

'Eight years.'

Keith finally found the paper he'd been searching for, and handed it over.

'I like London,' continued Simon as he started to read. 'Spent quite a while there myself when I was training . . .' The words trailed off as he took in the contents of the letter. Keith stared at the floor for several agonisingly silent minutes.

At last, taking his glasses off and placing them carefully on the desk in front of him, Simon leaned back in his chair.

'We don't get many cases of AIDS here.'

Keith said nothing.

'How long have you been HIV positive?'

'Just over four years.'

'And you've been getting treatment at this centre?' asked Simon, glancing down at the letter heading.

'For most of that time, yes.'

'Do you have a partner?'

'He died five weeks ago.' Keith's face was expressionless, his eyes bleak.

'Was he in a hospice?'

'At Mildmay in the East End, but only for the last month or so. Before that, I nursed him.'

'You lived together?'

'For five years.'

'What's brought you here?'

'Mum and Dad. I've come home.' He made an attempt to laugh, a guttural, choking sound that became a rasping cough. Simon waited quietly while the young man recovered.

'How's that working out? At home, I mean.'

A shrug of the shoulders was the only answer.

'Do your parents understand what you're dealing with?'

'You mean, do they know I've come home to die? My mum does. My dad doesn't speak to me, so I don't care what he thinks.'

'We've got a counsellor here, attached to the practice. Do you think she could help?'

Keith aimed a steady gaze at the doctor. 'Counselling would be wasted on my dad and I can take care of my mum. I don't need to talk to anyone. I'm fully aware of what's happening to me. I nursed Ian. I know the score.'

'You might be familiar with the physical symptoms,' Simon said gently, 'but what about your emotions? You're a very young man, just twenty-eight. Too young to be . . .'

'. . . ready to face my own death?' He paused, as if choosing from many painful thoughts. 'I've done exactly that each day of my life for the past four and a half years. I watched the man I loved fade before my eyes. I cleared up his vomit, mopped his diarrhoea, and washed away his tears with tears of my own. I'm not only ready to face my own death. I *want* it. I long to die – because without Ian, I have nothing to live for.'

Blazing in his eyes was defensive defiance, and a depth of sorrow which made Simon's heart lurch with pity. Plainly, this young man's wounds needed a great deal more than just physical tending.

'Keith, I can't tell you much you don't already know. What I can do is make sure that you get the treatment you need. There's a genito-urinary unit in Southampton which specialises in HIV care. There's so much that can be done now, with antibiotics and the triple therapy anti-retroviral drugs. I can organise for you to . . .'

'No. I'm not looking for a cure, and I have no wish to prolong my life. I'll just come to you for whatever I need to make it bearable. Apart from that, I don't want anything.'

Simon eyed him for a few seconds before speaking again. 'Well, we'll see how things go, but for the time being I'm happy to handle your treatment. I'll check you over today, to see how things stand. And let's do a blood test to find out how your T4 helper cell blood count is doing.'

Keith's expression didn't alter, but his shoulders visibly relaxed. 'OK,' he said, unbuttoning his shirt, 'let's get on with it.'

That Friday afternoon, Lynn got back from her house calls early enough to grab a few minutes over a cup of tea with Jill. In spite of the age difference, the two nurses had always got on well, especially as, years before, Jill had been a health visitor herself. It had suited her to adapt her job not only to the timetable of her children over the years, but to the demands of Michael's career and ambition. Since their marriage, they'd never been in a house for more than four years at a time. The move to this area three years before had been a very happy one for Jill. It was a lovely part of the country and a flourishing practice. And Simon was here.

It had been such a coincidence to bump into him again after so many years, on the day she'd come to be interviewed for the job. He'd enveloped her in a huge hug, surprised and delighted to see her. After that, her appointment had been a matter of formality, especially when Gerald and Patricia recognised her varied experience and first-class qualifications. Since then, her time at work had been nothing but pleasure. She'd enjoyed every moment of establishing her own clinics – asthma, diabetes, travel, immunisation, anti-smoking. And the company was good. After all, Simon was here.

Lynn kicked off her shoes as she slumped on to a chair, a steaming mug of tea in her hand. 'Aah, I've just got to sit down for five minutes. My feet are killing me.'

'Busy day?'

'I don't know what it is about May, but it's always such a bumper month for babies! I blame the summer holidays. Do you know, I've called on eight mums today?'

Jill grinned. 'Make you feel broody?'

'Not likely! It's enough to put you off for life! No, I've got the two best kids in the world, and that's fine for me. I must admit I enjoy them much more now they're a bit older.'

Jill dropped in a sweetener, and stirred her tea with a smile. 'I loved it when the children were small, but it's frightening how long ago that was. Jenny's twenty-five next month, with a daughter of her own. And Jonathan's getting married in about a year. I don't know where the time's gone.'

'Has he qualified yet?'

'Next summer, just before the wedding. Debbie's a lovely girl, and they both plan to stay on at the hospital when they're married. She loves the ward she works on – you know she's in paediatrics? And Jonathan gets on well with the consultant orthopaedic surgeon there, so he'd like to stay with the same team, if they'll have him.'

'Isn't he the spitting image of Michael? I thought it was uncanny when I last saw him.'

'In looks, yes. In personality, no. He's much more casual about everything, not as single-minded as his father. It's always irritated Michael beyond belief that Jonathan is so laid back about studying.'

'But he does well in exams, doesn't he?'

'Always.'

'So Michael must be proud of him?'

'You'd think so, wouldn't you,' agreed Jill with a sigh, 'but Michael's such a competitive animal. Even his own son is not allowed to match him, let alone beat him at his own game.'

'Does Jonathan mind?'

'He always talks about it as if it's a joke – but yes, deep down, I think he minds a lot.'

'Shame, in a way, that's he's chosen the same profession as his dad. It might have been better if he'd had a completely different career.'

'Perhaps. Maybe then Michael could behave like any other father, and be proud of him.'

★

'Everything all right, Alistair?'

Startled, the young doctor slammed shut the reception address book and turned to face Gerald with the most casual expression he could muster.

'Fine. Yes. Just on my way home really.'

'How it's working out with Mrs Briggs? Are you comfortable there?'

Alistair thought of her austere front room, with the family photographs in a neat row on the mantelpiece. He pictured his bedroom, with its salmon-coloured candlewick bedspread and Victorian street scene picture above the fireplace. He shivered at the thought of the bathroom, where the water was always cold and the window rattled.

'Fine,' he lied, thinking that the sooner he could escape and find his own place, the better.

'She's a marvellous woman, Doris Briggs. A great friend of my family for years. Does wonderful work with the WRVS, I understand.'

'So she tells me.' Endlessly . . .

Gerald leaned against the desk, apparently in the mood for a chat.

'And her house is such a convenient place for you to be based while you're doing your GP training year here. Home from home, really.'

'Umm,' agreed Alistair.

'And things are working out with Simon as your tutor? He's putting you right on everything you need to know?'

'He's terrific, thanks. Most helpful.'

'Good, I'm glad to hear it. And your father? How is he?'

'Fine, thank you. Always busy – you know what he's like.'

'And your mother?'

'Not so well, at the moment. A bout of shingles has laid her low for several weeks.'

'How very unfortunate – and painful. How's she managing?'

'My sister is just round the corner, and pops in every day. She's a nurse too, of course.'

'Quite a family, yours! Well, do give your father my regards. I can't recall how long James and I have known each other. The years have certainly flown by.'

'He often speaks of his days at medical college with great affection.'

'And your mother, of course. Please remember me to her.' Gerald's expression softened. 'She was a real beauty, you know. Thought about marrying her myself at one time!'

The smile on Alistair's lips was less than convincing. He glanced across at the clock on the wall behind Gerald, then bent down to pick up his bag.

'Well, must go.'

'Out tonight?'

'Hope so.'

Gerald smiled indulgently. 'Well, enjoy yourself. I'll lock up, if you care to make your way out first.'

Pulling on his leather jacket, Alistair headed for the back door.

And as he sped off in his elderly Escort, a cheery wave thrown over his shoulder in Gerald's direction, he wondered exactly how he would fill his evening. A pint down at the pub perhaps? He could join the other three people who were regulars there for a heart-stopping game of dominoes.

He sighed as he thought how different tonight *might* have been, if Gerald hadn't come in just as he was looking up Christine's home number in the address book. He might even have plucked up enough courage to ring her – and who knows what might have happened then?

Chapter Two

Brian Turner popped his head round the door and looked hopefully at Julie.

'On the phone, I'm afraid. Busy morning. Can you wait?'

'Yeah, I will, but I need to get out to Acorn Grove by eleven. The Building Inspector's coming.'

'Hang on then. I'll try and attract his attention, let him know you're here.'

As she opened his door Derek Ryder was sitting back in his seat, legs stretched out in front of him. His voice was booming as he spoke down the phone. It wasn't that he was shouting, although his shouting was something everyone in the place was well used to. It was just that, even in normal conversation, Derek's voice could fill a couple of rooms and the hallway too.

'Look, I'm not letting a *tree* get in the way of my deadline. The weather has held us up enough already, and *nothing* is going to stop us finishing on time now!'

The person at the other end was allowed a few seconds say before he interrupted again.

'Then nudge it! It looks pretty unsafe to me, a dangerous hazard for my men . . .'

Another short interval of listening, then he began again, the volume louder than ever.

'I take a pride, Frank, in bringing my jobs in on time. This is the first contract I've done for Arcadian Homes, and I don't intend it to be my last! And I refuse, *refuse*, to pay penalty payments when they can be avoided. Just clear that tree and get the equipment in, you hear me!'

Julie smiled as she pictured the expression on the face of their building site foreman, Frank Bateman, as he took this call. Frank and Derek were old mates. They spoke the same language. They fought each other like cat and dog, but stood shoulder to shoulder whenever the chips were down.

As Derek slammed home the receiver, Julie walked in. She'd been his secretary for more years than either of them cared to remember. When his short fuse and impatience got the better of him, she smoothed the ruffled feathers around him. And having danced at her wedding a few years back, he was the staunchest of comforters when her husband ran off with a lady bank manager. Derek even offered to run her ex down with one of his road rollers. In spite of her broken heart, Julie had laughed out loud at his suggestion – and she'd adored her boss ever since.

'Here's your tea. Godwins rang again. Why didn't you call them when I told you to yesterday? And that Mr Smith from Smith Brown Electrics wants you to ring back. Oh, and Brian's here, in a hurry.'

'Good, I want to see him.'

Brian was already at the door, and without a word of greeting strode in to pull up a chair on the other side of the desk. He shook his head when Derek offered him a cigarette, something he insisted on doing even though he knew Brian had given up smoking more than a year before. Derek lit his own, took a slurp of tea, and sat back in his chair again before he spoke.

'This tree at Acorn Grove. Is it going to be a problem if our JCB accidentally knocks it over?'

'It's got a preservation order on it.'

'Could we say it looked dangerous?'

'We could. It wouldn't be true though.'

'Can we work round it?'

'Difficult. It leaves that entrance too narrow now we've started on the house up at the end.'

'It's got to go then. I'll have a word with that tree preservation bloke over at the council, buy him a drink or two. That should smooth it.'

'Well, while you're on, ask him if he knows anything about the new school on Farthing Corner.'

Derek's eyebrows shot up.

'Are they making moves on that at last?'

'Heard a whisper this morning. They've got in Robbins as the architects, and they expect to be putting the plans out to tender within two months.'

'I want that contract. We need it.'

Brian nodded in agreement. 'Worth a lot of money.'

'Are we in with a chance?'

'Don't see why not. Baskins will make a bid, of course – and Wilkinsons, but I don't think they're in good enough shape to cope with such a big job now, with Joe Wilkinson having that heart attack.'

'Then we're going all out for this. Who do I need to talk to? Who's in charge at the council?'

'Well, that's the good news. I've heard it's Ken Baker who's contract manager, working to Gareth Walters.'

Derek relaxed into his seat with a smile. 'As good as ours then. Gareth may be chairman of the Building Committee, but he does owe me a favour for sorting out that business for him last year.'

'And Martin Balcombe is the architect.'

'Perfect! Haven't seen Martin in a while. Time we had a drink, I reckon.'

Brian got to his feet. 'Must go. The Building Inspector is due at Acorn in half an hour.'

'Well, drop into the conversation that you think that oak tree is unstable.'

'Will do.' Brian turned with one hand on the handle, a grin on his face.

'Hey, they won't be able to use the name Acorn Grove if the oak tree goes. They might have to rename it Ryder Road!'

That would be nice, thought Derek, as he picked up the phone to ring home.

Keith was asleep. Annie sat opposite him as he lay stretched out on the sofa, and watched him, with his shallow breathing and dark circles under his eyes. Sleep brought relaxation, making the deep creases which scored his thin face seem lighter, less intrusive. He lay curled up as he'd done as a small boy, his hands clasped between his knees. She glanced up at the framed picture on the shelf above his head. He'd looked so proud and grown-up that day, in his new uniform that had been bought to last the whole year. His lop-sided grin revealed the gap where his two bottom teeth should have been, and his brown leather satchel almost touched the floor, even though it was strapped as tightly as possible over one small shoulder. His first day at school – it seemed like yesterday. She'd never forgotten his excited face as she met him at the gate that afternoon. His knee-high socks were around his ankles, his smart black shoes scuffed, and his jersey inside out when she arrived to take him home.

She'd driven to London to bring him home too. Brought him home to die.

She stretched out her hand to stroke his hair, but then drew back in case she woke him. She loved his hair. When he was a toddler, it had been almost white. Even as a teenager, his straight blond hair had been the talk of the local girls. She'd wondered if one of them would catch his eye. And when none of the village girls had been picked out from the crowd, she waited for him to bring someone home from university. At last he did, his roommate John. They were lads together, drinking, driving too fast, laughing loudly, arms around each others' shoulders. And

when she'd found them that morning, heads touching, flaked
out on Keith's bed, she'd smiled to herself. Boys, she thought.
Nice to see they were such good friends.

John left the scene when Keith left university. Within weeks,
he'd met Ian. Ian loved Keith's blond hair too. It was as she
watched him reach out to touch it that she saw the expression
on her son's face. And at that moment, she knew the village girls
had never had a chance.

She jumped as the phone rang. Quickly, she leaned over to
pick it up, frightened it would wake him. It was her husband.

'I might be late tonight,' boomed Derek. 'Something's come
up. Someone I need to take out for a drink. Could be a big job
in the offing.'

'Shall I keep dinner for you?'

'Put mine in the oven.'

'Right. Keith needs to eat quite early, because of his medication.'

There was the briefest of pauses from Derek. And then, as if
she'd not spoken, he grunted goodbye and replaced the receiver.

Simon got the pasta out of the microwave and filled his glass
with what was left of the bottle of chablis. Grabbing the bowl
of salad, he hit the button on the television as he passed by and
sank down in his favourite armchair, balancing the plate of
pasta on his lap. He was a good cook. Over the years, cooking
had been a favourite and sociable pastime. This pasta might have
been left over from the night before, but it was still pretty good,
even if he did say so himself.

Good. He hadn't missed the News. As he rarely had time to
read a paper these days, watching the News was a small pleasure.
Mr Jackson's heart attack that evening had almost made him miss
it. Poor Fred Jackson. Things didn't look good. Simon wondered
if he'd make the night. He'd ring the hospital in the morning.

A quarter of an hour later, replete with pasta and mellow

with wine, Simon's eyelids began to droop as he tried to focus on the screen. Bed, he thought. That would be nice.

Shoving the dirty plates into the sink, he switched off the lights, and made his way upstairs. Within minutes, he was in bed and almost asleep when the phone rang. He groped out in the darkness to pick up the receiver.

'Doc?'

He recognised Bert's voice straight away.

'Need your help. I'm sort of stuck . . .'

'Stuck? Where?'

'In my chair. My back's seized up.'

'Have you got any of those relaxant tablets handy?'

'In my coat pocket.'

'Where's your coat?'

'In the shed.'

'That's a good place for it.'

'Do us a favour, doc. Come and sort me out.'

'Bert . . .'

'Oh, come on! I did all that weeding for you yesterday.'

'That's blackmail.'

'Really?'

'I'm in bed.'

'And bed's where I'd like to be. Doctor's orders. You said I should get lots of rest!'

'Bert Davies, you're fired as my gardener. Your back is a burden to us both.'

'You'll come over then?'

Simon groaned, burying his face in his pillow. 'OK. Give me ten minutes. Is the key still under the pot?'

'Same as usual. You pop over now – and I'll put some extra dahlias in for you next week.'

Traffic was slower than ever the following morning as Gerald and Patricia made their way into the surgery. Their converted farmhouse was little more than four miles away, but the construction of the new by-pass had been causing chaos for months, much to Gerald's annoyance. Most irritating of all was the fact that the new road would be of most use to the new estates which were mushrooming up around them, practically absorbing Berston into the outskirts of Southampton. Gerald tutted at the sound of the Radio 4 pips.

'That rep is going to be there before I am, the rate we're going!'

'Doubt it,' answered Patricia,' he's probably stuck in the same traffic jam as we are. Anyway, Simon can deal with him. That's why we have a group practice, so we can share the load.'

'Simon's always so rude to reps, have you noticed?'

Patricia laughed. 'Well, that's not necessarily a bad thing. He doesn't let them get away with sales jargon, our Simon! That certainly sorts out the ones who don't know what they're talking about.'

'He's a good man, no doubt about that, but he sets impossibly high standards for everyone around him.'

'Well, no one could possibly question your standards.'

He turned to smile at her. 'I should hope not! But you know what I mean. That business with Michael the other night – so unnecessary! What is it between those two? They always seem to be taking a dig at each other.'

'Chalk and cheese, I suppose. Both GPs, but they couldn't be more different in their approach.'

'And I can see right in both points of view. I often feel like a referee between the two of them, each trying to score points off the other, both as stubborn as mules.'

'It must be hard on Jill too, knowing how closely she works with Simon. His constant carping about her husband must get her down.'

Patricia chuckled. 'Oh, she's got the measure of them. She's brought up a couple of kids. She can certainly handle two daft men.'

Gerald fell silent for a while, listening to the news as the traffic ground once again to a halt.

'Odd really, isn't it? That Simon's never married?'

'Hmm. He's quite attractive, I suppose, in his own way – and the women all seem to adore him, if his patient list is anything to go by.'

'I asked him about it once, you know, when we were out playing golf.'

'And? What did he say?'

'Nothing really. He neatly sidestepped the question, and I was none the wiser.'

'What I reckon our Simon needs,' said Patricia, pulling down the visor so that she could check her hair in the mirror, 'is the love of a good woman.'

'Better still,' agreed Gerald, turning the car in the direction of the surgery, 'a very bad one!'

Dr Alistair Norris knew when he started work at this practice that he'd finally arrived where he belonged. He looked back on his years of studying and working at the large London teaching hospital where his father was the leading consultant surgeon, and realised that what he'd learned there was technical expertise. He was clinically proficient. He could make accurate diagnoses, and prescribe the most relevant treatment with precision and con-fidence. He could work his way through a line of patients in Accident and Emergency, or in the Ante-Natal Clinic, as efficiently as the best of them. In theory he excelled – but in practice what he lacked and missed was a real relationship with his patients. He had chosen to become a doctor because it was a caring profession, and he was a caring man. And he recognised that the relationship with patients he really longed for, he was unlikely to find in a huge hospital. He wanted to become a GP.

His father had been openly delighted when his youngest son had announced his intention to follow him into the medical profession. He had immediately taken Alistair out for a man-to-man talk about the many lucrative and challenging opportunities open to bright young doctors nowadays, especially if they had the right connections. Alistair had listened dutifully, and studied hard. Throughout his training years, his father had encouraged and cajoled and name-dropped. And when, at the end of his hospital studies, Alistair had announced his intention to train as a GP in an out-of-the-way South of England practice in somewhere that was little more than a village, his father bit his tongue and hoped that in time his son would mature enough to see sense.

That morning, Alistair was smiling reassuringly across his desk at Lily Gordon. This was the third time in as many weeks the elderly widow had come to see him. There she sat, small, frail and angelic – and he *knew* she was lying to him.

'Now, tell me again, Lily, how did you get all these cuts and scratches on your hands?'

'The knife slipped when I was peeling the carrots.'

'Uh-huh. And last week?'

'Pruning the roses. You should see the thorns on my climber!'

'Well, can't your son do difficult jobs like that for you?'

'Oh, Bernie's very good. He does all the gardening.'

'All the gardening – but not the pruning.'

'No, not that.'

'Well, what does he think about the way you keep injuring yourself?'

'He doesn't know.'

'He must do. Every week, I send you home with your hands in bandages. What does he say when he sees you?'

'I can't do the washing up with bandages on. I've taken them off before he comes home.'

'So, why do you bother to get me to dress them for you?'

'I just want you to clean them up for me. Your antiseptic is stronger than mine. They get better quicker.'

Alistair sighed. He was getting nowhere.

'Look, Lily, I can't help you much if you're not completely honest with me. I have to say these cuts don't look to me like the slip of a vegetable knife, or rose thorns. Perhaps if you tell me what's really going on I can help to prevent it happening again.'

Lily remained stubbornly silent.

'Is everything OK at home?'

'Fine.'

'No problems?'

The defiance in her expression didn't quite reach her eyes. 'None at all, thank you.'

'And do you think you've come to the end of these jobs around the house that are damaging you? Or am I likely to see you again next week?'

'Can't say,' she replied, getting up from her seat. 'Thank you, doctor.'

It was some hours before Alistair caught up with Simon to discuss the puzzling case of Lily's mysterious wounds with him. Since his arrival a few weeks before, Alistair had quickly come to realise just how fortunate he was to have Dr Simon Gatward designated to him during this year of GP training. As he watched Simon's patience, friendship, compassion and endless good humour with the fascinating cross section of humanity that arrived in his surgery, Alistair recognised in him the role model for the doctor he hoped to become. From Simon he would learn more than just putting the theory into practice. In him, he saw what a doctor should be.

Simon leaned against the filing cabinet as he listened to Alistair's concerns about Lily.

'What sort of wounds are these? Are they deep?'

'No. Mostly ragged, as if her skin's been ripped.'

'Any bruising?'

'Plenty of small bruises covering her hands and arms right up to the elbow.'

'Self-inflicted, do you think?'

'Probably not. But what – or who – could be causing this?'

Simon thought for a while. 'I've met her son a couple of times. He's been into the surgery once in a while when he's injured himself. He's a leading light in the local boxing circuit.'

Alistair's eyes widened. 'You don't think . . . ?'

'. . . that he's using his mum as a punch bag? I doubt it. He can be a bit unpredictable, especially when he's had a skinful – and he's probably not the brightest of men, but I really don't think he's into granny bashing.'

'I should hope not.'

'But,' added Simon thoughtfully, 'you never can tell, can you?'

'But you haven't had any breakfast!'

'I'm not hungry.'

'And what about your medication? Have you taken your pills this morning?'

'Yes.' Keith brushed past Annie on his way to the hall cupboard to fish out his jacket.

'You'll need a bigger coat than that. It's pouring outside.'

'Mum, I'll be all right. I've just got to get out for a while.'

'Keith, you know what that doctor at the London clinic said. Your resistance to infection is low. You catch a simple little bug, and you could be laid up for weeks!'

He turned to lay his hands on her arms. 'Look, I know the score. This is all new to you, but I've been living with it for years. Stop worrying.'

At that moment his father came down the stairs, putting his mobile phone into his coat pocket.

'Derek, talk to him please. You make him see sense.'

'I'm in Southampton at a meeting all day today,' he said, as if she hadn't spoken. 'And if I don't get back early enough, I'll go straight on to the club as usual tonight.'

'Look, can't you at least give him a lift? He really shouldn't be out in weather like this. He'll get soaked!'

He turned to give her a peck on the cheek and was almost out the front door as she shouted after him, 'Derek, you've got to deal with this! You can't go on acting as if your own son doesn't exist!'

'Why not?' asked Keith, his face without expression. 'He's right. The sooner I'm gone for good, the better.'

As a rule, Simon had Wednesday afternoon off. Occasionally urgent calls would get in the way, but on the whole it was his cherished oasis in a busy week. Not even the drizzle that morning could put him off. He was going fishing. He had his rod in the car, a fresh supply of maggots, three days' worth of newspapers to catch up on, a bottle of wine, a French loaf, a chunk of Brie, and a ready-made salad from the local super-market. And no phone! Heaven!

He nearly always chose the same spot, on a corner of the river about a mile and a half out of Berston. It wasn't a particu-larly good place to catch fish, but it was excellent for avoiding other fishermen – and the solitude was what he enjoyed most.

He parked the car, then trudged along the path to a sheltered stretch of the river bank. Sometimes he caught trout here, his favourite fish with its delicate rainbow colouring. He always put them back in, of course. It didn't occur to him to cook what he caught. It was simply the challenge and the chase, and the eyeball to eyeball contact with this elegant creature who was captured, but never completely conquered. Carefully, he set up his rod, arranged it in the rest, and lay back on the grass, savouring the cool warmth of May sunshine on his face. Above his head he could hear the lazy buzzing of early bees as they discovered the snow-white blossom of the hawthorn.

He was thinking about Bert, and the phone call he'd made just before leaving the surgery to Solar Landscapes whose cheerful advert he'd noticed in the local paper over many weeks. Yes, they'd be delighted to cut his lawn and dig over the beds. And of course a regular maintenance arrangement could be happily accommodated. Of course, it wasn't usual for a client to arrange for his own gardener to do the planting, especially when they had expert horticulturists on their team, and an all-inclusive deal was by far the most economic – but anything could be arranged.

He knew in his heart that less digging was the only solution to Bert's back problem, but persuading Bert to accept the solution would be a problem in itself.

His mind wandered as he became dimly aware of the sounds around him: a distant tractor, squabbling birds, someone hammering far away, those buzzing bees . . . Perhaps he dropped off. Perhaps his thoughts merely became muddled with memories of other trees on another late spring afternoon. A child giggling, calling. The ring of a phone. Hawthorn blossom. Blond hair. Bumble bees. The twenty-fourth of May. A rope ladder. The enormous, bulging eyes of a trout, eerie and dead . . .

He woke to the sound of his own cry, his breath coming in uneven gasps, his skin clammy and cold. Sitting up suddenly, he clasped his arms around his knees, hoping to calm his thumping heart and shaking limbs.

'Are you all right?'

His head shot up guiltily, aghast that anyone should see him so disoriented and vulnerable. Keith Ryder was crouching down just yards from him.

Simon recovered quickly enough to answer, 'Fine. I'm just fine.'

Keith said nothing, but to Simon's dismay he looked out towards the river and began to seat himself comfortably, laying a sketchpad down on the grass beside him.

'I have bad dreams too. Nightmares really. Sometimes, I'm too scared to close my eyes because I know it will come again.'

'It? Always the same dream?'

'Variations on a theme, but yes, mostly.'

'What triggers it off, do you know?'

'Grief, I suppose. Fear.'

'Is it any better now you're at home again?'

'I'm not at home here. I don't belong.'

'So, will you go back to London?'

'I don't belong there either.'

'What were you doing there? Working?'

'At a big publishing house in the West End, in the graphic design department. I really loved it.'

'And your partner?'

'Ian was my boss. I met him on the first day I arrived there, straight out of university, with my hopes high and knees knocking.'

'He was older than you then.'

'By ten years. That never mattered though.'

'Did you get involved straight away?'

Keith gazed at the river, a soft smile lighting up his face. 'Pretty much. I'd been at university in London, so shared a house with a few mates south of the river for the previous couple of years. But they'd all headed off to new jobs and I was left out on a limb, trying to decide where to live next. When I first met Ian I'd actually taken a room at the YMCA, because it was cheap and central and gave me time to sort out something better.'

'And Ian was something better?'

Keith grinned. 'He sure was. We hit it off from the very start. He was really great at helping me to settle in at work – and then, he suggested going out for a drink halfway through the first week. We sat in a bar just off Argyll Street, and talked and talked until they finally threw us out in the early hours. He was so interesting, so talented, like no one I'd ever come across before.' His eyes closed at the sweet memory. 'And I never slept at the YMCA again.'

'Was he your first partner?'

'No. There'd been someone special at college, John. We

were roommates for a year or so before we both felt we needed to branch out, play the field. I did the rounds a bit then.'

'How much did your parents know about all this?'

Keith started picking absently at the blades of grass in front of him. 'My mum knew. We never really spoke much about it, but when she saw me with Ian she knew I was happy, and that was fine for her. We used to meet up in London quite often, when she was in town selling her sculptures. She's really good at it. Makes a bit of money too.'

'And your father?'

A handful of grass was ripped out by its roots. 'My dad's a man's man, you know what I mean? I'm his son and heir, his pride and joy. At least, I was – until he found out I was gay.'

'Was it your mum who told him?'

'Unfortunately not. He turned up without warning one afternoon when Ian and I hadn't been together very long. He knew I shared a flat with a guy and all that, but he hadn't put two and two together. Ian and I were having a bath – you know, really relaxing with music, lots of bath oil, scented candles . . .'

'And your dad arrived in the middle of that?'

'Well, it was fairly obvious we were both dripping wet. It didn't take a genius to work out that we'd been in the bath together.'

'How did he react?'

Keith gave a small, hollow laugh. 'Actually, he didn't say a lot, which is quite unlike him. My dad's usually got an opinion on everything, but the blood just drained from his face. I thought he was going to faint. He glared at me, and then said, 'You've got ten minutes to detach yourself from your faggot friend, make yourself decent, and meet me in the pub across the road.'

Simon noticed the young man's hands were trembling as he went on.

'I don't think I've ever been so scared in my life. There I was – a grown man, with a degree, a great job, a partner, a future, a *life* – and I felt like a little boy caught red-handed stealing gobstoppers. Ian wanted to come down with me, of course. He was furious that anyone should treat me like that. He said I shouldn't stand for it . . .'

'. . . but?'

Keith turned to look at Simon. 'But he's my dad – my hero, really, for so many years. I knew I was his whole world, and the revelation about my sexuality would be a bombshell for him.'

Simon was silent, waiting for the young man to continue.

'He wasn't in the pub when I eventually found him. He was in his car, just sitting there staring at nothing. I got in beside him, and neither of us said anything for a while. Then he started. He said I'd been led astray, that Ian should be horsewhipped for corrupting a young innocent like me. He said I was just to pack my bags and come home, that he'd sort out a job for me locally through his club friends, and that I could put the whole episode behind me and start again. Well, I just blew up! He was treating me as if I were one of the minions at his building business who jump when he snaps out orders to them. I told him my living arrangements and choice of partner were my business, that I was more than capable of making my own decisions without his interference. And from there on, it got worse and worse. It ended up with him yelling that as long as I continued with "this gay nonsense", I was no son of his. Good, I thought. That suits me fine!'

Two hot splashes of anger coloured Keith's cheekbones as he spoke. 'And then, just as I was about to storm out of the car, his mood completely changed as he remembered why he'd made such an unexpected visit to the flat in the first place. My nan had died – his mother. He adored her. He must have been wrecked by that news, and he'd driven all the way to London to tell me himself, because he didn't want to upset me by telling me on the phone.'

Simon watched in helpless fascination as Keith buried his face in his hands. 'He cared that much. He'd been trying to protect me. But that's the problem. He's always trying to protect me, always wanting me to live my life his way. But from that moment on, we both knew the gulf between us was too wide.'

'I went home for Nan's funeral, of course, but Dad didn't speak to me. Mum pleaded with him, tried to act as go-between as far as she could, but he and I simply had nothing to talk about. I can't be the sporty, red-blooded son he wants me to be. I never was. And he can't be the supportive, open-minded father I need. Stalemate.'

'And now you have AIDS?'

'He's petrified, for himself, not me. He's terrified about living with me, that I'm using the towels, drinking from the cups, sitting on the toilet seat. But he's a big man, and real men don't admit they're scared. They just bark and shout and avoid discussion, anything to hide their fear.'

'But surely he's glad you're home? That's what he wanted.'

'Not any more. As far as he's concerned, I didn't jump to his order five years ago – and because of that, I became HIV positive. My own fault. Self-inflicted. He was right all along. I'm stupid and pitiful and whining for sympathy I don't deserve.'

'And yet from the little I know of you, sympathy seems to be the last thing you want.'

'Especially from him. He believes I have no one to blame but myself – and he's right! I'm not looking for anything, especially not from him.'

'How did you become infected? Through Ian?'

Keith nodded. 'He didn't know when I met him. He'd never have allowed me to get involved with him if he had. He'd been around a bit, had lots of partners. It could have been anyone. He may have been positive for a while.'

'How did you find out?'

'He must have suspected. Apparently he'd been feeling tired all the time and getting those white blotches on his gums. I wish he'd told me, but he didn't, not even when he finally got up the courage to go for a test. When I got home that night, he was sitting on the floor with a can of lager, crying. He was destroyed by the news – distraught for himself, devastated for me.'

'How long ago was that?'

'About four and a half years, within months of me moving in with him. I must have been just twenty-three then.'

'Did you go for a test yourself?'

'I didn't need to. I knew that this was something we were destined to share. I loved him. There was no question that I wouldn't stay with him. He needed me. I'd never leave him.'

'Very hard though, to watch someone you love go through a condition like that?'

'Worst of all, I think, was the fear – fear in the gay community, paranoia in the heterosexual world around us, and our own fear at the probability we would die as young men. That's very difficult to come to terms with. Ian wasn't even forty when I lost him. No age at all.'

'Did he have a supportive family?'

'He had a family. No dad, but a mum, and a couple of sisters. Occasionally they would descend in twittering swarms, telling him he should do this and do that. They'd never talk to me. Although I nursed him day and night, and knew him better than anyone in the world, to them I wasn't there. I was irrelevant.'

Simon watched as the young man's head went down, shoulders shuddering in his distress. 'I was alone with him when he died. He'd been unconscious for some time, but I was holding him, talking to him. It was wonderful – intimate and private and loving. I watched him struggling to breathe, until the gaps between each breath became unbearable – and then, there were no more. He just faded away, cradled in my arms.'

He wiped the back of his hand across his cheeks.

'That family of his took over then. They swooped down on

the hospital, wailing and demanding. This son they had shunned in life, they claimed in death. They organised his funeral, a big flashy affair at their family church in Dulwich.'

He turned his tear-filled eyes towards Simon.

'And do you know what? They never even invited me.'

Chapter Three

Ringing the hospital was always a long-winded business. After endless sessions of responding to disembodied voices giving lists of options, then holding on as she listened for the umpteenth time to Brahms' Lullaby, Christine eventually thumped the phone down and glanced guiltily up at the wall clock. Ten past three! She should have left quarter of an hour ago. Robbie would be standing tearfully at the school gates wondering if she'd abandoned him, if she didn't get a move on. Gathering up her bag, and yelling goodbye over her shoulder to the other girls in reception, she grabbed her coat and hurried towards the rear of the building. It took just one look at the back door, with its sophisticated security system which took umbrage and refused to work with reliable unpredictability, to know it wouldn't work for her now. She was absolutely right. After what seemed like an age of stabbing furiously at the keypad, she dropped her belongings in a heap on the floor and thumped her fists in angry frustration on the door. At that moment the door miraculously opened, and Alistair walked in to receive the full fury of her flailing fists. It was difficult to say who was more shocked but within seconds the two of them were giggling like schoolchildren as he clambered over her bag and coat to make his way in.

'I'm so sorry,' she gasped, 'this blessed door hates me! I'll swear it sees me coming. And I'm really late. I'll have to run like mad all the way!'

'Where? Can I help?'

Her expression suddenly became guarded. The habit of being defensive where her young son was concerned had become ingrained in her over the years. She didn't want to be known as someone who had timekeeping problems just because she was bringing up Robbie on her own. She was proud of him, and proud of her own achievement in organising their lives as well as she possibly could. Taking help, even when it was offered with the best of motives, had always been uncomfortable for her.

'No, I'm fine. It's OK, really.'

'Look, I've finished for today, and my trusty Escort is behaving itself for once. It's no trouble. In fact, it would be my pleasure . . .'

Doubt tussled with need in Christine's mind. She knew she'd never make the school in time by foot. She really had no choice. A sudden shyness crept over her as she nodded agreement. Alistair scooped up her bits and pieces and led the way to the car.

'Right, where to?'

'The Infants School. Do you know where that is?'

'Not exactly, but I know the road. Just yell if you see me going wrong.'

They drove off in silence, neither quite sure how to continue the small talk. She noticed he was wearing the same sporty sweatshirt today which she'd liked when he'd worn it previously. It looked good with his short light brown hair and round pleasant face. Heavens, she thought with a start. Fancy me even considering the way he looks! I'm off men, all of them! Aren't I?

'How old is your son?' His question broke the silence.

'Robbie's nearly five. He's only been at school since Easter.'

'How's he getting on?'

'Oh, he loves it. He's made lots of friends there, and he thinks his teacher is simply wonderful.'

'That must be a relief for you.'

'You're not kidding.'

Conversation stopped as she indicated the right turn they needed. The car slowed as they approached the school gates.

'There he is!'

'Can I say hello to him?'

Uncertainty flashed across her face, but good manners won the day.

'Of course. I'll go and get him.'

Parking on that road as school came out was almost impossible. By the time Alistair had driven up to the top of the street, and back to the gate again, steady drops of rain had begun pounding down on the windscreen. He leaned over to open the back door as Christine and Robbie approached.

'Hop in! I'll drive you home.'

'Really, it's no problem. We're only just round the corner . . .'

'And you'll be soaked by the time you get there. Come on, it won't take a minute.'

Robbie was already clambering into the car, his red hair standing on end in spite of its no-nonsense cut. A smart blue pullover, grey shorts and a rather fetching smear of green paint on his chin completed the picture.

'I got a star today!' he announced, as if he'd known Alistair forever. 'Mrs Whitely said my painting was the best in the class! And I'm doing country dancing at the village fete tomorrow. I've got to wear a hat.' He fiddled with the strap of his school bag thoughtfully. 'I hate hats. Only girls wear hats, and I'm not a girl.'

'No, I can see that,' agreed Alistair solemnly.

'It's got flowers on it, and we're going to have bells on our shoes. I don't mind the bells – but a hat with flowers on. Yuck!'

Christine climbed in beside him, hiding a smile as she

buckled up his seat belt. 'It's up to the end, turn right, then take the first on the left, Watson Avenue.'

'How many of you will be doing the dancing?' asked Alistair, pulling away from the kerb.

'Only the best dancers,' replied Robbie, 'and they're all in my class. I'm a very good dancer.'

'I bet you are.'

'You can come and watch me, if you like.'

Christine stiffened. She looked into the mirror, straight into Alistair's eyes.

'Well,' he replied casually, 'that would be great, Robbie, if your mum doesn't mind.'

'She won't. My mum never minds about anything.'

In the mirror, his eyes looked questioningly at her. Christine hugged Robbie to her. 'Well, Dr Norris is a very busy man. He has to make everyone who's sick feel better again. He probably won't have time.'

'Tomorrow's my day off.'

'We're first on,' announced Robbie proudly, 'even before the majorettes!'

'Then I'd better make sure I get there early.'

'And if we do really well, Mrs Whitely says she'll bring us all a surprise on Monday.'

'That OK with you?' Alistair turned to look directly at Christine as he spoke.

'Fine,' was the quick reply, as she recognised that the knot of trepidation in the pit of her stomach was practically drowned by the almost forgotten pleasure of sharing such a special occasion with a very nice man.

There was a voice of opinion in the village that mid-June was far too early for their village fete. The weather had never settled by then, and it was always touch and go whether the whole event would be ruined by a downpour.

'Baloney!' announced Bert, looking sagely at the gathering gloom the evening before. 'No rain tomorrow! Wrong clouds. Take your sunglasses. You'll need them!'

He was right. Saturday morning dawned bright and clear, although the grass was wet underfoot as Simon arrived at an unearthly hour with the back of his car full of borrowed PA equipment. He couldn't remember quite how he'd ended up on the Fete Committee, and over the past few weeks he'd sometimes wished he hadn't. That morning, though, as he looked around at the good-natured and enthusiastic team of neighbours who were putting up trestle tables, stoking up the fire under the hog roast, and struggling to erect brightly coloured, hardly-weatherproof displays, he felt a bubble of affection and pride for the small welcoming community of which he was now part.

At ten o'clock he was up a ladder fixing a speaker. By eleven he was covered in oil from the generator, and starving hungry. At midday some kind soul handed him a hot dog smothered in onions and mustard. At twelve thirty, as he helped assemble the coconut shy, he found a can of watery shandy to quench his thirst. And at one o'clock, just as a wayward labrador appeared from nowhere to cause chaos with the plant stall, the local councillor arrived to perform the grand opening ceremony and judge the fancy dress parade.

'Turned out nice again!' Simon joked, as he joined Bert at the edge of the arena. 'Do you fancy a cup of tea?'

Bert looked at him coldly. 'If I'm not good enough to dig your garden, then I think I'd prefer to take tea with someone who values my company. And Mrs Gibson says she's saving me a piece of her rich fruit cake too.'

'Oh, for heaven's sake, Bert, it's for your own good! You're still in charge of the flower beds!'

But Bert had already turned on his heel and headed off towards the tea stall.

'Hello.'

Alistair had stood behind Christine for some seconds before

he spoke, taking in her neat figure in blue jeans and a crisp white blouse, with her chin-length auburn hair gleaming in the sunshine. The familiar shyness came over her as she spun round to smile at him.

'Mum!' Robbie yelled, as a crocodile of children dressed as small Morris Men strode proudly into the arena. 'Mum, my hat's wobbly! Can I take it off!'

'No!' said Mrs Whitely firmly from the head of the line. 'Hats stay on heads!'

And with indulgent, affectionate smiles on both their faces, Alistair and Christine moved forward to watch the dancing begin.

'Look at that!'

From the shelter of the bottle stall, Moira nudged Joan in the ribs. 'Now isn't that interesting?'

As Joan followed her gaze, her face lit up at the sight of Alistair and Christine standing closely together.

'Told you he fancied her. I knew it!'

'Well, he could do a whole lot worse. She's a lovely girl. Quite lonely at times, I reckon.'

'And such a devoted mum . . .'

The two women smiled warmly in the direction of the totally oblivious couple on the other side of the field.

'I've got an idea.'

'Really?'

'Just in case Cupid needs a helping hand. Tell me what you think . . .'

Keith wondered why he'd come. Village fetes were hardly his scene. Too many people, none of whom he knew. Perhaps that's what he'd been looking for? A familiar face? Maybe someone from his barely remembered school days? A friend?

Stupid idea! He had no friends, not any longer. Who'd want to make friends with someone who had AIDS?

Then again, perhaps he'd simply come because he needed to get out of the house. His father was at home that morning.

When Keith could stand his indifference no longer, escape had seemed the only option. And now, surrounded by crowds of even more indifferent faces, his instinct was to scuttle back home again. There was no escape. He belonged nowhere.

He thought about buying a can of something. He was almost tempted by the smell of sausages on the barbecue. Then he saw the queue, and changed his mind. Instead he skirted round to the other side of the field where a makeshift adventure playground had been constructed for very small children. Soft inflatable and cushioned constructions had been laid out together so that toddlers could clamber over and through them. He positioned himself on a discarded wooden crate a few yards away from the sandpit in which one stockily-built youngster sat, his face creased with concentration as he ran the sand through his fingers.

Reaching into his jacket pocket, Keith pulled out his pencil and sketchpad, and got to work.

'Excuse me, are you in charge of announcements?'

Simon turned to find a very large, obviously harassed, lady blocking his path.

'Only, if you are, can you say we're closing the entries for the Name the Doll competition early, because we've got to leave at three? We're doing another stall at Holy Saviour's fete this afternoon. We're the Women's Institute over in the corner there. Can everyone come and make their guesses in the next half-hour please?'

'I'm not – but I know the man who is in charge of announcements,' smiled Simon in reply. 'Leave it to me.'

Andy, the man on the mike, was in his element that afternoon. As a hospital radio enthusiast, and sometime disco DJ, having the undivided attention of the whole village at once was practically a dream come true, a vital step on the road to fame. Simon passed on his message, checked all was well with the PA system, then decided he'd stroll round the stalls for a while. In fact that stroll took almost an hour, and in that time he barely managed to look at any of the stalls in detail. When you're a doctor in a small community, not only does everyone know you and seek your company, but they also seek your off-duty advice for everything from blisters on the heel to whether vanilla ice cream sold from a tub on such a hot day could be a health hazard for a one-year-old.

Simon didn't mind. He never minded when people came up and chatted to him. By the end of his tour round the field, he felt mellow and needed and surrounded by friendship. He was also parched. Joining the queue for the beer tent, he looked absent-mindedly about him. When he spied Keith sitting apart from everyone else over by the children's playground, on impulse he bought two beers rather than one and wandered over in his direction.

Keith was so engrossed in his sketching he didn't immediately notice he had company. Simon stood for some minutes at the young man's shoulder, marvelling at the speed with which he worked, the attention to detail which brought out mood and texture in the subject he was drawing. He'd captured exactly the earnestness of the little boy's expression as he piled handfuls of sand on top of each other, creating the castle he plainly saw in his mind's eye.

'You really are very talented.'

Keith turned with a start, his face relaxing into a smile when he realised who was speaking. He snapped the pad shut.

'Just a bit of nonsense. Nothing really.'

'Don't stop. It's a pleasure to watch you work. I wish I could draw like that!'

'Have you ever tried?'

Simon chuckled. 'No point really. I'm a typical doctor. People can't even decipher my handwriting, let alone my pictures. I simply admire the ability in others – and I must say, your drawings are brilliant, so lifelike.'

'It used to get me into trouble at school. If I got bored, I'd start drawing far-too-lifelike cartoons of the teachers. Sometimes the other lads would add rude, but very funny, captions to them, and hand them round the class. It was fine until we got caught. I remember my mate had to write a thousand times, "I must have respect for the teaching staff, because I have a lot to learn from them" – and they made me draw the school photograph! Twelve hundred pupils! It took me a whole week. They thought it was a dreadful punishment – and I loved it!'

'Now I've seen your work, I'm not at all surprised you chose to go into graphic design. I bet you were really good at your job.'

Keith shrugged dismissively as he looked down towards his sketchpad, but Simon could tell from the faint flush that coloured his cheeks the praise had pleased him.

'Actually,' added Simon thoughtfully, 'you might be able to do me a great favour. We could do with some posters for the surgery to make important points our patients need to know, but in an eye-catching way. Cartoons might be just the answer!'

Keith's gaze remained fixed on his sketchpad, but it was plain he was interested. 'A3 size,' continued Simon, his enthusiasm growing by the second, 'in different colours perhaps? There could be about six of them, maybe more. What do you think?'

'I don't mind.' If the answer was non-committal, Simon appeared not to notice.

'Look, I need to get my thoughts in order on this, but if you're willing to give it a try let's talk it over during the week. I could pop round to you, if that's easier. Wednesday afternoon is good for me. Are you about then?'

Keith looked up at him. 'I'm always about. Nothing else to do.'

'I'll soon sort that out!'

'Aren't you supposed to treat me like an invalid?'

'A bright young man like you? Certainly not!' replied Simon with a grin. 'See you on Wednesday then.' And with a cheery wave, he wandered off towards the arena.

'Now, you two,' said Moira, grabbing Alistair and Christine by the arm as if seeing them together was the most natural thing in the world. 'The Dinner and Dance tonight – I've got just two tickets left, and they're going like hot cakes.'

'I wonder where Robbie's got to?' said Christine, disentangling herself from Moira's grasp, only to walk straight into the homely embrace of Joan.

'Everyone says the Berston Fete Day Dinner and Dance is the best event of the year. Take Alistair along, Christine. Introduce him round a bit. Make him feel at home.'

If Alistair had an opinion on the matter he was wise enough to keep his mouth shut, recognising that these two determined women were likely to do the job for him. Christine flashed an appealing glance in his direction. He smiled innocently back at her.

'Lovely idea,' she agreed at last, 'Alistair should definitely go. Perhaps you could take him, Moira. You're always saying your John won't get up and dance.'

'Not tonight, I'm afraid. The in-laws are coming.'

'What a shame. I couldn't possibly go to something like that, of course, because of Robbie . . .'

'I'll babysit,' said Joan.

'Oh, no need for that! Besides, Robbie won't settle with anyone but me.'

'Young Robbie knows me well enough. We're good friends, your little man and I. I'd be glad to come!'

'Joan, that's really kind, but honestly, I . . .'

'Look, it's my hubby's bowls night, so I'll be glad of the chance to get out. I'd enjoy Robbie's company.'

'But the tickets are a bit pricey for me. I'm quite happy at home, really.'

Joan's face came close to hers. 'That's the trouble, pet. Moira and I are always saying you ought to get out and enjoy yourself a bit more! Here's your chance. No arguments. And there's no charge for your ticket, because Dr Norris is paying, aren't you, Alistair?'

His hand was already in his pocket, drawing out a couple of twenty-pound notes. He joined the other two in looking hopefully at Christine. With a sigh, she realised she was beaten.

'OK,' she laughed, 'you win. But I haven't got a thing to wear!'

Just me, thought Alistair happily. I'll keep you warm!

Because Ryder Construction was the main sponsor of the Berston Dinner and Dance, Derek and Brian planned to arrive early so they could position themselves in just the right place to greet particular guests on their arrival. Rumour had it that Martin Balcombe had bought tickets for the whole team at Robbins Architects and their wives. If so, this could be the perfect opportunity to bring up the subject of the new school contract. Derek glanced over at Annie. He was relying on her to keep Martin's wife happy so the men could get on with the real talking. In a detached way, he thought Annie looked very presentable that evening. She was in a neat black dress, topped by a sequinned jacket in midnight blue which captured the hue of her eyes. Her silvery blonde hair was not hanging loosely over her shoulders as usual, but swept up in a more sophisticated style that showed off the gleaming diamond studs in her ears. Not bad, he thought. She'll do.

Annie eyed the gathering crowd with little interest. Although she recognised many of the faces as neighbours she'd known for years, her mood was hardly right to enjoy an event like this. She'd left Keith at home alone. He'd insisted he was fine, but her instinct told her he was hiding his true feelings and fears. She knew her overwhelming desire to wrap him in cotton wool was smothering. She could feel herself doing it, and sense his irritation. What she couldn't do was stand back, although she knew she should. She was his mother. He was her only child. He was dying, and all she wanted to do was hold him close and never let him go.

She was dimly aware of one group of wives looking in her direction. She knew most of them by sight, if not name. They were talking about her. She smiled over at them and immediately their conversation stopped as they turned abruptly away.

They're saying that's the woman whose son has AIDS, she thought bleakly. They're wondering what it's like to live with someone who's gay, who's HIV positive. They're curious and judgemental and frightened.

Her fingernails dug angrily into the palm of her hand.

And who are they to judge? My son is worth the whole crowd of them put together! Damn them, with their knowing looks and smug expressions! Damn them!

At that moment, in the midst of a milling, laughing crowd, Annie felt a depth of loneliness that set her apart. She looked at Derek, with his booming voice and exaggerated laugh as he clasped the hand of some work colleague or another, his face animated with interest – and she wondered if she could pinpoint exactly when she had stopped loving him. More than that, as she coldly observed his movement towards yet another group of smartly-suited businessmen, she asked herself if she now felt even a shred of liking for him. She must have done once, when he was younger and kinder. She remembered being drawn not just to his rugby-player looks, but to his good nature and sense of humour – the way they'd talked into the early hours, the ridiculous private jokes they laughed at together which no one else could possibly understand. She recalled the admiration in his eyes, the warm comfort of his arms around her, the security and strength of him beside her.

Yes, she'd liked him well enough then, until she ached with love for him. But that was long ago, before he'd turned his back on Keith. They were two very different people now, living together but worlds apart. Their only son, who had tied them together in a practical sense for so many years, had become the cause of the gulf between them. No, she didn't love Derek. She despised him.

Alistair and Christine were almost the last to arrive. She felt ill-prepared and awkward, standing together at the doorway of the glittering hall filled with smartly dressed couples. His heart went out to her, as he sensed her shrink towards him with shyness.

'Without a doubt,' he whispered softly into her ear,' you are the most beautiful woman in this room. You look absolutely lovely – and I'm very proud to have you on my arm.'

She looked up at him then, her eyes shining with surprise and gratitude as he took her cold hand in his. She was dressed very simply in a knee-length rich red silk dress which accentuated her slim figure and caught the auburn lights in her hair.

I can't believe I'm really here, she thought to herself. All those years of saying she needed to be at home with Robbie, when in fact she knew she was too scared to be anywhere but home nowadays. She was unused to being in company, unfamiliar with the feeling of a man's hand in hers. She glanced up at Alistair, looking unfairly handsome in his dark suit, and knew she'd never been so scared in her life. She was almost twenty-five years old, a practical mature woman, a mother – yet she was terrified by the prospect of this evening. No, if she was honest, excitement fought for equal placing with terror in her muddled emotions at that moment.

Then, very gently, Alistair stretched his hand up to cup her face in a gesture that was unexpectedly caring. 'You look wonderful, Christine – really you do.' And he kissed her, the most featherlight of kisses that was over so quickly she almost wondered if she'd imagined it. As he tucked her arm safely in his to lead the way to the tables, she felt her confidence grow as a thrill of pure pleasure and anticipation bubbled up within her.

They deliberately didn't choose to join the crowd in which Simon, Gerald, Patricia, Jill, Michael and a few other medical acquaintances were already gathered. In fact there were no more seats at that table, which was a great relief for both of them as they selected places on the furthest side of the hall from their practice colleagues. Without discussion, they knew this evening was theirs alone. There'd be time later to share their new friendship with others. Their presence was however soon noted by Patricia, who smiled with delight as she grabbed Gerald's arm and pointed in their direction.

'Well, I never! He's a fast worker, our Alistair! Good for him!'

Michael wasn't listening. He was deeply, and loudly, in conversation with a GP from the Turpin Way Practice in Southampton whom he knew as a fellow member of the Local Medical Committee.

'The trouble is,' Michael was saying, 'they want much more time from me than I'm able to give. The clinic is booming with business, though – mostly abortions, of course, but vasectomies, fertility treatment, even cosmetic surgery. It's a very lucrative sideline, one I might consider taking up full-time in the future.'

Jill caught sight of Simon's expression. He said nothing. He didn't need to. She leaned over to touch his arm.

'Don't forget you promised to dance all the Sixties numbers with me tonight. You know how Michael hates dancing, and I refuse to sit here like a wallflower all evening!'

He looked at her with that expression of teasing fondness which had always turned her heart upside down.

'I'll never understand why you did it . . .'

'Did what?'

'Marry that moron.'

'Now, you behave, or you'll have to find another partner for the rock'n'roll!'

He threw his head back in delighted laughter. 'You heartless woman!' Putting his arm round her shoulders, he drew her to him in an affectionate hug, oblivious to the cold look from Michael.

For Christine, the evening was a whirl of good food, great company and mood-setting music. The occasional glass of light white wine loosened her nerves and her tongue. In fact she and Alistair didn't bother to talk much to anyone but each other. They sat with their heads close, their hands almost touching, as they chatted about everything from Robbie's favourite bedtime story to Alistair's passion for motorbikes; from the idiosyncracies and wasted expectations of their parents to their aspirations for themselves; from their lost childhood dreams to concerns about the future. And in the heartstopping moment when his eyes held hers in a gaze full of longing and promise, she knew she wasn't alone in hoping that night might be the start of something special. It was too early to put into words, too delicate for discussion – but they each savoured the thought. As he led her on to the floor to join couples dancing singly around them, he drew her close so that they swayed together, the length of their bodies touching, their lips not quite. That came later, when exhilarated and exhausted, he at last helped her out of the car and circled her shoulders with his arm as they walked to her door. Then he kissed her with a passion that took her breath away. She wondered about asking him in. She knew she wanted to – and she knew what would happen if she did. The last man she'd been with had been Robbie's father, and she hadn't seen him for more than four years. How wonderful it would be to give herself up to the headiness of her feelings, to respond as she wanted to, to feel Alistair's arms around her, his body beside hers in the darkness . . .

But then, there was Robbie – and she had been too hurt in the past to trust her feelings now.

Gently, she pulled away from him.

'Alistair, this evening has been wonderful, the best I can ever remember . . .'

He stopped her with a kiss, until lightheaded and smiling she drew back from him.

'Thank you so very, very much. I'll see you on Monday.'

'Oh, much sooner than that! I'll be back for you both at one o'clock tomorrow. I found a lovely country pub the other day with a great line in Sunday lunch and a massive children's playground.'

And before she could object he kissed her again, a leisurely tender embrace. 'Sleep tight, lovely Christine.' And blowing a kiss towards her, he walked to the gate and climbed into his car.

Chapter Four

Simon whistled softly to himself as he checked the number in Byron Close, then took in the expanse of neatly landscaped garden that led up to the imposing, although modern, house. Keith might not feel he belonged here but his home was anything but humble. Everything about it, from the elegant stone statue on the lawn to the expensive brass fitments on the front door, spoke of comfortable good taste.

To his surprise the door was answered not by Keith himself but by a slim, slightly built woman, with fair hair drawn back in a soft sweep towards her neck. Her finely boned face was almost classic in its beauty, her skin fresh and unlined although she was probably well into her forties. Her expression at that moment was questioning, and curiosity shone in her pale blue eyes. Keith's eyes. This must be his mother.

'Hello,' he began, 'I'm Dr Simon Gatward. Did Keith tell you I said I'd drop in to see him today?'

'I'm afraid he didn't. He's upstairs asleep at the moment, and he's only been there about a quarter of an hour. Have you got time for me to make us all a cup of tea, and I'll wake him in ten minutes or so?'

'Great idea,' he replied, stepping inside. 'I'm not here officially. At the fete the other day I saw what a wonderful artist he is, so I asked if he'd consider doing some information posters for the surgery – if you have no objection, that is.'

He noticed how her face lit up as she smiled towards him. 'I think it's a great idea! He *is* a terrific artist, and he's had so little to occupy his time lately. He really needs a project like that, and he'd do a good job, I'm sure.'

'Does he get his talent from you?' Simon perched himself on a kitchen stool from where he could watch her busying with the kettle. 'Didn't he tell me you're a sculptor?'

A flush of surprised pleasure coloured her face.

'Well, only in a small way . . .'

'But you exhibit in London?'

'Occasionally, yes. I've been very lucky.'

'What sort of work do you do?'

She glanced over to the shelves of the kitchen dresser, which he suddenly realised were filled with figures, some bronze, others in wood or stone, ranging in height from just a few inches to more than a foot.

Getting up, he walked over and picked up the piece nearest to him. It was of a pair of hands cupped together around a small bird, its eyes staring with fear, muscles poised for flight. Simon peered closely at the delicate carving, marvelling at the minute detail, the lifelike curve of fingers and feathers.

'This is exquisite,' he whispered almost to himself, 'absolutely beautiful.' His hand moved along the shelves, lifting first one statue, then another. 'They're all superb . . .'

She appeared not to hear him as she laid out a tray with fine bone china mugs. Simon moved over to stand beside her, carefully turning over in his hands the piece he was carrying. It was the statue of a young boy sitting comfortably on a fallen log, a sketchpad on his lap, his gaze concentrated ahead of him towards whatever it was he was drawing.

'How old was Keith when you did this?'

'About eleven.'

'Did he have to sit for you?'

'No. I work from photographs quite a lot, to get the precise detail of shape and line, but the rest I do by instinct. I'm not always looking for physical exactness. What I try to bring out is the essence of my subject – the emotion, the fear, the joy, the pain . . .'

'Not a lot of pain in his face. He looks like a young man full of expectation for a great life ahead of him.'

She leaned over to take the figure from his hands, studying it closely. 'He was, and so was I on his behalf. It's unbelievable how quickly things can change . . .' A strand of blonde hair escaped from the clip at her neck, masking the side of her face. As her shoulders slumped Simon almost reached out to reassure her, because he recognised her grief, understood her pain. Almost – but then he thought better of it.

Within seconds she had straightened, and tucking her hair behind her ear, turned to him.

'I know a bit about this illness from talking to the doctor in London, but Keith says so little nowadays. Will you tell me, because I need to know – how is he? What's likely to happen next? How can I help him most?'

'Well, he's asked me to supervise his care completely. I'm not totally happy about that, because I know he'd benefit from the specialist treatment that the genito–urinary unit in Southampton could offer him.'

'So why isn't he going there?'

'Because he doesn't want to.'

'What do you mean?'

'He was very explicit about it. He knows the score. He's familiar with the treatment available because of nursing Ian all those years. There are a whole range of options around now which could prolong his life for some time, but he's adamant he's not interested in any of them. He's plainly very bereaved for his partner, and life doesn't hold a great deal of appeal for him at the moment.'

'Are you saying he wants to die?'

'Look, you must ask him yourself. As his doctor, I've only

recently met him. I don't know him at all, and I'm sure he would tell you a great deal more than he would me – but he did speak of coming to terms with his own death.'

She covered her mouth with one hand, breathing deeply, holding back a forlorn wave of choking emotion.

'And with this new treatment, could he have real quality for what remains of his life?'

Simon chose his words carefully. 'He has AIDS, and eventually, one way or another, that will lead to his death. Medication can lessen the effect, and perhaps give him a few more years, but in the end the outcome will be the same.'

She shook her head sadly. 'And he'd want to get on with it. He'd hate being an invalid, I know that. That's why he's hardly bothering to eat anything. He wants it to end.'

She was crying. Embarrassed by her tears, she brushed her hand almost angrily across her face. 'I'm sorry. You don't need this. I'm so sorry.'

He did reach out towards her then, touching her arm gently as he spoke. 'Don't apologise. This is very hard on you – and I'm here not just for Keith, but you and your husband too.'

She shrugged. 'Derek doesn't need help. Not yours, and certainly not mine. He's detached himself from it all. He doesn't speak to Keith, and won't discuss any of this with me. Ignore it, and it will go away. And it will. Keith will die, and it won't touch him at all.'

'I doubt that's true. Ignoring the issue may be his way of dealing with it, but only on the surface. It sounds to me as if he needs help to sort out his feelings about what's happening. Would he see our counsellor, do you think?'

'No chance.'

'Would you like me to talk to him?'

'I don't think that would do any good.'

'Can I try?'

She looked at him thoughtfully before sighing with resignation. 'If you like, but I don't think you'll get anywhere.'

'Would he come and see me at the surgery?'

'Let me talk to him first.'

Across the kitchen surface, their eyes met. She smiled. And as he smiled in return, Simon realised his hand was still on her arm.

'Hi.'

They both turned at the sound of Keith's voice. 'I see you two have introduced yourselves. Is the kettle on?'

'Coming up!' smiled Annie, as she finished laying out the tray with sugar and biscuits. 'Keith, you've hardly eaten anything today. How about some soup, or a sandwich?'

'I'm not hungry, Mum.'

'Your medication will work much more effectively if it's taken with food. And your mum's right. A sensible diet is what you need to keep your strength up.'

Keith looked from one to the other, then grinned slowly at Simon. 'OK, I'll have whatever you're having.'

Simon looked at his watch. 'Well, I . . .'

'Come on, doc, you can't be on duty now. You came to talk to me about the posters. And my mum *does* make the best soup you've ever tasted.'

Annie flushed with embarrassment, avoiding Simon's eyes. 'Dr Gatward's wife is probably wondering where on earth he's got to. I expect she'll have a meal waiting for him.'

'No wife – and no homemade soup. So thank you, Keith. If your mum doesn't mind and you're having soup and a sandwich, then so will I.'

Two hours later, when Derek put his key in the door and walked into the house, he was intrigued by the animated discussion he heard coming from the lounge. Unnoticed, he put his head round the door, where an unexpected scene met his eye. Keith was stretched out on the floor surrounded by sheets of paper, sketching and in deep conversation with an older man who was on his knees beside him. Sitting on the floor alongside them both was Annie, warmed by the glow of the fire, her long hair falling in soft folds around her face. The coffee table above them was littered with dishes, mugs and the debris of a meal. Their concentration on Keith's drawing, the easy conversation, the laughter that punctuated their sentences, the way Annie was smiling at this total stranger – they all knotted into a tight possessive ball in the pit of Derek's stomach. He banged the lounge door shut as he walked in, his expression cold and controlled. Annie scrambled to her feet.

'Goodness, you're so late. This is Simon Gatward, Keith's doctor.'

Simon got to his feet too, holding out his hand in greeting to the newcomer. Derek ignored the gesture.

'And do you prefer to do your examinations not only on the floor, but after hours, doctor?'

'Derek . . .'

There was a hard edge to Simon's voice as he replied. 'Actually, Mr Ryder, your son has very kindly offered to lend his talents to producing some health information posters for the surgery. He has some wonderful ideas.'

'How could he possibly have anything to say about health education? He doesn't even know that men are *supposed* to go with women. He has such a lot to learn, doctor, I can assure you he has nothing whatsoever to offer you or your practice. That being the case, perhaps you would respect my family's privacy and organise any future consultations at your surgery – not rolling round on the floor with my wife.'

'Derek, that's enough!'

But Simon was already gathering up his coat and bag, and heading for the door. He didn't bother to look in Derek's direction.

'Please make an appointment to see me at the end of the week, Keith. Your blood test results should be in by then.'

Annie hurried after him as he made for the door, her eyes blazing with anger and indignation – so the warmth in his expression as he turned to say goodbye took her by surprise.

'Don't worry, Mrs Ryder. I do understand. Give me a ring any time if you need to talk.' Then without a backward glance he was gone.

With some relief, Joan turned the key on the surgery door at one o'clock precisely. One blessed hour of relative peace during which the practice team could grab a sandwich, catch up on notes and computer entries, and draw breath.

Moira looked up from the appointments book in surprise as Joan grabbed her arm and began to frogmarch her towards the kitchen. 'I've got a sample in my bag of the material I'm thinking of using for my dress for the wedding. I need your opinion. Come and see.'

Once outside the door, Joan released her friend. 'Didn't you notice? Alistair's hanging around like a big-eyed puppy, obviously hoping for a quiet word with Christine!'

'Really?'

'I think what we need is a *long* cup of tea. And you can even look at my material, if you like!'

Christine had her earphones on as she typed into the word processor the letters dictated after surgery that morning by the doctors. It wasn't until she felt Alistair's lips on the back of her neck that she even realised he was there. Flustered, she took off her earphones, checking with relief that they were alone.

'Alistair, you mustn't do that. You'll get me fired. I need this job.'

He came round to sit on the desk, looking down at her fondly.

'You're beautiful.'

'I'm busy. I need to get this finished. And I feel very strongly that we shouldn't mix work with . . .'

'Pleasure?'

'. . . out of work activities.'

'Quite right. Can I pop round tonight then?'

She hesitated.

'Oh, come on, you heartless woman! Your son thrashed me mercilessly at Snap on Sunday, and I vowed revenge. We men have our pride! I'll be taking no prisoners in the return match this evening. And I've told him – if I don't win, I'll cry!'

She couldn't help but laugh. He leaned forward then to take her hand.

'And I'm rather hoping for a return match with his mum too.'

'Alistair, I . . .'

He stroked a stray strand of hair away from her forehead.

'Yes?'

'This is all moving too fast.'

He tilted up her chin to look into her eyes.

'Yes – and doesn't it feel wonderful?'

'I'm just not sure . . .'

'That you're allowed to be happy? That it's OK to relax with someone who really treasures your company? That it's even more of a bonus if we're wildly attracted to each other?'

She pulled her hand out of his.

'I've been on my own so long. I had the stuffing knocked out of my confidence when Robbie's father left.'

'And now you can't trust anyone?'

She was silent.

'I promise you, Christine, you can trust me. And however long it takes, I will prove that to you.'

She looked at him then, a long searching gaze full of unspoken questions.

'So, Robbie and I have this evening all planned. I bring in the fish and chips, you provide the ketchup. Then you discreetly disappear while we men do battle. And when one triumphant little chap finally gives in and goes to bed, this big chap will play it whatever way you like. I'll take my defeat on the chin and leave if you say so – but I hope you'll want me to stay, at least long enough to reassure you that you *can* trust me.' He grinned. 'I'm a doctor!'

And in spite of herself, she grinned too.

Along the corridor, Simon and Jill had joined Patricia in her office. Spread out on the desk in front of them were a selection of the poster ideas Keith had come up with the previous evening.

'These are really good,' said Patricia, sifting through them. 'So witty, but simple too.'

'Well, they've got to be simple if they're going to work,' added Jill. 'They need to be eye-catching, with just one straight-forward thought on each poster for people to remember them.'

'Do you like his cartoon characters? I thought the idea of having the same family featured in all of them works very well.'

'Hmm,' agreed Patricia, 'it's great. And I think we could expand the concept to cover a few more topics, perhaps to advertise the specialist clinics we run?'

'Well, Keith's got a lot of time on his hands at the moment, and he seems very keen to be asked to use his talent in this way.'

Jill walked over to sink into a chair on the other side of the desk.

'Is this therapy then?'

Simon eyed her thoughtfully. 'Perhaps it is. He's certainly got a lot to contend with at home.'

'His parents?'

'His father. He's a dreadful man! He practically threw me out the house when he arrived to find us discussing these last night.'

Patricia's brow furrowed. 'Then perhaps we shouldn't antag-onise him. After all, his son is very ill. If I were Keith's parent, I might well think that by asking him to do things like this, we're taking advantage of him. I don't think his father's reaction is surprising at all. It's out of love.'

'Out of fear – and ill-informed, bigoted, bloodymindedness!'

Patricia's eyes narrowed. 'Be careful, Simon. Stand back from this. I know we don't see many AIDS patients in a small place like Berston, which is all the more reason for us to act in a perfectly professional way.'

'Of course I'm professional! How could you ever doubt that?'

Jill leaned forward to place a steadying arm on his. 'Patricia's right. I've met Derek Ryder a few times. He's a member of the same club as Michael. He's not someone you can ignore. He makes his presence felt wherever he goes, and he's a man of some influence around here. Just be careful. Treat the patient. Let the family sort themselves out.'

'I couldn't agree with you more about the father – but the mum . . .'

'I've met her too, I think. A rather bohemian-looking woman with long hair? Some sort of artist, isn't she?'

Simon nodded. 'A sculptor. A very good one.'

Jill eyed him curiously. 'You've seen her work?'

'She showed me some stunning pieces last night. Without a doubt, Keith gets his artistic eye from her.'

'How's she coping with her son's illness?'

'She's very pragmatic. She wants to know all the facts. She's frightened for him, longs to protect him. She's tearful some-times, strong at others. She's quite a woman.'

Jill watched his face and said nothing.

'It would be a shame not to have these posters though,' mused Patricia, rearranging them in front of her. 'They could do so much good.'

'Well,' said Simon, gathering up the papers and scooping them into his briefcase, 'we're all agreed then. Providing Keith Ryder himself is happy – and he is, after all, an intelligent, artic-ulate adult – then we would very much appreciate his help with our poster campaign. I'll let you know how it develops from here. Excuse me, I've got some calls to make.'

And as the door swung shut behind him, the two women looked at each other in mild surprise.

Behind the sanctuary of his own surgery door Simon sat down heavily, then picked up the phone, thumping in a number. As he waited for the line to connect, he thought back over the conversation they'd just had.

Why did I get so angry, he wondered to himself.

But he knew the answer. In Annie Ryder's eyes he'd glimpsed the same despair and pain that lurked deeply hidden in his own heart.

'Derek, long time no see! How's business?'

Michael moved along the club bar to shake Derek's outstretched hand. The two men were more acquaintances than friends, but with golf and club activities in common, their paths had crossed very amicably over the years.

'Nice to see you. Well, I can't complain. Things are looking rather good at the moment.'

'Oh?'

'The new school on Farthing Corner. The tender's out in a couple of weeks.'

'And you're in with a chance?'

Derek paused to take a gulp of beer, then with a knowing smile leaned nearer to Michael. 'Well, it's who you know, isn't it? And we know the right people.'

'That job should be worth a bob or two.'

'Well, we could certainly do with it. Things have been a bit quiet lately. In fact, I'm already planning my retirement in the sun on the strength of getting this contract. A little villa in Spain perhaps?'

'I bet your family would like that.'

Derek's expression clouded. 'Well, Annie looks good with a suntan. I think a change would do her good.'

Something clicked in Michael's memory, a faint recollection of a conversation he'd had with Jill.

'Oh, how thoughtless of me. Jill told me about your son. How is he?'

Derek stiffened, pausing to take another mouthful before he spoke. 'He's fine.'

'Come on, I'm a doctor. I know he's not fine, but is he coping? Are you?'

'He's doing all right. He keeps pretty much to himself.'

'He'll be getting the very best care from the specialist unit in Southampton. They can do wonders these days. It's not the life sentence it used to be.'

There was no answer.

'Just let me know if there's anything I can do, push things along a bit, perhaps? When lists are long, it might help to talk to the right people.'

Still no reply.

'Well, you know where I am. I see my guest has arrived. Do you know him? Matthew Benson? He's a solicitor, of course, but he's just become a local councillor too. Clever chap. Must go. Keep in touch.'

Derek stayed at the bar for some minutes, apparently deep in thought. Suddenly, he looked up towards the door. He'd arrived! His face beaming welcome, Derek moved over to greet Ken Baker, the council contracts manager for the Farthing Corner site, then led the way through to the discreet corner table he'd booked for lunch.

Simon frowned with concern as he listened to the young woman who'd just joined him in the surgery. He'd known the Claymores for some time, not just as their doctor, but also as social acquaintances rather than close friends. With her twentieth birthday looming, Debbie was the brightest of the three children, but also a quiet, shy girl who preferred to be at the back of the crowd rather than in the limelight. It had come as no surprise to her parents when she decided against going off to university in favour of an administrative post in the local solicitors' office. As her confidence and responsibilities at work had expanded, so had the warmth of her personality. She'd emerged from schoolgirl gaucheness to the elegant style of a young office worker, complete with smart suits and modern haircut. Her life stretched with promise ahead of her – or at least it had until today. Debbie was pregnant.

'Have you told your parents?'

'No.'

'What do you think their reaction will be?'

'I'm not sure. Disappointed, I suppose.'

'And the baby's father?'

'I've told him.'

'And?'

'And nothing. He wasn't exactly pleased.'

'Do you think you'll stay together?'

She looked at him levelly. 'I don't think his wife would think much of that, do you?'

'Nevertheless, this baby is his responsibility too. You both need to make proper arrangements for its future.'

'The baby won't have a future if he has anything to do with it. He wants me to have an abortion.'

'And you? What do you want?'

The confident façade crumpled as tears filled her eyes. 'I don't know what I want. I love him. I thought he loved me. He said he did. But he's cooled off so much, I just don't know what to think.'

'But is your instinct that you'd like to keep this baby?'

Her face was etched with dilemma and exhaustion. 'I don't want to kill it. I can't.'

'Well, there's no reason why you shouldn't bring up the child on your own. Plenty of young women do.'

'I don't know what he'd think about that. He'd worry about what people might say. His reputation means a lot to him.'

'But your health, and his baby's welfare, are more important than his reputation. He must have known there was the risk you'd get pregnant.'

'He said it was my fault.'

'It takes two, Debbie.'

She fell silent, shoulders slumped, head down.

'Would it help if I talked to your mum and dad?'

'No. I'll do it.'

'I'm sure they'd help you come to the right decision. But we also have a counsellor here, and she could talk over the various options with you. Can I make you an appointment to see her?'

'No, thanks. I don't want to talk to anyone else. I'll come and see you again when I've decided what to do.'

'Don't leave it too long. And Debbie, don't allow yourself to be pushed into anything you're not entirely happy with. It's your body and your baby. It's quite natural that maternal instinct should take over to protect your unborn child. Having a baby at this time in your life may not be what you planned, but it doesn't have to be a disaster. It might even be the very best thing that ever happened to you.'

Her smile was watery and half-hearted as she rose from the seat. 'Thanks. I'll think it over. And I'll come back when I'm feeling more sure about all this.'

As usual, the roast beef at the club restaurant was cooked to perfection, pink and tender. Throughout the starter course Derek and Ken had kept their conversation light and general. As the horseradish arrived, they got to the subject they both knew they were there to discuss.

'Are Wilkinsons completely out of it?'

'Not heard a word from them. I don't think there's anyone properly in charge there now that Joe's ill, and from what I hear, his wife is trying to persuade him to retire completely. And that daft son of his isn't likely to get his act together for a big contract like this one.'

'So, what about Baskins? Are they planning a bid?'

'Almost certainly. George Baskin popped into my office earlier this week and gave me a grilling about what we're looking for. Mind you, I don't think he needs to ask me. He's thick as thieves with Gareth Walters these days.'

Derek's brow shot up. 'Really? I wouldn't have thought they had much in common, although I suppose now Gareth is chairman of the Building Committee, George has made it his business to creep round him.'

'He's a slimy sod, that Gareth. Why the council gave him that post I'll never know, but he seems to run the Building Committee as if it's his own business. I don't trust him an inch.'

Ken's wine glass hovered in the air, fixing his eyes on Derek as he spoke.

'I don't think he'll be a problem. He's got too many skeletons he'd prefer to keep in the cupboard.'

A slow smile spread across Derek's face. 'Well, I'm very grateful to hear that, and naturally I'm prepared to show my gratitude for any tips you can give me in the usual way . . .'

'Naturally.'

The two men continued their meal in silence for a while, until at last Ken pushed away his plate and sat back in his chair with a sigh.

'Actually, I don't think Gareth's mind is on work much at all at the moment. His daughter's getting married in a couple of months. Do you know her? Mandy? Tall girl, long hair, a bit of a looker?'

Derek shook his head. 'Can't say I do.'

'Well, you'd think it was the social event of the year. It's his wife, of course. Carole Walters was always a bit of a social climber – all down to the fact she's American, I reckon. She's got a superiority complex.'

'Perhaps they might need a bit of extra cash to help with the expenses of the wedding then? Costly business, weddings. What do you reckon?'

'Hmm. Something towards the reception? Or maybe just a contribution towards soothing the tattered nerves of the bride's parents . . .'

'Can you pick your time to have a word in his ear?'

'Consider it done.' Ken raised his glass. 'Here's to Farthing Corner!'

Across the room, Michael laughed loudly at the end of a long and convoluted story from his lunch companion, Matthew, about a divorce case he'd been working on. The two men got on well. The doctor recognised the professional in the solicitor, so that the occasional contact through work had led to a social link between the two families. Jill and Matthew's wife, Linda, often took themselves off on shopping trips, or for a day of pampering at the local health farm. And every now and then Michael remembered to let Matthew beat him at golf.

Almost imperceptibly, Matthew drew in his chair and lowered his voice as he leaned in towards Michael.

'Actually, there's a little matter I'd like your advice on.'

'Oh?'

'Are you still involved with that private clinic?'

'Elmside? Yes, I'm on the board there.'

'Do they do abortions?'

Michael took a sip of wine and eyed his companion carefully.

'Every day. Why?'

'I have a friend who needs one.'

'Do I know her?'

'She works in our office.'

'And she's sure about this?'

'She will be.'

'What about the father? Is that what he wants?'

'Yes, Michael, I most certainly do.'

Michael whistled quietly under his breath.

'Yours? Does Linda know about this?'

'Are you kidding? Of course not. This time she'd definitely

leave me, and take everything I own with her.' He looked down as he turned the saltcellar round with his fingers. 'Look, I'm a man. You know how it is. When it's offered on a plate, why not? The silly little girl practically threw herself at me.'

'Has she been to see a doctor yet?'

'I don't know. I shouldn't think so.'

'Could you get her to come and see me?'

'I was hoping you'd say that. Yes, I'll arrange it. She'll do as she's told.'

'Well, do it soon. Give me a ring at Roxborough's later this afternoon. We can fix an appointment.'

'And this can be kept completely discreet?'

Michael smiled reassuringly. 'Absolutely. Leave it to me.'

Jill happened to be standing behind the counter in the reception area when Keith checked in, then chose his chair in the waiting room, trying not to notice the steady glare he was given by the little boy sitting on his mother's lap on the seat beside him.

'What's that?' the youngster asked, pointing a chubby finger at one of the reddish blotches on Keith's face.

Keith grabbed a magazine from the pile on the table, and tried to look absorbed in the cookery recipes of a six-month-old copy of *Woman's Weekly*.

'Is that a spot?' The youngster was relentless. 'Or did you fall over? I fell over. Do you want to see my scab? I've nearly picked it off now.'

'Shh,' whispered his embarrassed mother, although Keith could feel her eyeing the telltale Kaposi Sarcoma lesions that had not only started appearing on his face, but were now all over his body.

'I've got to have my tonsils out. Look!' The boy grabbed Keith's arm as he opened his mouth wide for inspection.

'Leave the gentleman alone, Matthew. Come on, let's move.'

She knows, thought Keith. She knows I've got AIDS, and she's afraid.

'But why does he look like that, Mum? Has he got a rash like I had?'

Faces turned in his direction. Jill watched with pity as interested looks became curious stares. Finally Keith slammed down the magazine and headed for the door. It wasn't until he reached the corner of the building and leaned back against the wall to get his breath back, that he felt hot tears rolling down his cheek.

Simon was the last to leave the practice that evening. He secured the lock on the back door, and turning his collar up against the steady drizzle that had hardly stopped all day, he made for his car. It was only when he heard someone call his name that he realised a figure was squatting hunched into the shadows on the low wall which enclosed the rather neglected flower bed.

'Keith! Good Lord, you're soaked. Whatever are you doing here?'

'I need to see you.'

'You missed your appointment. Why didn't you just come in the front door like everybody else?'

'Because I'm not like everybody else – and they make sure I know that.'

'Hop in the car. I'll take you home.'

'No. I don't want to go there.'

'Why not?'

Keith shrugged.

'Does your mum know you're here?'

'I told her I was seeing you.'

'Home's the best place for you.'

'Look, Dad's there tonight, so I don't want to be.' Suddenly he spun round and began to walk wearily towards the exit of the car park. 'Oh, for heaven's sake, just forget it!'

'Have you eaten?'

Keith stopped, but said nothing.

'Right, will spaghetti do? Come and dry out at my house, then we can chat and get you fed before I take you home.'

Without waiting for an answer, Simon walked over to unlock the car. A few seconds later, Keith lowered himself into the passenger seat.

An hour later, Simon eyed the young man with concern as he handed him a plate of steaming bolognese. He watched as Keith pushed the food around with his fork, until eventually he gave up the pretence and shoved the tray away.

'No appetite?'

'Food just churns up my insides. It will only reappear with a vengeance at one end or the other.'

'I can give you something for that.'

'Fine, except whatever you give me, I'll bring up again.'

'Just make sure you keep up your fluid intake.'

'Drinking is worst of all. Mouth ulcers . . .'

'That medication didn't help?'

'My mouth is covered in deep, septic patches. Anything that's either hot or cold is agony. Even water seems like sand-paper scraping raw flesh. My tongue feels so tender and swollen, there's hardly room for it.'

'You don't have to suffer like this. You know there's so much more we can do for you . . .'

'No.'

'Keith, you're a young man. You have talent. You have a family who love you. You have real worth.'

'No.'

'Would Ian want you to throw your life away like this?'

'I think the knowledge that he'd passed this on to me was the hardest thing for him to bear. He was so angry, wild with fury that a stupid little thing like a virus which can't even be seen by the human eye, which can't live in the open air, and which can be killed by household bleach, should be taking his life – and that it would eventually kill the person he loved most!' His face was drawn with forlorn sadness as he turned towards Simon. 'You know, I'd never known such love until I met him. He was the reflection of my own soul. He made me complete. Without him, I have nothing left to live for.'

'Oh, Keith, that's so untrue.'

'It's true for me. I just want to get this over, and be with him.'

'And so you will be, but you don't have to accelerate that process or make it more painful than it needs to be. You might have a very reasonable life for years with all the new medication available nowadays. You'd have time to explore your talent, make more friends, experience new love . . .'

'How? When mothers move their children away for fear of touching me? When my own father is paranoid that I might have contaminated even the cutlery in the house? Who'd want to put their arms around me, or kiss me, or make love with me? No one. No one at all. And that's the loneliest feeling in the world.' His voice trembled with choking despair, so that his words came out in slow, painful gulps. 'I am so lonely. Alone among people, alone in our house. On my own, and frightened as hell. And it's only the thought that once this is over I'll be with Ian forever that gets me through.'

He broke down then as wrenching sobs tore through his body. Moving over beside him, Simon drew the shaking boy towards him, resting his head on the mop of blond hair, as he murmured soft inadequate words of comfort.

It was shortly after eight the next morning when the bell went. Simon was surprised to find Jill on the doorstep.

'Hi. I know you're not due in until later this morning, and as I'm on the road today, I wanted to catch you before I left. Have you got a moment?'

'Sure. Come in. I'm just making tea. Do you want one?'

Simon strode off into the kitchen, not noticing the slow progress Jill made to follow him. En route she had glanced into the lounge. Stretched out sound asleep on the settee, warmly covered by a duvet, was Keith Ryder.

'Simon, for God's sake, what are you doing? Why is he here?'

'He was waiting for me outside the surgery last night. He wouldn't let me take him home. He was soaked and exhausted. I couldn't just leave him there, so this seemed the best place for him. He's all in, poor kid.'

'But why didn't you take him home? Or ring his parents to come and collect him?'

'I did speak to his mum, but that was only after he'd got very emotional and upset and I had no choice but to sedate him. I wanted to keep an eye on him anyway. She's coming to collect him in an hour or so.'

'Simon, you shouldn't do this. This is your private space, and Keith Ryder is simply work. You have to detach yourself. Why are you involving yourself in this way?'

'I don't know what you mean.'

'Yes you do – and it's me you're talking to. I've never known you like this before, taking it all so personally. Why? What is it about this case?'

'Jill, I really don't know. There's just something about him, something about his despair and his courage, his talent and the fact he's so young. His life's hardly begun, yet he can't wait to die.'

'But you've dealt with terminal illness in patients younger this, and not reacted the same way. What's happening?'

'Look, I became a doctor because I care about people when they're hurt and frightened. I've always cared about my patients, and this one is no exception.'

'You haven't always brought them here to spend the night in your home.'

'I had no choice.'

'You did, and you made it. It wouldn't look so bad if you had a wife here . . .'

He stared at her.

'I can't believe you said that.'

'Simon, you've got to see it as others will.'

'It would take pretty warped minds to read something into this.'

'People have got warped minds when it comes to AIDS. You know that. They're ignorant and prejudiced and frightened.'

'And they're wrong! That doesn't mean I have to act wrongly too.'

'Precisely. So you must be extra careful. Please Simon, I couldn't bear this to backfire on you.' Her expression softened as she walked over to put her arms around him. He gathered her close, relaxing against her. Together they stood for some time, no more words needed. Finally, he pulled back enough to tip her face up towards his.

'Thank you for caring,' he said softly. Then he bent his head to brush her cheek with the gentlest of kisses before drawing her head down on to his shoulder.

Chapter Five

The damp cool summer became an early autumn as watery September sunshine tinged the leaves with gold and rust. Alistair pulled his collar closer round his neck as he parked the car, and started down the pavement, checking the number of the house he was due to visit as he went. Number 43, that was it. He turned up the path towards a block of four maisonettes. Harry Gordon apparently lived in the bottom flat. The sound of coughing greeted his ring of the bell, as someone made their slow way to answer the door. It was opened by a short, muscular man with thinning hair and a nose that had obviously lost an argument with something hard earlier in its life.

Ten minutes and an examination later, Alistair confirmed what Harry already suspected. It was bronchitis, for which the remedy was plenty of rest, steam inhalation and a course of strong antibiotics.

'Is there anyone here to look after you?'

'My mum. She's not home at the moment.'

Glancing at Harry's broad torso, with its misshapen collar bone and bulging biceps, recollection clicked.

'Your Mum's not *Lily* Gordon?'

'That's right. Why?'

Alistair smiled. 'Well, in that case, you could help me solve a little mystery that's been puzzling me for quite some time!'

★

Annie's fingers worked skilfully, smoothing life and shape into the form on the bench before her. With practised accuracy, her sculptor's hands enticed into being the creation she saw in her mind's eye. This piece was special. Her heart was in this one. This was for Keith. And while she busied herself with wood and tools, her mind roamed free.

She was angry with Derek – not just angry, but since the embarrassment of his outburst in front of Dr Gatward, seething with cold, disbelieving fury. He was no longer someone she knew or understood. She wondered who had changed. Was it her? Had she always known he was a bigot and a bully, and accepted it? She thought back over their early years of marriage, how they'd worked together to establish his building business, she keeping the accounts and running the office, while he at first did the work himself, then later employed others with skills that would enhance his good name.

Keith's difficult birth had brought an end to her role in the office, as their son not only arrived two months early but was frail and worrying for the first year of his life. She remembered the dark night-time hours as he snuffled and wheezed while she slept beside him, checking the warmth of his skin, listening for each precious breath. She had longed to share her fear with her husband, but his business was building, his reputation growing, so his working hours extended, and his time at home was spent either sleeping or catching up on phone calls and paperwork. Derek was plainly perplexed by his delicate, beautiful son. As other toddlers grew to romp and fight and argue, so Keith preferred to stand on the edge of any crowd, his eyes enormous, his pale skin and golden hair giving him an angelic appearance. Never mind, thought Derek. Our next boy will be more like me. But there never was another boy. Try as they might, there was no other baby at all.

Over the years, the only arguments they'd ever had were

over Keith. Derek was determined to toughen him up. He bought him a football to go with the goal net he erected in the garden. He made him join a martial arts club. He even bribed the sports master to get Keith a place in the school rugby team. It wasn't until they got a call from the hospital to say that their son had been taken there with his leg broken during rugby practice that Annie put her foot down. No more! Derek was trying to make their boy something he wasn't. He could never be in the same sporting mould as his father. He was like his mum, gentle, shy and artistic – and Derek had never forgiven him for that.

Over the years Derek accused her of mollycoddling the boy, so she constantly checked herself if she thought she was being over-protective or smothering. She simply allowed him to be himself which, for Keith, often meant solitary activities. He'd spend hours making little wooden or clay models, which he painted with painstaking precision and concentration. He liked to grow things, whether sunflowers on his windowsill or runner beans up gangly canes in the garden. Even before he started school he would perch high on the piano stool where his feet couldn't touch the ground, and pick out tunes he'd either heard on the radio or dreamed up himself. And he began to draw. Pencil outlines that were instantly recognisable as his parents, his favourite soft toy or his teacher began to appear on the corners of every scrap of paper he laid hands on. For Annie, who was an artist herself, the wonder of his doodlings wasn't just their accuracy, but their humour. In fact, doodles soon became an entertaining form of communication between mother and son. Why bother with words or written notes, when 'Sorry', 'Thank you' or 'You drive me mad but I still love you' could be expressed more eloquently in the comical expression of a cartoon character?

Biting her lip with concentration as she shaped away at a corner of the sculpture, Annie was warmed by the thought of the closeness she'd always shared with Keith. Throughout it all

– his leaving home for university, her acknowledgement of his sexuality which at heart she'd probably always known, the dreadful time of the death of her mother-in-law, and Derek's fury at discovering his son was gay – her closeness to Keith had remained.

And soon, she would be losing him.

Her vision clouded over as mist filled her eyes. It's getting dark, she thought. Perhaps I'll work on this again tomorrow.

Simon trudged up the garden path and ignored the bell beside the door. He knew it hadn't worked for years. Bert wasn't one for mending things. A couple of loud thumps brought no response. He yelled through the letter box, then peered through the grubby side window, but the house looked and sounded deserted. Clutching the brown paper bag with its precious bottle of whisky closely to him, he made his way round to the back of the building in case Bert was to be found where he was always happiest, in his garden. But no, there was no sign of him.

'He's out.'

The neighbour's head appeared over the side fence. She was a small woman, wearing the kind of wraparound apron his mother had always worn for housework.

'Probably at Ivy Gibson's. She's been giving him dinner. Feeds him all the time, she does.'

'Good for Ivy,' grinned Simon. 'That's just what he needs!'

'Got an eye for him, I reckon.'

'What, for Bert?'

'Her husband's not been in his grave a year, and already she's got another man with his feet under the table.'

'Well, she'll not have much to worry about if it's Bert she's feeding. He wouldn't even think to take his wellies off!'

'She always was a hussy, that one. Knew her at school. She was a proper little madam even then.'

Simon nodded wordlessly, trying to keep a straight face at

the thought of a 'hussy' throwing her hat in Bert's direction. Don't suppose he'd even notice!

'His garden's gone all to pot. He's not dug up his new potatoes, and you know how he loves them – and just look at his runner beans. Ruined!' She sniffed. 'I hear her lawn's immaculate these days . . .'

Actually, Simon thought the beans didn't look bad at all, but then, as Bert never tired of telling him, for a doctor he was a hopeless gardener.

The woman drew her lips together in a tight thin line. 'She's after him, you mark my words.'

'Well, I just came by on the off chance. Perhaps if I write a note I could ask you to pop this round to him when he gets back.'

With the slightest nod of agreement, the woman didn't bother to reply as Simon drew a pad and pen out of his pocket, and began to scribble.

> Bert,
>   Sorry not to catch you in. I called round with this little
> peace offering – strictly medicinal, you understand! I miss
> you, you old goat! Give me a ring when you can.
>   Simon Gatward

'I'll make sure he gets it,' said the neighbour, showing great self-control in not peering into the paper bag, even though he knew she'd examine it thoroughly the moment he'd gone. 'And I'll tell him you called.'

With that, her small pale face, with its neat white curled hair, disappeared below the fence.

From the moment he'd spotted her name on his surgery list, Alistair had been waiting for her to appear round his door. Mrs Gordon bustled in and sat down beside his desk.

'Another cut on your hand, Lily?'

'Not really. It's just the one from last week. It's not healed up very well. Gone a bit septic, I think. Would you take a look at it for me?'

'And what did you say caused this?' he asked, gently peeling off the plaster she'd placed over the wound.

Her expression became vague. 'Something in the garden, I think.'

'You think?'

'Hmm.'

'Funny really,' he continued, looking closely at the red welt, 'only this looks like a dog bite to me.'

She didn't reply.

'You've got a dog, haven't you, Lily?'

She looked straight at him, her eyes suddenly glassy and defensive.

'What if I have?'

'Was it your dog that did this to you? Has it been your dog all along?'

'He's a good boy, a very good boy! He just gets a bit excited now and then . . .'

'But if he's becoming vicious and hurting you, we've got to do something about it.'

'No! He doesn't mean it!'

'What?'

'He thinks I'm playing with him, you see.'

'Playing?'

The old lady's shoulders slumped. 'It's the sticks. He's always loved sticks, so he just thinks I get the sticks out for him to play with.'

'What sticks?'

'The kindling sticks for the fire. I like a real fire in the grate in the evenings, even in the summer. It brightens up the place somehow.'

'And whenever you take a stick out of the bundle, and try to put it on the fire . . .'

'. . . he bites me. Well, he's aiming for the stick, of course, but his eyesight's no better than mine, so he keeps missing.'

'Lily, that's dreadful. Why ever do you put up with him? Dogs carry all sorts of diseases. No wonder these cuts keep on going septic, if he's sinking his teeth into you all the time!'

'He can't help it. He doesn't understand. It's my own stupid fault.'

'But why didn't you tell me? Why didn't you at least ask your son for help? He wondered if it might have something to do with the dog, but he hadn't worked out the whole story.'

The old lady's eyes filled with tears. 'I knew this would happen!' she sobbed. 'You'll make them take him away, won't you, and I couldn't bear that. Scamp is my best friend in all the world. He loves me. He just doesn't understand. And neither do you!'

Alistair moved round to the front of the desk where he placed a comforting arm about the frail shoulders.

'Look, Lily, no one is talking about taking Scamp away. I'm sure we can come up with a solution to this.' Lily continued to sob pitifully as Alistair murmured comforting noises, hoping that would help.

Of course there's a solution to this, he thought grimly. It's just that right at the moment, I can't think of one. But I will. I most certainly will.

Jill was ironing, her least favourite job, but a task she found mechanical and undemanding, so that as she automatically moved on from shirt collar to cuff her thoughts were free to move along their own path.

She was thinking about Michael. Her husband was a complex self-contained man, not warm, not demonstrative, not in obvious need of emotional bolstering from any direction. Perhaps that was because of his years growing up in a military family where his mother and father travelled the world and the offspring were shipped home to boarding school in England. Whatever the reason, in all the years of their marriage Michael had never used the word 'love', not even in the first heady days of their romance. It was almost as if he couldn't truly understand its meaning and was, therefore, unable to commit himself to a term he couldn't define. His reticence on the subject had warned her away from speaking of her own feelings for him, knowing it would bring down a wall of silence between them. She learned to look for actions rather than words. In every way, he was a loyal and caring man, a loving husband – but the expression of that love remained unspoken between them.

There was something about this lack of definition in their relationship that Jill had always found oddly acceptable. The bond between them was built on years of mutual respect, commitment, friendship, success and family life. Their partnership worked. She had recognised in him a strength and stability that could provide her with a secure and comfortable life. They each knew their role, and played their part well. No fuss. No hysterics. No ups and downs.

None of the passion she'd always felt for Simon. His kiss the other day, however lightly and innocently meant, had re-awakened old feelings she'd thought the years had let fade. He didn't know, of course. He couldn't. Their teasing, affectionate friendship had grown through liking, shared interest, and years of knowing each other well. It wouldn't occur to him to speak of love. He had no need to. Perhaps, like Michael, it was a word he never used. But whereas with her husband she had no wish to change their reserve about emotional matters, she found herself savouring the thought that one day she might speak freely of love to Simon. She dreamed of the moment, turning the dialogue over in her mind, rehearsing her speech and imagining his surprised, delighted reaction. It was a dream that warmed her to the very depths of her being. But it was only a dream.

She sighed, picking out yet another shirt from the ironing basket. How foolish and fanciful she was becoming as she slipped into middle age. Her children had flown the nest, her husband had his time and thoughts occupied by his demanding profession and a busy social life – and all the while, she was growing older. She felt useless and unattractive and superfluous. Glancing over towards the kitchen mirror, she stood the iron on its end and walked over to peer critically at the face staring back at her from the glass. Her skin was good, her hazel eyes bright and her neat trimmed cut made the most of her thick wavy hair and oval face. But round the eyes were crow's feet, deep ridges lined the sides of her mouth, and her cheeks and chin were definitely showing the effects of gravity. Running fingers through her cropped hair, silver glowed among the brown at her temples and along her fringe. In the mornings, her back ached. By evening, her big toe joint nagged with pain.

At gone fifty, she was almost through middle age. And if passion was what she'd missed in her marriage to Michael, who in their right mind would ever think of her as an object of passion now? No one. Certainly not someone as eligible and likable as Simon. He could have anyone he chose. So why had he never made a choice? Why was there no one sharing his life?

That question often occupied Jill's thoughts. Why had Simon never married? He was attractive, intelligent, sensitive, reasonably well off. She was aware of the glances many of their lady patients threw in his direction. She watched from the sidelines as he kindly defused their attention, disentangling himself in a way that never offended or embarrassed. Of course, there had been occasions when he'd chosen a partner to accompany him to this 'do' or that event – but it was always casual, always short-lived, never apparently more than friendly. Each time, Jill held her breath until he reappeared alone again. It was selfish of her to want him that way, but the thought of him falling in love with someone – anyone – was more than she could bear.

Moving away from the mirror she reached over towards the kettle and flicked on the switch before leaning up for the coffee and a mug. Staring absent-mindedly at the work surface, her thoughts returned to the other morning. She'd been shocked and disturbed to find Keith Ryder asleep in Simon's house. He seemed uncharacteristically oblivious to the dangers of such a situation. It was quite enough to have invited a patient to stay in his own home. That was professionally compromising in itself.

But Keith was gay, and HIV positive. And Simon was a single man, a bachelor. It didn't take much imagination to work out what people might think. Foolish, ignorant people, of course. But Simon was too intelligent not to realise how dangerous foolish gossip could be.

Steam billowed into her face as the kettle boiled. It was tempting to sit for a while with her cup of coffee, but the pile of ironing stared accusingly at her. Best get it done. Michael needed his evening shirt for their visit to the theatre that night. He looked extremely handsome in his dinner suit, a striking elegant man. How fortunate she was to be married to him. So many women would envy her!

Why, then, did she feel such emptiness gnawing away at the depths of her heart?

'Are you still here? I thought you'd have gone ages ago.'

Derek hadn't expected to find Julie still working at half past six when he finally made his way back to the office from his meeting with Martin Balcombe.

Smiling at him, she pushed her chair back and headed for the coffee pot which constantly simmered on a shelf in the corner. 'I wanted to know how you got on. How was it? Are we in with a chance?'

The expression on his face almost replied for him. 'It's a big job, a very big job. That's why we need it so much. It will take some organising for us to do it well. I'll have to take on quite a few new people, get the best possible team together.'

'Did he give you the impression the job's ours then?'

'Well, he's only the architect, of course, and hasn't got the final say. That's down to Gareth Walters and the council Building Committee.'

'But Martin has a lot of influence, hasn't he? And he's worked with you enough in the past to know they'll get the job done properly.'

Derek smiled knowingly as he took the cup of steaming coffee she offered him. 'Nothing official, of course, but he thinks we'll walk away with it.'

'Has he talked to Gareth then?'

'You know Gareth Walters. He's always got his own agenda. Whatever he says to your face, you can never be sure what he's really up to.'

'He didn't ring back, you know. I asked his secretary several days ago to arrange a meeting for you. I'll give her another call tomorrow.'

'Good girl, Jules. Sort it out for me. I really must get to see him as soon as possible, especially since Ken told me at lunch the other day that George Baskin has already been sniffing round.'

'Too big a job for him, surely?'

'I hope so, but he always did have eyes bigger than his ability to deliver.'

'But if he's been in to talk to Gareth . . .'

'. . . and Gareth isn't returning our calls about an appointment . . .'

Derek sat back in his seat, gulping down several mouthfuls of coffee before drawing a packet of cigarettes out of his pocket and lighting up. He leaned forward then, rubbing his eyes wearily.

'Tired?'

'Exhausted. I'll be glad when this job's sewn up, and I can just get on with it.'

Quietly Julie walked over to stand behind him, her voice soft as she spoke. 'You look like a man who needs his shoulders rubbed.'

He leaned back against her, closing his eyes with a sigh as his shoulders relaxed. For minutes he stayed perfectly still, luxuriating in the comfort of her gently massaging hands.

'How are things at home?'

He shrugged. 'The same. No, that's not true. They're worse. I found Annie cavorting round the floor with Keith's doctor the other night.'

'What? I don't believe it!'

'Doing something for the surgery, she said. Apparently, Keith offered to make up some cartoon posters for them.'

'He'll be good at that.'

'He's good at nothing. Good *for* nothing.'

'Derek, that's not true.'

'Look, don't you start! I get enough of this at home.'

'He's your son! He's ill. He needs your love and support. So does Annie.'

His eyes shot open, staring up at her as she stood behind him. 'Jules, I just can't. I know it's hard for you to understand, but I can't think of that person as my son. I've never seen anything of me in him. He's always been ill and delicate, into stupid girly pastimes like drawing and music. If I didn't know Annie better, I'd say his existence had nothing whatever to do with me.'

'That's ridiculous!'

His face grew suddenly bleak. 'Of course it is, but I still can't help the way I am.'

'But you do love him. I know you do.'

'I'm not sure what I feel. I'm not certain any more if I'm capable of feeling anything.'

'Can't you talk to Annie about it? She must be desperate, especially if you keep pushing her away.'

'That's nothing new.'

'What do you mean?'

He thought for a few moments before replying. Her hands were still on his shoulders.

'Keith was born twenty-eight years ago – and from the

moment he came into our lives he has been a wedge between Annie and me. The woman who had been my wife suddenly became a mother, and nothing else seemed to matter to her. Oh, I know I was busy too, building up the business in those early days – but you know, even though she'd worked in the office with me when I first began, she lost all interest when Keith came along.'

'But he was ill, wasn't he? He needed all her care, for a few years at least.'

'Well, he got it, and she's never stopped putting him first.'

Julie's hands began moving again, stroking his shoulders with barely moving fingers.

'I don't understand how she could be like that, with a wonderful husband like you. The marriage came before the family. A woman should always be a wife first. Otherwise, how can the family survive?'

'That's something I wonder about a great deal these days.'

Her fingers hovered again. 'Oh?'

'There really doesn't seem to be much left between Annie and me.'

'Oh, Derek, you poor man. I'm so sorry . . .'

'After all these years, I can't believe I've come to the point where I'm thinking I might be happier on my own.'

'You wouldn't be on your own.'

Again, his eyes looked up into hers. 'I wouldn't?'

'You've always been a wonderful friend to me, Derek. And if ever you need a shoulder to cry on, just remember I'm here for you.'

He held her gaze for a second or two before stretching up to cover her hand on his shoulder.

'I'll remember that, Jules. I certainly will.'

'And Alistair says if I practise a lot, I'll need a proper kit. A Manchester United shirt and everything!'

'Wow!' Christine smiled encouragingly at Robbie as his words tumbled out so fast he barely had time to draw breath.

'And he's going to show me how to be a goalie. He says I need to be a bit bigger to be a really good goalie, but because I'm strong, he still thinks I'll be all right. He tested my muscles and everything, and he says they're so good that when I grow up I'll be a really great footballer. Then I'll be rich, Mum, and I can buy you a red car that doesn't break down all the time!'

He stopped just long enough to insert a couple of sticky fingers into the tube of Smarties he was holding, then draw out a bright orange chocolate bean. Crunching it noisily between his teeth, his brow creased with thought.

'He's a brilliant kicker, Mum. I've never seen anyone kick a ball that high before. He says he's going to teach me all about foot control, only I need a proper pair of boots first. When can we go and get my new boots?'

'We'll have to see, Robbie. Boots are very expensive, you know.'

'But I've got to have them, Mum. Alistair says.'

'Well, Alistair doesn't have to find the money for them. I do. You must understand, Robbie, that I can't afford everything you'd like just because you want it. I have to save up for things, just like you do in your money box.'

Robbie's face fell. 'How long then? I need them now!'

'Sweetheart, I know how much you like football, and I promise I'll try and sort out a pair for you. But you can use your trainers in the mean time. I've seen how fast you run in those.'

'I can't kick though. How am I ever going to be a proper footballer if I haven't got the right boots?'

Just look what you've done, Alistair Norris! It's all right for you. You're educated and qualified, and earn a decent wage. What do you know about trying to make ends meet? It's nothing to you to whip up a little boy's trust and enthusiasm. Not so easy for me to pay for it all!

'Don't worry, Mum. I'll ask Alistair. He'll get me some boots. He knows what I need.'

'No! You mustn't ask him for anything. That would be very rude. Do you hear me?'

The little boy looked puzzled. 'He won't mind. Alistair never minds about anything. He's brill, Mum.'

She reached out to pull him into the circle of her arms. 'Yes, love, I know.' He *is* brilliant, she thought. He's funny and enthusiastic and encouraging. He's filled Robbie's head with ideas which will probably never come true. And he's filled my life with fun and affection and hope for something that can't ever be. He's from a different world, a well-off influential family. And look at me, a single mum who's hidden in a safe little shell for all these years.

She closed her eyes, burying her head in her son's soft hair that smelt of shampoo and chocolate.

Take care, Alistair. It would be so easy to hurt us. Please, take great care.

'You haven't forgotten the meeting tonight, have you?'

Patricia's head appeared round Alistair's surgery door just as the last patient was walking away down the corridor.

'Certainly not. I'll just clear up here, and be with you.'

'By the way, here's that number I promised you. David's an old friend. I'm sure he'll come up with something helpful.'

'Great! I'll ring straight away and join you in a moment.' Alistair turned to the phone, and dialled the number. For Lily Gordon's sake, he hoped this worked.

By the time he reached the others the tea was made and biscuits being handed round. Most of the team were there. Gerald and Patricia sat at the front of the room, with Simon and Jill deep in conversation by the window. Moira, Joan and Christine represented the reception staff, while midwife Wendy had just arrived along with the practice counsellor, Jackie.

'Right,' began Gerald, 'thanks for coming. There are quite a few matters we need to talk through together, and I know several of you have information you'd like to share with the rest of the team. However, the main topic needing urgent discussion is whether we should make a definite decision to expand our premises. I don't need to tell you how cramped we are at present. There's a desperate lack of examination rooms, and the nurses really do need a dedicated area of their own, bearing in mind the growing number of specialist clinics we run. And with Jackie now working here so often, it's simply not acceptable for her to handle delicate counselling sessions with patients when other members of staff have no choice but to march in and out for supplies all the time.'

Patricia took over at that point. 'The problem is that our patient list has almost doubled in number over the past two years, with all the new housing developments that have mushroomed up around Berston. And now, with the new city by-pass practically on our doorstep, we can no longer think of ourselves as a village practice, but as a service for a growing outer-city conurbation. If the population around us is growing, we must expand too. So, you've all had time to see the rough plans we drew up. What do you think about them? Any ideas?'

Conversation was lively and constructive. Half an hour later they had all agreed on the possibility of a two-storey extension into the car park area at the back of their building, which could house a couple of new consulting rooms, a quiet room which would be suitable for counselling and other sessions, a store cupboard, a new kitchen, and a shower room with toilet.

'Well, I'm pleased to report,' said Patricia, 'that we've been given the green light as far as funding is concerned. So the next step is for me to contact an architect. I only know of Robbins locally. Does anyone know anything about them?'

'I've played the odd round of golf with Martin Balcombe,' offered Simon, 'and I think he's the chief honcho there. Seems a nice enough chap. Do you want me to give him a ring?'

'Why not? Ask if he can pop over and take a look around, just for a general chat initially. Now, is there any other business?'

It was a full hour before finally the meeting broke up, and as people began to gather their bits and pieces together, Christine became of aware of Alistair at her elbow.

'I'm starving. Shall I pick up a Chinese and be at your place in half an hour?'

'I've got to go and get Robbie first. He stayed at his friend's for tea.'

'An hour then? Is that enough time for you to get him home and spruce him up for bed?'

'I don't want to put you to any trouble . . .'

'No trouble. It's a pleasure.'

It certainly is for me, she thought as he winked at her before walking away. I'm growing to like this too much – and it scares me.

It was half past eleven. Robbie was safely tucked up in bed as they sat in the glow of the gas fire, the remains of their Chinese meal strewn across the coffee table. They felt no need for conversation. With a tape softly playing in the background, they were stretched out along the settee, Christine's head resting snugly under Alistair's chin.

She felt his lips touch her hair, small light kisses that worked their way over her forehead and down the length of her nose. Then, catching sight of her expression, he stopped.

'Penny for them?'

'Perhaps they're not worth sharing.'

'Try me and see.'

When she didn't reply, he leaned his head down towards her until their lips touched. Then, as he drew back, he was surprised to see that her eyes had filled with tears.

'Christine, whatever's the matter? Are you OK?'

Embarrassment flooded over her. She pulled away from him, sitting up abruptly.

'I'm sorry. You must think me an idiot.'

'I think a lot of things about you. That isn't one of them.'

Rubbing her eyes hastily with her fingers, she didn't reply.

'What's wrong, Chris? Is it me?'

'No. There's nothing wrong with you at all. That's the problem.'

'Why?'

Her eyes became glassy again, as a note of despair crept into her voice.

'Because you're just wonderful. You're clever and good looking and . . .'

'I am?'

'. . . and Robbie adores you, and I . . .'

'. . . and you?'

Flustered, she dropped her gaze to her hands.

'And you, Chris? How do you feel?'

She looked straight into his eyes. 'Too much, I think. Far more than I should, and it terrifies me.'

He grinned. 'I don't think I've ever managed to frighten anyone before.'

'I don't mean you frighten me. I mean this whole situation does. You being here. All these cosy nights in with supper and firelight and soft music, and Robbie asleep next door. No one has ever wanted to be with us like this before, and it's bowled us over. But, Alistair, this isn't right for you, and I know that. You have such a wonderful life and career ahead of you, so I understand you're just passing through on your way up and out. And when you go, it will break Robbie's heart!'

'Only Robbie's?'

'Don't patronise me, please. I know I'm making a fool of myself. I shouldn't be saying any of this, but I'm not a lovesick teenager any more. I'm a grown woman, and a mum, and I just can't go through all that pain again, getting to know and want someone, then have them walk away without a backward glance. And I know you'll walk away in the end. Of course you must . . .'

He silenced her by taking her face in both his hands and looking deeply into her eyes.

'Chris, I'm not going anywhere.'

Her face was almost touching his. He could feel her shaking as he held her.

'Why not? I have so little to offer you. I'm not clever or sophisticated. Why would you want me?'

He kissed her then with gentle tenderness. 'You are the most beautiful person I've ever met. I noticed you the first day I arrived at the surgery, looking so efficient and neat in reception. I thought you were tough and organised – but you're not at all. But when I saw you with Robbie, and began to understand the reason for your toughness, I found myself wanting to making things better for you. I know you've been hurt. I know you're scared. I know that when Robbie's dad walked out, you felt you could never trust any man again. But I'm not just anyone, Chris. I'm here with you because I want to be. And I'm not leaving.'

She looked at him in sheer, stunned amazement, her eyes bright with fresh tears. Then she laughed. 'I told you I'm an idiot. Look at me! Over the moon with happiness, and all I can do is bawl my eyes out!'

Chapter Six

'Have you got a moment?'

Seeing what she thought was probably that evening's last patient leave Simon's surgery. Jill popped her head around his door.

'For you, always!' Simon stretched back in his chair, rubbing his neck wearily. 'Has this been a really long day, or am I just getting old and grouchy?'

'You're getting old and grouchy.'

He grinned. 'Only my best friend could tell me that.'

'Your best friend often opens her mouth without thinking first. I'm sorry about the other morning. I had no right to speak out as I did, in your own home too!'

He sighed. 'Jill, I know you're right. You usually are. I just hate the fact that my free time should be dictated by protocol. I like Keith Ryder. I feel immensely moved by his situation. He's a talented, sensitive, interesting young man, and anyone can see he's frightened and hurt by what's happening to him. Of course I respond perfectly professionally as a doctor – but on a different level, I can't help reacting as a human being too. Is that so very wrong?'

'Of course not. You are what you are, thank goodness.' She moved across to perch on the desk in front of his chair. 'Just take care though. You're too good a doctor not to understand how this might look.'

'Do you know, I really don't care what other people think. If they're so petty-minded that they don't know me better, I don't give a damn about them. But I *do* care about him.'

'Why? Why should this patient, among all the many others, matter so much?'

For a moment, a shadow fell across his face, a painfilled bleakness Jill knew she'd glimpsed on occasions in the past.

'Simon, what's the matter? Talk to me.'

He stretched out to push a stray wisp of hair away from her face, giving himself time to gather his thoughts before he spoke.

'One day, I promise I'll tell you. But not now.'

'What happened to you in those years when we lost touch? You went off to Cardiff, I know that much. Weren't you happy?'

'Mostly.'

'Was it work? Did you have some problem there?'

'Work was fine.'

'In your private life then? Did something happen that hurt you, something that haunts you even now?'

He didn't answer. She could see he was holding back some deeply-felt emotion.

'One day, Jill,' he said at last, squeezing her hand. 'Just don't give up on me. You're very special, more than you know.'

Before she had time to think, Jill leaned forward and kissed him. For seconds her lips touched his in a kiss that spoke of much more than friendship. She pulled back, appalled at her indiscretion, hardly daring to meet his eyes for fear of what she might see there. It seemed an age before he finally spoke.

'What about you? How are things at home?'

'Fine.'

'You and Michael getting on OK?'

Her only reply was a non-committal shrug of the shoulders. 'Jill?'

'What can I say? We muddle along. You'll never believe it,

but he's a good husband. I'm very fortunate, I know I am.'

'But you're unhappy.'

'I can't say that.' She looked directly at him. 'I just know I could be so much happier.'

'Jill, I . . .'

'I nearly forgot what I came in to tell you.' She got abruptly to her feet. 'Pauline Gregory, do you remember her? She and her husband, Dave, had trouble conceiving, and eventually had IVF treatment?'

'Lovely couple. Lovely baby too. How is she?'

'Pauline brought Naomi in for a check-up this afternoon.'

'And?'

'I think she may be deaf.'

'Oh no. Was there any response at all?'

'During the test, very little. Of course, there could be lots of reasons for that, but when I asked Pauline about it, she'd plainly been worried for some time about Naomi, thinking perhaps she was a slow developer. It hadn't occurred to her that the baby's hearing might be at fault. I'd like to have her properly tested though. I've made an appointment for you to see her in the week. I just wanted to have a word with you before they come in.'

'What a shame. They went through so much to have her, it would be a tragedy if anything went wrong after all the joy she's brought to them.'

'Right! Must go.' Her smile was distant and professional, hiding the tangle of emotions within her. 'See you in the morning.'

'Jill!'

She turned at the door. There was real tenderness in his expression as he called her.

'Thank you.'

This time her smile was warm and instant as, with a spring in her step, she disappeared down the corridor.

★

Joan put down the phone and glanced at the wall clock. Nearly half past ten. The queues in the waiting room were thinning out as the doctors worked their way through their lists for morning surgery. The phone started ringing again. She sighed as she reached for the receiver. 'If I don't have a cup of tea and at least three chocolate biscuits very soon, I'm going to keel over. This diet will be the death of me.'

'Well, brace yourself!' grinned Moira at her elbow. 'Here comes Dolly!'

The waiting room door flew open, and in waddled the portly figure of Dolly Williams, her beaming gappy smile stretching from ear to ear.

'Is he in? I've come for my hug.'

'He's with a patient at the moment, Dolly. Will I do?'

Alistair, who'd just wandered into the reception area, watched in amazement as Joan opened the door to the waiting room, holding her breath as she was enveloped tightly in vice-like arms, practically disappearing into the folds of Dolly's matronly bosom.

'Good Lord,' he whispered into Christine's ear, 'Do we all get that treatment?'

'Just Joan, Moira – and Simon, of course.'

'Is she ill? What's she come in for?'

'A hug. That always makes her feel much better, and it's cheaper than a prescription.'

At that moment, Dolly's beady eyes focused on Alistair. 'You must be the new doctor. Oh, what a sweetheart! Let me give you a hug!'

'Delighted, Dolly – but not now!' he mumbled. 'I've just got to . . . Well, I'm needed in the surgery.'

'Hang on,' yelled Moira, 'there's someone waiting to see you!'

She nodded her head in the direction of the familiar figure sitting in the far corner of the waiting room. It was Lily Gordon.

'Send her straight in to see me!' And with the sound of the

girls' delighted laughter ringing in his ears, he disappeared.

Knocking quietly on his door, Lily came in smiling and took the seat next to Alistair.

'Well, are you a little miracle worker or what!'

'Really?'

'It was a brainwave sending that David Watkins along to see me. Not my usual vet, of course, but what a nice man!'

'Was he able to help?'

'Gave Scamp a complete going-over. Well, he's almost twelve now, poor old chap. His hair keeps falling out, and his breath smells horrible – but that was the interesting bit. Apparently, his bad breath is all because of his teeth. Rotten, they are, and probably causing him a lot of pain which is why he wants to chew sticks all the time, like a baby teething.'

'So?'

'So Mr Watkins took them out, every last one of them. Now if he fancies fighting for my kindling sticks, the most he can do is stick his tongue out at me!'

'Lily, that's wonderful!'

'Apart from that he says Scamp's in quite good nick, and should see out a fair few years yet.'

'So your hands should be in good nick from now on too!'

'Barely a scratch on them – and all thanks to you.'

'I'm absolutely delighted.'

'And,' she began, digging into her voluminous shopping bag for something that was plainly hidden right at the bottom, 'because I can use them again, I knitted you this, just to say thank you.'

Alistair took the plastic carrier bag from her hand and peered inside.

'I hope it fits.'

Out of the bag came a thick, multicoloured bobble hat, obviously made from whatever remnants of wool Lily happened to have in her cupboard. With a grin, he popped it on his head. It was enormous. It covered his ears and most of his face too.

'Good!' she beamed. 'It's not too small then. I hate hats that are tight.'

Feeling that he could easily share it with a friend and there'd still be room left over, Alistair nodded enthusiastically, until he realised that brought the woollen rim completely down over his eyes.

'Thanks Lily. It's great.'

'Well, if you like it so much, I'll knit you gloves to match. I've got enough of that mauve left to do one at least. Hold out your hand, let me have a look at the size.'

She turned his palm over from one side to the other. 'Nice neat hands you've got. A sign of breeding, my mother always said. Must go. I'll be in touch!' And gathering up her bag, she bustled out the door with a wave that, if it wasn't for the hat, he might have seen.

Down the corridor, Simon's phone rang.

'I've done the posters.' Keith Ryder's voice was instantly recognisable. 'Can I drop them in tomorrow morning?'

'Wednesday. My day off. You could leave them at reception though.'

'Or I could bring them round to your house, if that's easier?'

Simon hesitated.

'Doc?'

'I'm here. It's just that I planned to disappear for the day tomorrow.'

'Fishing?'

'Weather permitting. I'm a fair-weather fisherman – hibernate at the first sign of winter.'

'Mind if I join you?'

'Fishing?'

'Sketching. That stretch of river where we met up the other week has always been a favourite of mine.'

What had Jill said? This is a patient, not a friend. And his response to that? Keith was a patient, yes, but also a young man who appeared to *have* no friends, not round here anyway.

'Fine, I'd be glad of the company. It would probably be best if I picked you up from home, say about half past nine, so I can take a look at the posters first. Mind you, that rather depends on your father. Call me a coward, but I really don't fancy meeting him that early in the morning.'

'No chance. He's always in the office by eight.'

'OK, see you then.'

Replacing the receiver, Simon remembered that some time that day he needed to see Jill. In fact, it wasn't until the end of the afternoon that their paths crossed.

'Here you are!' she said with a grin. 'A love letter for you! Someone left it at reception.'

The envelope was pale blue, with Simon's name scrawled in spidery letters across the front. He grinned. 'Certainly not a love letter, more likely a ticking-off. It's from Bert.'

Missed me, eh? I'm not surprised. Your roses are covered with greenfly and your lawn's cut far too short. What do you expect from youngsters who've hardly spent five minutes in the gardening business? When you get fed up with them, I'll come and sort you out. I won't even say I told you so — well, not much anyway. Thanks for the whisky. I'm not allowed to drink alone, doctor's orders. I keep falling over, and it hurts my back. Get in the ginger, and I'll bring the bottle.
   Bert

Laughing out loud, he handed the note over to Jill. 'I'm glad you popped in. I wanted to ask you about the Claymores. You and Michael know them quite well, don't you? Have you seen Debbie lately by any chance?'

'Funnily enough she rang Michael just the other evening, and I never got round to asking him why. I thought she sounded a bit upset.'

'Debbie did?'

'Yes, it was a bit odd, come to think of it. Why? What's happening?'

'I'm not quite sure. Nothing, I hope.'

'Is she ill?'

'Difficult to say really. Look, forget I asked. Perhaps I'll give her a ring myself.'

Jill eyed his distraction with curiosity. 'How are you?' she asked at last. 'Good day?'

'OK. Busy. And you?'

'I'm leaving a bit early tonight. It's our anniversary.'

His expression was faintly mocking. 'Well, that must be cause for celebration.'

'Don't, Simon.'

'How many years?'

'Twenty-eight.'

'Well, I have to say you carry the burden of living with that awful man extremely well.'

She got up abruptly, weary of the conversation.

'You're boring.'

'And you're terrific. Have a lovely evening.'

'You don't mean that.'

'Believe me, Jill, I never wish *you* anything but the very best.'

The posters were stunning. Their simplicity, humour and the lifelike expressions of the cartoon characters all added up to a display that was both eye-catching and informative. Simon pored over them with admiration, finally glancing across the table towards Annie.

'Talented son you have here.'

'She knows,' grinned Keith, 'I get it all from her.'

'In fact, these are so good I reckon we ought to copy them for circulation to other practices in the area. Would you have any objection to that?'

'None at all. Great!'

'I'll take them with me now. Just look at the time, nearly ten o'clock already!'

'Cup of coffee first, to help you on your way?'

'Those fish don't hang around, you know! We ought to get going, Mrs Ryder, but thanks all the same for the offer.'

'Annie – please call me Annie.' She was standing silhouetted against the French windows, autumn light picking out the gold in her hair. Simon returned the warmth of her smile.

'Thanks Annie. I'll look after him.'

'I know you will,' was her soft reply as Keith scooped up his sketching materials and followed Simon to the car.

It was Gerald who had shown Martin Balcombe around when he was first invited to take a look over their practice building. The two men had talked extensively about the limitations of the present premises and the initial suggestions for extension and improvement. Martin had then spent some weeks talking to individual members of staff, watching them work, taking their problems and thoughts on board. That morning he was to deliver the culmination of his work so far, the draft copy of his plans for the new building.

One by one, they filed into Gerald's office to look over the drawings, exclaiming over this good idea or that excellent feature. Martin stayed around long enough to answer queries and discuss concerns. By the end of the morning, he was more relieved than anyone that for the most part, reaction was favourable.

Patricia held out a cup of coffee for him as she came back into the office. 'Well, that seemed to go well. General approval all round.'

'So, what happens next?'

'Next,' said Gerald from his seat behind the desk, 'we get final agreement from the Local Health Authority, but I don't think there'll be any problem there because this facility is so badly needed. And as far as we can tell at the moment, there's no reason why everything shouldn't go ahead smoothly.'

'Right, I'll make up a final copy of these plans, with the few slight alterations suggested this morning, for you to submit as necessary. And then we must think about approaching the right builder.'

'Anyone in mind?'

'There are a few companies to choose from locally, some better than others. There's Baskins, of course, and Ryders.'

'Derek Ryder?'

'Do you know him?'

'Vaguely. Seems a nice enough chap.'

'He's good at his job, that's the main thing. If I had to recommend anyone, I think he's probably our man.'

'Who approaches him? You or us?'

'When you're sure you want to go ahead, let me know and I bring him over to discuss the project fully with you.'

'That's wonderful,' said Gerald, rising from his chair to shake Martin's hand. 'You've done a splendid job. We're very grateful.'

'I'll have the plans finished by the morning, all being well, and get them dropped over to you by four at the latest.'

And the moment Martin had gathered up the plans and left the office closing the door behind him, Gerald and Patricia fell into each other's arms for a hug of excitement and mutual congratulation.

When Derek's mobile phone rang, he was in the car heading for his long-awaited meeting with Gareth Walters. The Chairman of the Building Committee had proved very elusive when it came to pinning down an exact appointment. But today was the day and Derek was well prepared. He pressed the button on his phone and spoke into the remote mike just above the sun visor.

'Derek Ryder.'

'Martin here. Thought I'd ring you with a bit of news.'

'About Farthing Corner?'

'Afraid not. You haven't heard anything then?'

'Well, I might have more to report in an hour or two. I'm on my way to see Gareth now.'

'Really? He did mention on the phone the other day the contract will be out for tender very shortly.'

'This is only a first meeting, of course, and they probably don't realise how much I already know about the complexity of the thing from my discussions with you, but a proper chat with him will give me an idea what sort of budget and timescale they have in mind.'

'Well, good luck with that.'

'Thanks, I'll let you know how it goes. And your news?'

'You know Gerald and Patricia Bryant, don't you?'

'The doctors at the surgery?'

'I've just come back from there with drawings for the extension they're planning, which all looks very promising. Providing they get the go-ahead from the Health Authority – and they don't seem to think that's a problem – they plan to start building as soon as possible.'

'And we're in with a chance for the contract?'

'I recommended you.'

'Martin, I owe you one. Several thousand "ones", if we get the school contract too . . .'

'How well we understand each other . . .'

'I'll ring you later then, after I leave Gareth.'

And as the line clicked dead, a broad smile crept across Derek's face.

They laughed a lot that morning. It all started when Simon lost his footing on the bank and landed in an inelegant heap with one foot in the river. Quick as a flash Keith reached out, not to help Simon up, but to make sure the sandwich box was safely rescued – and suddenly they were both laughing like children. Then they settled down, one with a rod, the other with his sketchpad, sometimes chatting easily like long-time friends, sometimes sitting in companionable silence.

After an hour or so hunger set in. They broke open the Thermos flask and attacked cheese sandwiches, bags of crisps and a whole packet of chocolate Bourbons with ravenous enthusiasm. They swapped stories of childhood and news headlines and local gossip. They compared the worst winters they could recall, the most embarrassing memories of school days, their special fulfilling moments at work. They spoke of music and films and places they loved. And they never mentioned AIDS at all.

Simon felt a tug on his line, and for a few exciting minutes he concentrated on pulling in his catch, with Keith cheering encouragement at his elbow. When the fish which fought like an Amazon turned out to be a rather undersized trout, the two men looked into its eyes, then each other's – and threw it back in. It was the only sight of a fish they had all afternoon.

Each sat with his own thoughts for a while after that, until Simon became vaguely aware that the scratching of Keith's pencil on his sketchpad had stopped. Looking around, he smiled to see that in minutes Keith had fallen soundly asleep. The face that had just been alight with life and interest had crumpled and sagged in slumber, so that the gaunt lines, red blotches and dark shadows stood out starkly on his pale skin. In sleep, he had the look of an old man.

With professional efficiency, Simon quickly checked to make sure his pulse and breathing were normal, then laid a padded jacket gently over the silent form. Just as he turned back to re-thread his rod, he brushed against the sketchpad which had fallen unnoticed from Keith's hand. Staring out at him from the open page was a picture of himself – his face, his expression, his personality captured in light, skilful pencil lines. Looking at the drawing was almost like eavesdropping, catching a glimpse of himself as Keith saw him – a little older, a bit thinner on top, somewhat kinder than he ever imagined himself to be. Drawn with more affection and insight than strict accuracy, the image was curiously touching.

Simon reached out to tuck the jacket snugly round Keith's shoulders. But for the next few minutes, as he stared down at the slight sleeping figure, the image in his mind was of a different face altogether.

The evenings were drawing in. In a couple of weeks the clocks would go back, children would be trick or treating, and crowds would gather at bonfire parties on the fifth of November. Simon felt the chill as he walked down the long path from the Ryders' front door towards his car. Looking back to give a wave as he turned the key, an unexpected knot of emotion tightened inside him at the sight of Keith and Annie framed in the doorway. He was leaning against her, drawing support from her arm around his waist, head almost on her shoulder. Exhaustion was plain in the slump of his body, yet his face was alive with . . . what was it? Friendliness? Gratitude? The desperate longing for company that only the most lonely know? Yes, all of those – along with the isolation, stigma and resignation which all made their mark in the lines of Keith's face. And then there was Annie. Smiling as she waved goodbye, she turned to draw her son closer to her with fragile dignity that made Simon's heart lurch with pity.

The journey home took little more than ten minutes, but swinging into the drive he stopped the car abruptly, his mouth dry, breathing stilled. Someone was in the house. There was a light burning in the kitchen. And there shouldn't be.

He switched off the engine and got out, closing the car door as quietly as possible behind him. With cautious steps he covered the ground to the front door, silently turning the key in the lock, his heart pounding. The television was on. There was a faint stench of cigarette smoke. Whoever it was had made themselves at home. In seconds he'd covered the few yards to the kitchen door.

'Hello doc. I've started without you. Grab yourself a glass!'

With a grin, Simon did just that. Bert might be the most infuriating man he knew, but it certainly was good to have him back in his kitchen – and his hair – again!

Michael was late home that evening, not an unusual occurrence bearing in mind the number of committees he sat on. Jill had already taken herself off to bed with a cup of Horlicks and the last part of a thriller series on the television. The news was almost over before she heard his key in the door.

He didn't come up immediately, although he knew she was in. She heard him head towards his study, knowing that on the way he would have scooped up his mail from the hallstand. Some time later, her eyes heavy with sleep, she became aware of his footsteps on the stair before the bedroom door opened.

'Put the light on. I'm awake.'

'I read Jonathan's letter. Sounds like they're going to get that house after all.'

'I hope so. They've got their heart set on it.'

'Is my cream shirt ironed for tomorrow?'

'In the airing cupboard. Have you eaten?'

'I grabbed a sandwich at the club this evening before the meeting. I was with Matthew Benson, by the way. He sends his love.'

'That's nice. How's he enjoying being a local councillor? I'd have thought being a solicitor keeps him busy enough.'

'Apparently not. He seems to find time to squeeze in a few of the pleasures of life.'

'Pleasures?'

'Oh, you know Matthew, always had an eye for the ladies . . .'

'No, I don't know. What do you mean?'

Michael hesitated, looking directly at her for the first time since entering the room.

'Doesn't matter. Do you want a drink before you go to sleep?'

'Don't change the subject. What's Matthew been up to?'

He shrugged. 'Nothing much. Just a little problem I was able to help with.'

'A medical problem?'

'In a manner of speaking.'

'He's ill?'

'Not him.'

Jill looked at him steadily for a moment, her mind racing until the penny dropped.

'He's got someone pregnant.'

Michael was unbuttoning his shirt as he walked into the bathroom.

'It's sorted now.'

'You organised an abortion.'

'I was glad to help out a friend. Being in business is all about having friends.'

'And the girl? I assume it was a girl, because he'd never had the gumption to go for a grown-up. Did she have a choice?'

'She had exactly the same advice and options given to her that anyone visiting the clinic would have. Her decision was her own.'

'Did you see her? Was she all right?'

'Seemed to be.'

'Do we know her?'

He was cleaning his teeth. Perhaps he didn't hear.

'I'm leaving early in the morning,' he said, reappearing from the bathroom. 'Meeting in London.'

'Oh?'

'Quite interesting really. Do you remember James Turnbull? He was a couple of years ahead of me at Guy's?'

'I didn't know you two had kept in touch.'

'We haven't. He just rang me out of the blue a couple of days ago. Wanted a quiet chat, all very mysterious.'

'What's he doing now?'

'He's a big noise in the pharmaceutical world. Extremely well connected.'

'A job, do you think?'

'It must be.'

'Are you interested?'

His smile was slow and confident. 'You know me. Always up for bigger and better things.'

'I don't want to move again, Michael.'

'It may not mean a move.'

'If you're based in London, we'd have to.'

'For heaven's sake, Jill, I've no idea what the meeting's about. It could be nothing.'

'I'm happy here.'

'So am I, but let's keep an open mind, shall we?'

He pulled back the covers and climbed in beside her, leaning over to give her an affectionate peck on the cheek before snapping off the bedside lamp.

'Sleep tight, darling.' And rolling away from her, he was asleep in seconds.

But sleep eluded Jill as she lay stretched out on her back, staring towards the ceiling. She couldn't leave. She loved her home here. She loved her job. She loved . . . Deliberately, she stopped that notion in its tracks, although as Simon's image flashed ahead of her in the darkness another line of thought wormed its way into her mind.

Matthew Benson was a solicitor. Debbie Claymore worked in his office. It was a clearly distressed Debbie who'd rung Michael here at home just a few days before – and a plainly worried Simon had asked her about Debbie too. What a co-incidence – except that after years of living with Michael, she knew there was no such thing.

★

Derek was late home that night too, very late. The meeting with Brian Turner and Frank Bateman to discuss the various projects on which Ryder Construction was currently working had begun over a quick drink after work, eventually stretching to an Indian meal and several bottles of wine. He shouldn't have driven home, but then he shouldn't have drunk so much that he couldn't. Alcohol doesn't affect me as it does other people, he thought. I can hold my drink.

He let himself into the house and headed straight upstairs to the loo. To his surprise, the light was on and the door open. Keith was squatting in front of the toilet being violently sick. Derek reeled back at the sight and stench, clutching his mouth as nausea hit the curry already sitting heavily in his stomach. Staggering into the adjacent bathroom, he hung over the sink, grabbing the rim with both hands to steady himself. Some minutes later he slumped on to the edge of the bath, head down to quell the dizziness that engulfed him every time he tried to open his eyes. He felt rather than saw Keith come into the room. He heard the tap run and a glass being filled. And when Keith sat down beside him, Derek had nowhere to go, and no strength to move.

'You're disgusting.' His voice was filled with loathing.

'I'm ill. You're drunk. That makes you pretty disgusting too.'

'But by morning, I'll be back to normal. You were never normal. Never will be. You can't even support yourself. Why should you, when you can just laze around here and live off me?'

'You've no idea how much I'd love to be working. I hate being here, but I don't have a choice. You do! You're a grown man, and you're still getting drunk like a teenager! Whenever you drink too much, you always feel like this.'

'Oh, you had a choice too! I brought you up with everything. I gave you chances. I taught you right from wrong, and a fat lot of good it did you. You can't even decide if you're a man or a woman!'

Keith's head snapped round towards him, eyes blazing black in his deathly pale face. 'You'll never understand, will you! You're not capable of understanding that being gay isn't a choice, it's a fact! I can't be anything else. Nothing to blame, no one's fault – it's just what I am. I'm not stupid. It's got nothing to do with upbringing or schooling. It's not just to annoy you. This is nothing to do with *you*. Just me! I'm gay, and I'm not ashamed of it!'

Colour flooded into Derek's face as he tried to get up with his legs buckling beneath him. Hanging on to the door to stop himself swaying, he turned back to Keith.

'Well, you bloody should be!'

'Dad!' Keith's voice broke as he called after him. 'Dad, please! I need you! Please, *please*, don't keep turning your back on me! I love you, Dad – PLEASE!'

But the only response was the sound of the bathroom door slamming shut.

Chapter Seven

Alistair hated his digs. Mrs Briggs' fussy, pristine rooms and her rigid house rules hardly combined to create a homely atmosphere. He'd mused on the thought of moving, perhaps in answer to one of the adverts in the evening paper, but mostly the flats were miles away in Southampton, or they were looking for someone to share, and he honestly felt he'd had enough of gregarious living during his years of studying. What he really wanted was to buy his own place, put down roots at last – but much as he liked Berston his contract was only for a year, and beyond that the future was uncertain. He loved his work in the practice. He enjoyed being a doctor in this small community where names were starting to match faces, and patients become friends. Most of all, he was growing fond of the practice staff with whom he worked – their company, their banter, their patience and compassion with the frail, the frightened and the downright difficult. And then, of course, there was Christine. He smiled to himself as he walked down the road, his sports bag slung jauntily over his shoulder. Going to the gym was becoming a habit, a pleasant one in spite of his aching muscles and his left ankle weakened by an old football injury. At first he'd popped in for a visit just to get out of the house, but as he grew more confident on the equipment, and started to recognise other regulars enough to join them afterwards in the bar, he found himself looking forward more and more to his sessions there. With a friendly wave in the vague direction of a couple of fellow sufferers, he headed first for the treadmill. He always felt better once he'd got a mile or two under his belt.

'Sorry! I'm not going to last much longer on this, I can tell you! Give me a couple of minutes, and you can have it.'

The girl marching purposefully on the treadmill was a stunner, her dark hair scooped back into a pony tail caught in a tie that matched not just her poster-blue leotard but the exact hue of her eyes.

Alistair grinned. 'No hurry. I'll go on the multi-gym instead. That will hurt just as much!'

'Why do we do this?' she replied, with a smile that took his breath away.

'Because we meet a good class of people here. I'm Alistair Norris, *Doctor* Alistair Norris, so if you keel over I'm handy for a spot of resuscitation!'

'Actually, I think a lager would be nicer.' The speed of the treadmill slowed as she eyed him through long dark lashes. 'And I'm Wendy, by the way.'

'Well, Wendy, let's work up a thirst, then the lagers are on me!'

The phone rang in Simon's surgery.

'Hello. It's Annie Ryder.'

'Annie! How are you?'

'I'm fine, but Keith really isn't.' He could hear a note of despair in her voice.

'Has something happened?'

'Physically, he's going downhill all the time. We can all see that, and I know it's self-inflicted to a large degree. He doesn't take his medication unless I stand over him . . .'

'And without it, he must be feeling lousy, so his emotional state is rock bottom too.'

'That's the most heartbreaking of all. It's the depression that's killing him as much as anything and . . .' Her voice faltered. In the silence, Simon knew she was crying.

'I'll come round.' He quickly leafed through his bookings for that day. 'I've a clinic to do at eleven, then a few calls I must make. Yours can be the last – about three o'clock?'

'Oh, thank you.' Her relief was plain.

'Hang on, Annie. I'll be there as soon as I can.'

He thought she spoke again, but he didn't catch her words – and then the line went dead.

'He's upstairs.'

Simon eyed Annie with concern as he followed her into the kitchen. She looked worn out, her hair lank, her face drawn with fatigue and despair.

'Sit down,' he ordered. 'Have you eaten anything today?'

When she didn't reply he opened the bread bin, took out two wholemeal slices and dropped them into the toaster. He filled the kettle, pulled up a stool in front of the one on which she was sitting and took her hands in his.

'Annie, you can't look after Keith unless you take care of yourself. You look all in, and that won't help him.'

Closing her eyes to stem a fresh flow of tears, her head went down in forlorn defeat.

'What am I going to do? I love him so much. He's all the world to me. He's killing himself, and I can't do a thing to stop him.'

His voice was gentle in reply. 'The trouble is he's so wrapped up in his own pain and misery, he can't see the worry around him.'

'Can you talk to him? Can't you persuade him that his life *is* precious? That so much can be done with medication now-adays? He could live for months, perhaps years! He doesn't have to die. He *mustn't* die! Please Simon, don't let him! You're a doctor. You can save him!'

Her whole body was shuddering as she clutched his hands. To his surprise, the distress of this lovely woman moved him beyond words. He simply leaned forward and drew her towards him, until her head rested against his. There they stayed until the shuddering sobs subsided and she slumped in exhaustion.

'I promise you, Annie, I'll do all I can. In the end though, the decision is his. I've offered him everything. I've prescribed what he needs to deal with his symptoms, but it's up to him to take it.'

'We can't just stand by and watch him die.'

'We're not. We won't. But he has to work with us.'

'Then why won't he? For pity's sake, he can't *want* to die.'

'This is more about not wanting to live. He saw Ian through all of this. He watched someone he loved die of AIDS, and that's heartbreaking enough – but to know he's going to follow in the same way is simply unbearable. It's living with that knowledge that's so hard for him.'

Her whole body sagged in helpless frustration. At that moment, the toast popped noisily out of the toaster.

He tilted up her chin. 'I'm going to butter this toast for you, and sit you in the front room with a cup of tea while I go up and see Keith. Right?'

Her smile was watery, but her gratitude genuine. 'Right.'

Minutes later, with a cup in each hand, he pushed open the door of Keith's bedroom, which was filled with the rich tones of an orchestra accompanying what sounded like an all-male choir. Keith was stretched out on the bed, eyes closed, totally absorbed in the music around him. His appearance had changed considerably from the last time Simon had seen him. He looked thinner, his face gaunt, the Kaposi Sarcoma lesions standing out angrily on the skin of his arms and neck. As the doctor lowered himself down on to the side of the bed, Keith's eyes opened and he smiled, exposing the row of white ulcers that lined the edge of his swollen lips.

'I love this track.'

'Yes, but I don't recognise the singers.'

'It was Ian's favourite. He played this CD all the time. They're the New York City Gay Men's Choir. All these songs are not just dedicated to, but sung by people like Ian and me, people who've loved and lost partners and friends. We listened to this on the last day he spoke, three days before he died.'

Sometimes when we touch
The honesty's too much,
And I have to close my eyes and hide,
I want to hold you till I die,
Till we both break down and cry,
I want to hold you till the fear in me subsides . . .

'What about fear in you, Keith? Aren't you afraid of the way you're feeling at the moment? Let me do more to help you with the symptoms, ease the pain.'

The thin face turned towards him. 'You mean well. I know it isn't easy for you to deal with a patient who simply wants to die. Don't feel compromised by it, Simon. You're a good doctor, but be an even better friend. Let me die as I want to, with dignity. I'm not asking you to help me, simply let me do this my own way.'

'What does that mean?'

'I'm tired. I hurt everywhere. I miss Ian, God, I miss him so much! I've had enough.'

'And what about the people who love you, who are just as hurt to see you suffering like this as you were to watch Ian go through it?'

'My world's become very small. There won't be many people to cry beside my grave.'

'Your mum? What about her?'

Keith's expression softened. 'She doesn't understand.'

'I think she does. She just can't accept that her only son won't fight for the life she gave you. Keith, there are new advances in medicine happening every day. Who knows? If you take what's available now, allow yourself to live, perhaps next year they'll find a cure for this awful condition? Give yourself a chance! Surely Ian would want that for you. You have such talent, so much to live for. Don't throw it away!'

'With dignity. My own way.' Thin fingers gripped Simon's hand. 'Please, just see me through it – and hope the end comes soon.'

Derek emptied his coffee cup, with a last glance over his notes.

'That seems to be all then. I've studied Martin's plans of course, and everything seems quite straightforward. I'll have my people draw up a cost estimate in the morning and get back to you immediately.'

Gerald rose to show his visitor out, but with his hand on the doorknob, he turned. 'By the way, I was sad to hear about your son. Tragic news.'

'Thanks,' was the gruff reply, as Derek continued to repack his briefcase.

'How is he?'

'Fine.'

'I haven't treated him myself, of course. Dr Gatward is in charge of his case, so he's in the most capable hands.'

'Really?'

'Absolutely. And I know Simon's concerned that when one member of a family suffers from such a condition, the whole family is likely to be in need of support and advice.'

'Oh, he does, does he?'

'Correct me if I'm wrong, but Keith is your only son, I understand.'

'That's right.'

'This must be a dreadful sadness for you then.'

Derek snapped his case shut. 'Right, Gerald, we'll speak tomorrow.'

'I'll look forward to it. And please remember, Derek, if you and your family have any questions or concerns during this difficult time, you only have to . . .'

'Goodbye till then!' And without a backward glance, Derek strode from the surgery.

'Well, what do you think? I must accept, of course. It would be professional madness to turn down an opportunity like this!'

Michael picked up the letter for the umpteenth time, to read and reread the unbelievable offer it contained. Medical adviser to one of the largest pharmaceutical companies in the country, which was in turn a major player in the world market! They wanted him to oversee the marketing of a new line of anti-depressant drugs. His job would be to publicise the product to the general public, and promote an image which would appeal to them so much that patients would ask their doctors for it by name.

'This is a wonderful opportunity for us!'

'For you,' corrected Jill.

'Just look at the salary!'

'Money isn't everything.'

'You could have the sort of house you've always wanted.'

'I've got the house I've always wanted, and a job I love too. Michael, I know you're over the moon about this, and you're right to feel very proud they've asked you – but I can't pretend I'm as happy about it as you are.'

'Darling, just think about it – the people we'd meet, the circles we'd be moving in. You'd love it, I know you would.'

'Then you don't know me at all!'

'I must ring Gordon and tell him. He'll have to find someone to take over my role at the clinic. And whoever would be acceptable to Roxborough's after me? They'll be furious to hear I'm leaving. They had to work so hard to get me to join in the first place.'

Jill watched as he picked up the phone, punching in a number. Then she grabbed her car keys from the hook, reached for her jacket and walked out of the house knowing he simply wouldn't notice. Driving off at speed, she was more than a mile away before it struck her she had no idea where she was going. It wasn't until she pulled up outside Simon's door that she realised she'd known all along.

The house was in complete darkness. He wasn't home. Choking back her disappointment, she dug into her bag for her mobile and tapped in his number. Relief flooded through her as she finally heard him answer.

'Simon, it's Jill. I need to talk to you.'

'Of course. Can we meet up at the surgery early in the morning, if it's urgent?'

'No, now! I need to talk now!'

'For heaven's sake, Jill, whatever's wrong? You sound dreadful.'

'Things are happening at home. I need a friend.'

'Well, that's me! Only thing is I can't come just at the moment. I'm with a patient.'

'Where? Will you be long?'

'Byron Close.'

'You're with Keith?'

'Yes, and Annie. They're both rather upset.'

'His mother? You're on first-name terms now, are you?'

'Don't be like that, Jill.'

'You're getting too involved, Simon – and I'm sorry I disturbed you. See you tomorrow. Goodbye.'

And before he could say another word, she cut the line dead and switched off her phone.

Simon still hadn't managed his chat with Jill the following morning when Pauline Gregory sat across the desk from him, her small daughter cuddled up on her lap. At his words, tears sprang to Pauline's eyes. Burying her head in Naomi's soft golden curls, she was unable to speak, but simply drew her baby close as if to protect her from the implications of the news she'd just received.

'Look, this doesn't have to be as bad as it sounds. The General Hospital has a first-class reputation for dealing with deafness, and they can do so much nowadays. And as Naomi's still very young, her youth and health work in her favour.'

'It's just so unfair, after all we've been through.'

'Yes, but at the moment, we don't know exactly what the problem is. It depends on the cause. As I said, it doesn't look to me as if it's a conductive problem, which would probably be glue ear. That means the cause may well be neuronal, suggesting some nerve damage to the inner ear so that sounds aren't being transmitted to the brain. The important thing now is for Naomi to see the consultant at the General, let them run a few more tests and find out exactly what's happening.'

'We waited years. We went through all the indignity of fertility treatment. It nearly broke our marriage, do you know that? And then that unsuccessful IVF treatment which got our hopes up only to dash them again, and finally the wonderful moment when we heard Naomi was really on the way.'

'She's beautiful, Pauline.'

'I can't bear the thought she's different. You know what kids are like. They'll laugh at her if she's not like them, if they see she's got something wrong with her.'

'This has been a great shock to you, I know, but you're panicking more than you need. Now, when's her appointment at the General, did you say?'

'Next Tuesday.'

'They'll write to me fairly quickly after that – but why don't you book yourselves in to see me on Wednesday, so we can talk over what happened?'

She nodded, running her fingers through Naomi's hair. 'You must think I'm a real wimp. I just can't take it in.'

'Perhaps you don't need to at the moment. Seeing the consultant is simply a precaution. Try not to worry too much.'

'Easier said than done.' She struggled to smile as she gathered together baby and handbag and got to her feet. 'Thank you, doctor. I'll see you next Wednesday then.'

Simon followed her out of the door, but turned in the opposite direction down the corridor towards the nurses' room. Good, Jill was there and alone. He shut the door behind him as he walked in to join her, noting her guarded expression as she turned to greet him.

'Are you all right? I tried to ring you back last night.'

'It didn't matter.'

'But you sounded so upset. What happened?'

'Nothing worth talking about now. Did you want something?'

His expression was grim as he handed her a letter. 'Have you seen this, or do you know about it anyway?'

The wording was curt and formal. The letter was headed with the address of the Elmside Clinic in Southampton, where Dr Michael Dunbar was proudly listed as senior medical consultant. It simply stated that a patient of Dr Simon Gatward, Miss Deborah Claymore, had undergone a termination of pregnancy at the clinic, that everything had gone smoothly, and she had returned home the same day.

'She didn't want to have an abortion, Jill. She made that very clear to me. She intended to come back to talk over her options, and I was very concerned when she didn't make another appointment. That's why I asked you about her the other day.'

Jill nodded, still staring at the letter.

'She told me the father was a married man, someone she worked with. Did Michael know that? Did he organise a nice convenient abortion, because her pregnancy was an embarrassment to a pal of his? Is that what happened?'

'I have no idea.'

'But isn't that just the sort of favour Michael would be glad to arrange, seeing he's such a useful man to know?'

She sighed wearily, handing the letter back to him. 'I don't know. This is all news to me.'

'Really?'

'Anyway, she's twenty. She's a grown-up. She'd have been offered professional counselling at the clinic. The decision must have been her own.'

'So how come she's been in my surgery in tears this morning, overcome with guilt and depression?'

'Is she OK?'

'Depends what you mean. She feels she's compounded one mistake with another. It's clear that tremendous pressure was put on her, and eventually she gave in. She had a termination which was against her wishes and her principles.'

'Michael only pops in there a couple of times a week. He probably didn't know anything about it.'

'He handled the whole thing personally, even did the operation himself. That's why she rang him at home the other night. It had to be discreet because he was doing it as a favour for one of his business cronies, wasn't he?'

Jill's face was flushed as she snapped out a reply. 'Look, I don't know why you feel you have a monopoly on the moral high ground! It's done now. She'll get over it. Why can't you?'

He stared at her coldly.

'How strange. You were always the one person I thought would understand, because your instincts and ethics are the same as mine. I see now that you're a better partner for Michael than I ever realised.'

As the door banged behind him Jill steadied herself against her desk, sick with shock at the look of contempt and dismissal she'd seen in the face she'd held so dear for so long.

'More roast potatoes?'

Ivy needn't have asked. Bert was already helping himself

not only to another huge mound of potatoes, but two more Yorkshire puddings as well.

'It's so nice to cook for someone who enjoys his food. Fred was never a big eater, you know. He was always complimenting me on my cooking of course, but he never did it justice.' She sighed. 'Oh, I *do* miss him. Such a very upright man, God rest him. Had principles. I never had a moment's worry with him.'

Bert nodded, his mouth too full to answer.

'Always concerned for me, he was, couldn't do enough. I could tell in those last few days, he wasn't scared for himself, just for me. He was in turmoil thinking I'd never be able to manage without him to look after me. Such a wonderful husband was my Fred.'

There was another nod from Bert, who was preoccupied with the tricky problem of gathering freshly-popped peas on to his fork.

'Not an hour goes by when I don't think of him, may he rest in peace.' She sighed sadly to herself, her gaze fixed on some invisible image in her mind. 'And he always used to say, "Ivy, if anything happens to me, you'll need someone to look after you. I'd never rest in my grave if I thought you weren't cared for." What a wonderful thing to say? Don't you think that's wonderful, Bert?'

'Wonderful!' was the compliant reply, as Bert deflated a gravy-laden Yorkshire with a stab of his knife.

'He'd want me to marry again. He wouldn't want me to be alone.'

'Hmm.' Bert's grunt could have been addressed to her, or perhaps it was simply an expression of pleasure as the Yorkshire hit his palate.

'Do you ever think about marrying again, Bert?'

That question did stop him in his tracks. His fork hung in mid-air.

'Never got on much with marriage.'

'How long were you together, you and your wife?'

'Three years.'

'And why exactly did she leave?'

'Market gardener up the road. He was filling more than her freezer. Came to nothing of course. Left her six months later for a farmer's wife in Hambledon.'

Tutting sympathetically, she leaned forward to lay a comforting hand on his arm. 'How dreadful for you, you poor man.'

'Not dreadful at all. Never liked her much anyway.'

'So why did you marry her?'

'Can't remember now. Oh yes, I can. She had a car.'

'And that was it?'

He grinned. 'Afraid so.'

A rebuke was on the tip of her tongue, but she thought better of it and sniffed daintily instead.

'All worked out OK in the end though. She left, and I kept the car.'

A few minutes' silence followed, during which he munched his way through the remains of his dinner and she traced an outline with her index finger round the embroidered flowers on the tablecloth.

'So that's put you off the whole idea of marrying again then, has it?' she asked at last.

He looked at her with mild surprise. 'No.'

'Really?'

'Haven't ruled it out. Haven't thought about it. Who'd have me anyway?'

Her smile was sweet and sincere. 'Now, how do you like your crumble? With tutti-frutti ice cream – or homemade custard?'

It was much later, as they sat in front of the television, a card table between them on which were balanced a plate of sponge fingers and two delicate bone-china mugs of tea, that she brought up the subject of marriage again.

'Your friend, Dr Gatward? He never married, did he?'

Bert's mind was on *Home and Away*. 'No,' he replied, eyes not leaving the screen.

'Funny that, a good-looking man like him.'

Bert didn't seem to think a reply was needed. Reaching for another sponge finger, he settled himself more comfortably in the chair.

'OK, is he?'

He turned to her then. 'Yep. He's fine.'

'Bert, I'm not talking about his health. He's obviously *fine*. What I mean is, is he OK?'

He looked at her blankly.

'Only,' she continued, picking her words carefully, 'he's been seen lately.'

'Seen?'

'Down at the river the other day. And of course, we saw them at the summer fete too, don't you remember?'

Bert plainly didn't.

'With that young man, you know, the Ryders' boy – the one with AIDS.'

'Oh, him! They're friends. I've seen him at Simon's house. They know each other.'

'Really?' She picked a minuscule piece of dust off her skirt. 'Now, why ever should those two be friends? An odd relationship, don't you think?'

His gaze went back to the television screen, as if he'd stopped listening – not that that mattered to Ivy.

'How old is the doctor? Fifty? And that boy's only in his twenties. What would they have to talk about? Unless, of course, it's not talk they're interested in . . .'

Still no response.

'All I can say, Bert, is that if he's your friend, you ought to have a word in his ear. A single chap like him – and a gay young man. People will talk. Someone even mentioned it down at the Eventide Club last Friday. You ought to tell him.'

Bert looked at her sharply. 'Lovely cup of tea you make, Ivy. Any more in the pot? And I wouldn't say no to one of your cup cakes either.'

★

Derek was on the phone to Brian at the Acorn Grove site when Julie looked in at his door.

'Gareth Walters calling for you on line two.'

Hurriedly hanging up on Brian, he waved his crossed fingers at her as she smiled and closed the door behind her.

'Derek,' Gareth began, 'could you manage a little get-together some time this week? Nothing formal, you understand. Perhaps a drink one evening?'

Derek's grin was broad, his voice calm.

'This week? I'm quite tied up, I know. Let me just check with my secretary.' He clicked the line back to Julie.

'Jules, what have I got coming up? Any meetings booked for later this week?'

'None at all. Quite a slack time really.'

He clicked back to Gareth. 'Tonight's out, I'm afraid, and my secretary tells me the end of the week is particularly busy. Tuesday looks like the only option. Would half past six in the King's Head suit you?'

'Somewhere a little more out of the way perhaps? The Bull Hotel around the same time?'

'I'll see you there. And Gareth? Do I need to bring anything?'

'That's entirely up to you. Until tomorrow night then.'

Derek hurried through to the other office the moment he put the phone down. Julie was standing by the coffee machine pouring out a cup for each of them, when he grabbed her by the waist and pulled her into his arms to dance round the floor with him.

'We did it! We did it! We did it!'

'We've got the job?'

'He hasn't said so in so many words, but he wants to meet up. And he insisted on somewhere discreet. What else could that mean? The job's ours, and he wants to know what's in it for him.'

'That's wonderful!'

'Isn't it just! About time things started looking up for us.'

'You deserve that, Derek. No one could deserve it more.'

He stopped twirling to look down at her as she stood breathless in his arms, face alight with excitement and affection. For one surprising moment, it occurred to him to bend his head and kiss her full on the lips. They stared at each other with matching smiles of delight and partnership – and the moment passed. Instead he planted a peck on both her cheeks and hugged her to him – so he never saw the look of disappointment that flashed across her face for just a second, then was gone.

'Well? Is that what happened?'

Michael's expression didn't change one bit as he returned her glare. 'Jill, I really don't understand what you're so upset about, and frankly I find this a bit tedious. Yes, Debbie came to see me. Yes, she agreed that a termination would be best. And yes, I performed the operation myself. So what?'

'And it was Matthew Benson who was the father?'

'It really wasn't my place to ask. Maybe not. She works in his office, you know. Perhaps he was just taking a fatherly interest.'

'Oh, I think a fatherly interest was the very last thing he had in mind.'

'For heaven's sake, Jill, why should you care anyway?'

'Because Debbie Claymore is the daughter of a family we know as friends. Because she had made it quite clear to Simon that she wasn't happy at all about the idea of an abortion. She intended to keep her child but with your help Matthew changed her mind. And this morning, that poor girl was back in the surgery desperately unhappy, in floods of tears.'

Michael's laugh was hollow and derisory. 'Oh, I might have known Saint Simon would have his nose in here somewhere. So he objects, does he? Once again, I'm the villain of the piece, tying the poor innocent girl to the operating table, forcing her baby away from her against her will! Her pregnancy was nothing to do with her, of course. She was just a victim in all this, and I'm Dr Death! Is that really what you think of me, Jill? Is it?'

She sat down heavily, elbows on the kitchen table, head in hands. 'I don't know what to think.'

'You think I have no scruples, because Simon says so. And whatever Simon says is gospel to you. Tell me, Jill, how come you married me? If it was always him you wanted, why did you settle for less? I'll tell you! You married me because he didn't care enough to ask you, and I could offer you the lifestyle you coveted. And you've got it, haven't you. Look around you. Big house, money in the bank, friends that matter! You've got it all. And what's he got? An empty house, an empty bed – and a clear conscience! Well, he's welcome to it. And he's welcome to you too, if that's what you want!'

If he said more, Jill didn't hear it. Slowly, deliberately, her face pale, she rose from the seat and walked wordlessly from the room.

Chapter Eight

Derek was deliberately late arriving at the Bull. It wouldn't do to appear too keen, too available. In fact, he was parked on the road outside the hotel early enough to see Gareth's car pull into the driveway. He listened to the radio and watched the digital display on his dashboard count out ten whole minutes before he switched on the engine and drove up to the entrance.

Gareth had chosen a quiet corner tucked away at one end of the lounge bar. He didn't rise to greet Derek who, understanding the unspoken agreement for discretion, sank silently into the high-backed chair beside him.

'Gareth, nice to see you. How are things?'

'Busy time, as I'm sure you'll appreciate. We've got several contracts on the go at the moment. Plenty for me to keep my eye on.'

'Drink?'

'Thank you. Another whisky would go down well.'

Derek signalled to a hovering waiter, who promptly returned minutes later with two matching doubles.

Gareth downed what was left in his first glass and cleared his throat.

'I wanted to have a quiet chat with you before the end of the month when the tenders are due in. Are you quite clear about what's required: the budget, the timescale, the sensitive politics surrounding this school project?'

'I think it's all pretty clear. To complete in time for the start of the academic year in September will be a tall order, of course, and the budget's far too tight – but I would say that, wouldn't I? As for the politics, well, I understand that to get the new school built will be a major feather in the cap of this council. I imagine a few of the councillors' seats will depend on it. But then, Gareth, I've never been in the business of overrunning on contracts, either on time deadlines or price. If I say we'll do it, we'll do it as planned. You know me well enough to know I'm reliable.'

'It's a big job. You'll need to take on more men.'

'That goes without saying.'

'Skilled men, mind. The quality of work is paramount. That's what will swing the committee when it comes to making a decision.'

'That, and of course you, Gareth. I realise your opinion counts for a lot, and quite rightly so.'

'And you must expect real competition for this contract.'

'Naturally.'

'It's attracted interest from some very capable companies.'

'Like who?'

'Well, it would be indiscreet of me to name names . . .'

'Absolutely, but I hope you will anyway.'

'A couple of the big boys from Southampton . . .'

Derek's eyebrows shot up.

'But because employment is a hot issue round here, we probably would prefer to choose a local contender.'

'Wilkinsons?'

'Possibly.'

'Baskins?'

'Probably.'

'And how do we fit in?'

'Very nicely, I should think.'

'So what are you saying? That we're in with a chance? You'll put your weight behind us?'

'I can't say anything at all. You know that. I just thought an idea of the competition might be helpful to you.'

Derek sat back in the chair, took a swig from his glass and eyed Gareth thoughtfully. When he finally spoke, it was to change the subject.

'How's the family?'

Gareth's face lit up with pride and affection. 'Nice of you to ask. They're fine. Well, Carole has had a few back problems lately, not to mention the extra headache of organising Mandy's wedding. The beginning of December is a funny time to have a wedding, if you ask me – but then, no one asks the father of the bride for his opinion, just his cheque book.'

'A stressful time.'

'It certainly is.'

'Expensive too.'

'You can say that again.'

Derek leaned down to his briefcase, from which he carefully drew out a large brown envelope.

'I brought this for you. Our new catalogue. It might interest you. And there's a little something extra in there too. A small personal thank-you for your support and encouragement, with my best wishes to you and your family.'

'How very thoughtful! Thanks.' Gareth slipped the envelope into his own case without opening it. 'My, is that the time? Must fly. Carole's invited Mandy's future in-laws for dinner this evening.'

'Who's she marrying? Do I know him?'

Gareth hesitated for one moment. 'I don't think so. Mark comes from the Brighton area. Nice family though, with local connections.'

'Well, I hope it all goes well, Gareth. And our tender will be in on time at the end of the month, you can rest assured of that.'

'And you understand, of course, that this meeting never took place.'

'What meeting?'

They didn't shake hands. Gareth simply rose and left, and it wasn't until he reached the safety of his car that he opened the envelope. What a pleasant surprise! Inside was a sealed white package containing a bundle of crisp fifty-pound notes, two thousand pounds in all. With a grateful smile he started up the car and headed for home.

The phone hadn't stopped ringing all morning. The waiting room was packed, the weather outside awful, and Joan had a headache – all of which contributed to the rather curt response she gave to the telephone caller who was lucky enough to get through to the surgery in spite of the mayhem.

'Hi!' said a light, very girly voice at the other end of the line. 'Can I speak to Alistair please?'

'Alistair?'

'Sorry, I mean Dr Norris.'

'I'm afraid he's in surgery. Do you need an appointment?'

The girl giggled. 'Not for his surgery! No, I'll be seeing him tonight anyway. I just need to talk to him first. Can you put me through?'

Joan shot a glance across at Christine, who was sitting with her back to the reception area, facing her computer screen. Joan's lips pursed with disapproval as she spoke again.

'He's busy now. Can I give him a message?'

'Just ask him to call me, would you? It's Wendy. He knows the number.'

Does he now? Joan's thoughts were murderous.

'I'll tell him.' Oh, I most certainly *will*! 'Goodbye.' And she slammed down the phone, only for it to start ringing again. Joan ignored it. Walking over to Moira who was sorting out appointment bookings at the counter, she hissed urgently in her ear. 'We need a cup of coffee and a chat. Half an hour's time in the back room? You'll never believe the phone call I just had!' Moira took one look at her friend's stormy expression and knew she'd be bursting with curiosity for the next thirty minutes.

Simon had a full house that morning. The coming of the winter months had brought the usual batch of flu, sickness and bad chests, as patient after patient came in snuffling and wheezing from the virus they were probably all sharing and spreading. His last appointment was without doubt his most taxing. He'd known Janet Wharton ever since he'd joined the practice, both before the birth of young Sam just over four years earlier and during her pregnancy with twins Janie and Timmy, who had recently celebrated their first birthday. Janet always cheered him up, with her ready smile and good humour. She'd taken to being a mum as if she'd been born for it, and to meet her and her youngsters was always a pleasure. Today, though, there was no smile. She looked pale and worn out, as she balanced a twin on each knee, and tried in vain to keep the ever-curious Sam under control.

'How does this work?' Sam asked, plonking two sticky fingers on the only key he could reach on Simon's computer. It was the Delete button. Instantly, all the records relating to the family, which Simon had taken minutes to access, disappeared from the screen.

His mother was mortified and profuse in her apologies, plainly close to tears. Simon eyed her with concern. Something was badly wrong here. Janet wouldn't usually react so extremely when children were simply being children.

'You see what I mean?' she was saying. 'I just can't control him. He's on the go all the time, into everything, meddling, fiddling, arguing, asking questions . . .'

'He's an inquisitive, intelligent little lad, I can see that.'

'Look, I don't know what hyperactive really means, but I think it's the right word to describe him. He's wearing me out! Could it be what I'm feeding him? Might he be allergic to something? I'm at the end of my tether. He's driving me mad!'

At that moment Janie, who had been sitting quietly on her mum's lap, pulled a sticky sweet out of her mouth and dropped it on the floor in front of her. It was in Sam's hand, and popped into his mouth in no time. Appalled that his big brother had beaten him to it, Timmy started to wail.

Simon picked up the phone. When Jill answered, he asked if she could help out by taking charge of three noisy youngsters just for a minute or two? Without hesitation she agreed and within minutes Sam and the twins were whisked away to explore the rest of the building.

'Now,' said Simon, the surgery blissfully quiet after their departure, 'how are *you*?'

She sighed, her fingers intertwining nervously as she spoke. 'I'm OK. Tired, that's all.'

'Are you sleeping all right?'

'Sometimes.'

'What's keeping you awake? The children?'

'No, they're quite good these days. Sam never wants to go to bed, of course, but once I've got rid of him, about ten o'clock usually, I just conk out.'

'But you don't stay asleep.'

'I always seem to wake up about one, and then lie there for hours.'

'Why? Are you worrying about something?'

She didn't reply.'

'Janet?'

'I've found a lump . . .'

'On your breast?'

'It seemed to come from nowhere. I mean, I'm used to having lumpy breasts, what with feeding the twins for so long, but I just didn't notice this.'

'There's probably nothing to worry about. Most lumps on

the breast are quite benign. Let me take a look, and perhaps I can put your mind at rest.'

'I've been really frightened. The kids are so young. How could they ever manage without me? Malcolm would go to pieces if there were anything wrong with me . . .'

'Janet, you're worrying too much too soon. But let's check it over, just as a precaution.'

'My mum died of breast cancer, did I tell you that? And my elder sister had a lump removed just a couple of years ago.'

Simon's express didn't change, but those two facts were immediately logged. Minutes later after a thorough examination he gently explained that he was arranging an immediate appointment for her with the consultant surgeon and consultant radiologist at the General Hospital Breast Clinic. 'They'll explain all the possibilities to you, and arrange for an x-ray and ultrasound. Then they'll write to me with the results, and we can take it from there.'

Her eyes were huge and shiny with unshed tears. She picked nervously at one of her nails as she tried to take in what he was saying. Gently he helped her to her feet, then with his arm around her shoulders, they both walked down the corridor to the nurses' room where Jill was just coming to the end of the story she was reading to Janet's youngsters.

'Come on,' said Jill kindly, 'I'll help you out to your car.'

'Thanks, Jill,' whispered Simon as she passed him. 'There are a few things we need to catch up on. Can you come in and see me when you've finished?' She nodded as the small group made their way towards the back door.

When she finally joined him she was carrying a couple of cups of coffee and a packet of biscuits. He looked at her carefully, noting the dark circles under her eyes.

'Are you OK?'

'A bit tired, that's all.'

He gazed at her for some seconds before coming round to the front of the desk to stand close beside her.

'And what else?'

'Nothing else.'

'Jill, I've known you a long time, long enough to know when something's worrying you.'

'It's nothing you can help with.'

'Try me.'

'It would take too long.'

'Then we'll make time. How about this evening? Have you got any plans?'

'A hot date with the washing machine.'

'Well, before you start, how about a drink? Could you manage that?'

'What? In a pub?'

'That would be OK, wouldn't it? Or would dear Michael object to two colleagues having a drink together after work?'

She closed her eyes to block out his words, then turned away from him.

'Oh, I see. It's about Michael, is it? We mustn't be seen gossiping about him in public.'

When she didn't answer, something in the sag of her shoulders made him gently pull her back round to face him.

'You're crying. I've never seen you cry before.'

She laid her face against him so that her voice was muffled by the rough fabric of his jacket.

'Can I just pop round and see you at home? Straight after work? I'd feel safer talking there.'

'Of course, my love. Jill, I've never seen you so upset. What can I do to help?'

'What I'd like you to do would probably be no help at all. I'll see you about six.' And he watched after her as she slipped from his grasp back to the safety of her room.

It was a couple of hours later when Simon headed out on his rounds. As part of Alistair's GP training he had asked the younger doctor to accompany him. In particular he planned to introduce him to Mr and Mrs 'Martyr to her Joints' Brown. Hetty Brown's insistence on regular home visits from Simon was becoming unreasonable and inconvenient, and it had been decided within the practice that the load should be shared among the three doctors. As Alistair wandered into the reception area to collect Harry and Hetty's notes, he found his way barred by a stormy-looking Joan.

'Here's a message for you. She said she'd see you tonight, and you'd know her number.'

Alistair glanced down at the scrap of paper to see Wendy's name, and grinned.

'Oh great, thanks!'

It was on the tip of Joan's tongue to demand who she was, and what *exactly* was he up to, when he moved over quickly to whisper in Christine's ear as she sat at the computer.

'Hiya gorgeous, how are you?'

She turned, face alight with the pleasure of seeing him.

'You've got that school meeting this evening, haven't you,' he went on, 'so I'll try and give you a ring later. Otherwise, are you still all right for tomorrow?'

'Looking forward to it. Are you sure Simon doesn't mind me tagging along?'

'Not at all. There's quite a group going, I think, so everyone's welcome. Events like this are usually well-supported because they're in aid of the Hospital Appeal Fund. I reckon you'll know quite a few people when you get there.'

'What do I wear? Is it a posh affair?'

'Smart casual, that's what Simon says. I think that's a nice way of telling me not to wear my jeans.'

Her eyes flashed flirtatiously. 'Well, I think you look very tasty in jeans . . .'

'Do you now? I'd like to hear more about that . . .'

'Ready, Alistair? I'll meet you out by the car!' Simon's voice cut into their conversation.

'One minute! Just need to update this patient's notes!'

Alistair looked businesslike as he reached for a surgery notepad, and drew out a pen from his pocket. His face serious, he wrote something she couldn't quite see then folded the paper and handed it to her.

' 'Bye then,' he said cheerily, ignoring the meaningful look exchanged between Moira and Joan as they watched Christine carefully open the note. 'To be continued . . .' it read. 'Miss you till then!' It was signed with a heart and two kisses. The contentment on her face was unmistakable, while the concern on the matching faces of her two older colleagues was totally lost on her.

'Going out tonight, are you?' Moira asked at last.

Christine was still smiling as she turned. 'Parent-teachers' meeting at the school. I think Robbie's doing OK, but it will be good to hear what his teacher has to say.'

'Oh, so you're not seeing Alistair then? What's he going to do all by himself?'

'I don't know. Stay in and watch telly, I expect. It won't hurt him to miss me for one evening, now will it?'

Christine didn't notice Moira's sharp intake of breath, although Joan certainly did as the two women returned to their posts at the reception desk, both bristling with indignation at the heartlessness of men.

It took several minutes for their knock at the Browns' door to be answered. Harry's slow, shuffling footsteps could be heard approaching for what seemed an age before bolts were drawn back, locks turned and the door opened.

'Good morning, doctor,' was the polite greeting. 'Oh, not on your own today?'

'This is my colleague, Dr Norris. He may well be coming to see you both from time to time in the future.'

'How nice. You're welcome, Dr Norris. Come through!'

With Harry leading the way at the same painful shaky pace, Alistair had time to take a good look at the portrait gallery of family pictures that lined the narrow hallway. Finally they emerged into the overheated, dimly-lit back room, where Hetty sat queenlike beside the heavily-draped and drawn curtains.

'Who's this?' she snapped. 'I don't like strangers.'

'Well, Dr Norris won't be a stranger for long, Hetty,' said Simon soothingly. 'You may be seeing quite a bit of him from now on.'

'I don't want a beginner. My medical condition is far too delicate and complicated for that. I need a man of experience. I need *you*!'

He smiled sweetly as he drew up a chair in front of her. 'And I'm not going anywhere. It's just that Dr Bryant and I feel that the more heads considering your condition, the better. You're very lucky to have a man of Dr Norris's calibre available to you!'

She grunted, and with an exaggerated groan of pain settled back into the cloud of cushions stuffed around her in the huge armchair.

'Harold, haven't you got the kettle on yet? Whatever are you thinking of? And Dr Gatward only likes the plain chocolate biscuits. Don't make the same silly mistake you made last time!' With a guilty smile in Simon's direction, Harry tottered off to do as he was told.

'How are you, Hetty?'

'Well, I don't complain, you know, but the pain has been shocking, just shocking. My hips, both knees, the small of my back, my shoulders, and now my wrists! I couldn't even write Harold's shopping list yesterday without being in agony, agony!'

'What do you think of those new pills? Did they help?'

Her smile was tight and martyred. 'Well, *you* know that nothing's going to help me much now. I have no choice but simply to bear it. Sometimes I think I can't go on, and the thought that this pain will be a burden I must carry for the rest of my life is dreadful, quite dreadful.' She wiped her hand across her forehead in a gesture of distress. 'Although I realise, of course, that the rest of my life may be very short indeed . . .'

Standing to one side, Alistair struggled to hide a grin, although Simon's face was warmly sympathetic as he dug into his bag for a stethoscope. 'Right, well, let's check you over, shall we?'

'And now,' she continued to announce, 'I've got blood pressure!'

Alistair groped in his pocket for a hankie with which to cover his quivering mouth. Even Simon was having trouble controlling his expression.

'Well, I'm very glad to hear it. You'd be in trouble without it! Let's start by checking how high it is, shall we?'

Five minutes later, the examination over, Harry made his uncertain way back into the room carrying a flowery tray covered in a doily, on which stood a teapot with knitted cosy, matching cups and saucers and a plate of plain chocolate digestives. Alarmed by the violent shaking of Harry's hands as he struggled with the heavy load, Alistair stretched out to take the tray from him.

'Right, Alistair, you pour,' said Simon, getting to his feet. 'I want to take a look at Harry.'

The look of indignation on Hetty's face to think that even for a short while she might not be the centre of attention stayed with Simon as later the two doctors made their way back to the car.

'What do you think?' asked Alistair. 'Parkinson's?'

'I'm afraid so, and he's got so much worse in just a few weeks.'

'She'll never forgive him if he's got more wrong with him than she has.'

'She'll never forgive me either! Come on, I think we've got time for a quick sandwich at the pub before our next call.' And to Alistair, whose mind never strayed far from food, that seemed a great idea.

★

Keith was feeling better. He'd learned during Ian's illness to expect good times and bad patches. His bad bout of the previous week seemed to have passed, leaving him physically stronger but low and depressed in spirit. Nevertheless he'd been looking forward to Simon's visit that afternoon, although he was somewhat surprised to see that he was accompanied by a younger colleague. His natural shyness returned as he ushered in the newcomer, knowing that his ease in Simon's company would be strained in the presence of someone he didn't know. Simon, on the other hand, was as relaxed and friendly as ever as he carried out his examination. This was the first case of advanced AIDS Alistair had ever been involved with, and his interest was evident as Simon discussed Keith's progress and prognosis. Finally, Simon sat back on the settee to write a prescription.

'You'll have to come into the surgery next week. There are a few tests I'd like to do there.'

Keith didn't answer.

'Look, I know you feel uncomfortable about other patients at the surgery, but it's where you must be if I'm to give you the appropriate treatment.'

'I've told you. I only want to be monitored. I don't want treatment.'

'I need to know how things are progressing, and so do you. The T4 helper cell blood count is the only way to do that. I want you to come and see me at the surgery next week. Agreed?

Still silence. Alistair watched as Simon went over to sit right beside Keith, their shoulders touching.

'Keith, this test is important. I understand your feelings, and I will keep my promise to see you here at home whenever possible. But I have to know what's happening with your condition. As your friend as well as your doctor, I intend to do my best for you. Meet me halfway on this.'

Keith's eyes reflected a mixture of resignation and affection as he covered Simon's hand with his own. It was a curiously intimate gesture which Alistair noted with some surprise.

'OK,' Keith agreed at last with a half-hearted nod of the head.

'Right,' said Simon, standing abruptly. 'We must be going. Where's your mum, by the way?'

'She takes a sculpting class on Tuesday afternoons.'

'Is she a teacher?'

'Her classes have always got a waiting list of students wanting to join.'

'I'm not at all surprised. Give her my best wishes, and I'll see you next week. I'll get reception to ring you just to make sure you have an appointment.'

And as the two doctors gathered up their belongings and made their way out of the house, Alistair realised that Keith's eyes never left Simon until the door was finally closed behind them.

Bert was in the back garden when Simon got home. It was strictly forbidden for him to mow the lawn, but he had resumed his familiar pastime of pottering in the greenhouse, checking that the tender favourites plucked from the garden to over-winter in warmth were doing nicely. Having seen Simon arrive, he left it no longer than five minutes to make his way to the kitchen, knowing the tea would be brewed by then.

'What's all this I hear about you keeping company with a lady?' asked Simon with a teasing grin, as he spooned three sugars into Bert's mug. He couldn't be sure, bearing in mind the natural ruddiness of the gardener's complexion, but he could have sworn Bert blushed.

'Well, I wouldn't call it "keeping company" exactly. She likes to show off her cooking. I'm the guinea pig.'

'That's nice.'

'And I help out a bit in her garden.'

'That's nice too.'

'Nothing in it.'

'It might be rather good for you if there were!'

'What? With Ivy Gibson?'

'She's not so bad. Perfectly respectable. Keeps a good house. Likes cooking. Obviously adores you! What more could you want?'

Bert guffawed into his mug. 'Not me. What do you think I am? Soft?'

'Yes, I think you probably are, however crusty you try to be. Everyone likes a few home comforts. Why shouldn't you?'

Bert sniffed and sipped his tea at the same time. 'Well, if it's such a good idea, how come you haven't got a woman to look after you?'

The old man's eyes were probably not sharp enough to notice the shadow that passed over Simon's face. 'No one would have me, Bert. Besides, I can cook for myself.'

'That won't keep your feet warm!'

'Well, I won't ask you how you're keeping your feet warm these days. All I can say is good for you!'

'Double rations of socks in my wellies! Don't you worry about me. I worry about you though. You're a reasonable fella. Sort of nice-looking, I suppose. How come you've not been hooked by a wife, then?'

Simon shrugged. Don't want one, Bert.'

'Why not?'

'Oh, I don't know. And you've got to drink up because I've got someone coming to see me at half past six.'

'Not that boy, the one with AIDS?'

'No. Now, come on, scram! That dinner Ivy's cooking you will be stone cold!'

If Bert intended to say more, he chose not to. Emptying his cup and grabbing one more biscuit from the tin, he ambled out of the kitchen.

In the end, it was more like seven before Jill arrived. Her

expression was guarded as he took her coat, grabbed two glasses and a cold bottle of dry white wine from the fridge, then led her through to the lounge.

'I'm late. I'm sorry.'

'No need to be, except if it means you're watching the clock because you can't stay long.'

'No.'

'When's Michael home?'

'I have no idea.'

He looked at her closely. 'You say that as if you don't much care if he's home or not.'

She returned his gaze. 'At the moment, I'm not sure I do.'

He opened the bottle and poured out a glass for each of them, handing one to her. Then he settled down beside her, waiting for her to speak.

'I don't know what I'm doing here,' she said at last.

'When you're unhappy, you need a friend. I've been your friend a very long time.'

Almost absent-mindedly, she threaded her fingers through his. 'I owe you an apology for the way I reacted about Debbie Claymore the other day.'

'It was true then.'

'Yes. He organised the whole thing. He did it as a favour for Matthew Benson, you know, the solicitor she works for? Debbie was very reluctant even to go to Elmside, and the only person she spoke to there was Michael. All very hush-hush, you see. He can be extremely persuasive when he puts his mind to it. The poor girl didn't stand a chance. She was in and having the operation before the week was out.'

'Have you talked to him about this? What does he say?'

'Not much. He doesn't accept there's any issue here. She was unmarried. The father had no wish to make the pregnancy public, or even stand by her. From Michael's point of view, it would simply be foolhardy to allow a baby to be born into such a situation.'

'And you? What do you think?'

'Well, I'm a mum. My children mean the world to me. Why should Debbie's mean any less to her, whatever the circumstances?'

'Have you told Michael that?'

'No. His mind is too full of other things to listen to me at the moment.'

'Oh?'

'He's been offered another job, one he's very excited about. Do you remember James Turnbull? He was training several years ahead of us, but Michael knew him reasonably well. He was always a bright cookie, very ambitious. He went straight into commercial medicine and is now high up in the pharmaceutical business.'

'Our paths never really crossed then,' replied Simon, frowning as he tried to recall the face, 'but I know him by reputation. He's the one who's masterminded the development of that anti-depressant Michael's always on about.'

'That's the one. And he's obviously spotted a kindred spirit in Michael, because he's asked him to join the team marketing the new drug to the general public. Michael's task will be to make it a household name which patients will ask their doctors for specifically.'

'It's overpriced, and it makes claims that are simply not proven. There are several generic products already on the market which are much cheaper. To my mind, creating a market for what is nothing more than a designer drug is unethical, at the very least.'

'The job is based in London.'

He looked at her then, noticing the brightness of her eyes, the bleakness of her expression.

'He could commute from here.'

'He doesn't want to. He wants us to move back and buy a house there. He says now the kids are grown up and gone, there's nothing to stop us.'

'But you love it here. I know you do.'

'You know. He doesn't.'

He laid down his glass, putting his arm around her shoulders to draw her to him.

'So let him go if that's what he wants. You stay here.'

'Break up the marriage, is that what you mean?'

'Is that what you want?'

'Well, that depends.'

'On what?'

'On whether what I decide matters to you.'

'Of course it matters. I can't bear to see you unhappy. And that man has made you unhappy for years.'

'That's not what I mean.'

He didn't answer – and she knew he understood exactly what she meant.

'I am about to make a fool of myself, and probably the biggest mistake of my life, but I just have to be honest about how I feel. I love you, Simon. I've always loved you. And what's more, I believe you love me. I think we fit together like two halves of a whole.'

She didn't dare look up at him, and was too scared of his reaction to stop talking. 'I've known you for years. I feel total empathy with you – yet in many ways, I don't know you at all. I have no idea how you feel about me, not really. I've always been aware of your affection and loyalty. I have no doubt that you *like* me. But I want so much more than that. I want to be with you. I want us to share more than just a few hours at the surgery. I want to watch television with you, have breakfast together, wash your back in the bath, worry over the bills, grumble about the weather, buy your socks, iron your shirts. I want to go to bed with you and not care if we get no sleep at all. I love you. And I can't go on without you knowing that.'

She felt his arm tighten around her shoulders. She watched as his fingers gripped hers. But still he didn't answer. He simply drew her tense body back against the settee, where he held her close as the shadows lengthened and the world beyond that room slipped away.

At exactly quarter to seven that evening, Christine planted a kiss on Robbie's newly-washed hair and pulled the door shut behind her. Mary, her next-door neighbour, had been happy to babysit for a couple of hours while she went off to the school for the parent-teachers' evening.

And at exactly quarter to seven, Alistair's car pulled up outside a flat on the edge of Berston. He sounded the horn twice to attract her attention, and within minutes he was holding open the passenger door as Wendy lowered herself inside to join him.

Chapter Nine

Christine was nervous. She clutched Alistair's hand tightly as they made their way through to the bar where a crowd she mostly recognised were already gathered. Dr Bryant and his wife Patricia were there, and although she felt perfectly at home with the practice manager, she'd always been a little on edge with Gerald. They were talking to Dr Gatward, and he was nice. Best of all, Lynn the health visitor had arrived with her husband. Christine had never met David, but knew she'd like him from everything she'd heard about him. Bearing in mind that members of the practice spent so many daytime hours in each other's company, social gatherings like this were few and far between. Without Alistair's friendship, Christine knew she would never have been invited along to this particular event, especially as the Musical Moments fund-raising evening for the General Hospital Appeal Fund was a highlight in the medical calendar. Glancing down at her programme she saw that the entertainment was described as 'a sparkling array of performances by a talented selection of local musicians and soloists'. She didn't recognise their names, but that didn't matter. It was just a thrill to be here. Terrifying, but thrilling too.

'You look lovely. That jacket really suits you.'

Christine spun round to find Lynn at her elbow, and smiled with relief.

'Well, that's not surprising! It's yours! Really, Lynn, I'm so grateful. My wardrobe just doesn't stretch to occasions like this.'

'Did Alistair like it?'

Christine's eyes sparkled. 'Oh you know, he's always one for the compliments, but I could tell he really meant it this time. Does this outfit have the same effect on David when you wear it?'

Lynn grinned. 'Why do you think I lent it to you? I *knew* it would do the trick!'

The two women reached out to help themselves to the glass of wine offered to them by a passing waiter. Sipping slowly, Christine looked around at the people near her.

Alistair was in his element. He was looking particularly smart in a navy woollen jacket worn with dark trousers. She watched him fondly as he joined in the conversation with Gerald and Patricia, making them all laugh with his convoluted tale of a patient he'd seen that afternoon. Alistair was instantly at home in whatever company he found himself. How she envied him for that.

Her eyes moved on then to Simon Gatward. He was standing with their group, but his mind was plainly elsewhere. Following his gaze she realised that it was Jill Dunbar who had caught his eye, and that she was looking in his direction too. Jill and her husband were making their way towards their group, bringing another couple with them. Michael was smiling warmly as he shook Gerald's hand, and kissed Patricia on both cheeks.

'You're looking wonderful. Has that husband of yours put you on HRT?'

'No need. He's already given himself a dose of Viagra!'

'You know Matthew Benson, don't you, and his wife Linda?'

The new couple worked their way round the group shaking hands with each member in turn. Rather pointedly, Simon clasped Linda's hand warmly, but totally ignored her husband.

Michael glanced at his wife curiously, but was unable to get Jill's attention as she looked at the floor, wincing with embarrassment. Suddenly, the bell rang announcing that the performance would start in three minutes.

'Are you OK?' Alistair's lips brushed her ear as he spoke. Christine turned to face him, her heart overflowing with pride and happiness to be the partner of such a dear and attractive man.

'Couldn't be better. Shall we go in?'

'Am I allowed a bag of sweeties to munch, just in case the music's lost on me?'

'Toffees?'

'Now you're talking!'

'How did I know you'd ask? I've a packet of your favourites in my bag.'

'You're a wonderful woman, do you know that?'

'You bet! And don't you forget it!'

Simon hung behind as the group began to move in towards the auditorium. At last he was alongside Michael as he followed Jill, Linda and Matthew.

'Michael, long time no see.'

Michael's expression was guarded. 'Simon.'

'Funnily enough, I was thinking about you today. A patient of mine mentioned your name. Debbie Claymore. Very distressed she was. Something about an abortion. Perhaps you remember her?'

At the sound of Debbie's name Matthew's head snapped round in their direction, then back towards his wife to see if she'd also overheard. With his hand beneath her elbow, he propelled her at surprising speed towards their seats. Meanwhile Michael had stopped in his tracks and turned to face Simon, his expression cold and threatening.

'Simon, for someone who prides himself on taking the high moral ground, that was a mean, insensitive thing to do.'

'As mean and insensitive as persuading a young girl to have an abortion she really doesn't want?'

At once, Jill was between them. 'Stop this, both of you! The concert's starting. We need to go in.'

The two men glared at each other like gladiators, until finally Simon turned away and marched off. Michael looked down at Jill with anger in his eyes.

'You told him.'

'Not now, Michael, please.'

'That was unprofessional and indiscreet.'

'He's her doctor. Of course he knows.'

'But who told him of Matthew Benson's involvement? You, of course. Pillow talk, was it?'

For one fleeting moment, Jill's hand was poised to slap him hard across the face, but in her moment of hesitation he had turned away from her, weaving his way angrily through the auditorium to take his seat.

As the lights dimmed and the music began, Alistair reached out in the darkness to take Christine's hand with a smile for her that was so tender, she thought her heart would burst with contentment.

The opening orchestral piece was familiar and soothing, but it did nothing to calm Simon's fury. Along the line he could just make out Jill's profile, her face pale and unsmiling. Applause rippled around him as the orchestra reached the end of their first piece to an enthusiastic reception. As the chairman of the Appeal Trustees walked up to the microphone to announce the purpose of the evening, Simon turned his attention with some determination to the proceedings on stage. But while his eyes were focused, his thoughts were still on the exchange with Michael.

Why do I care so much? Why does that man irritate me so? Because everything about him is alien to me – his principles, his approach to medicine, his attitude to patients. And most of all because he's married to Jill.

Jill. At the thought of her Simon closed his eyes, blocking out the confusion that had engulfed him since her revelation the evening before. He wanted that man out of her life because he was wrong for her. He had always been wrong. But what then? Jill plainly saw a future for herself without her husband, but with Simon. So what sort of future did *he* see?

He opened his eyes to drag himself back into the right frame of mind, but once again found both his thoughts and gaze wandering. But when he caught sight of the person sitting further along his row on the other side of the aisle, he knew in whose company he'd like to spend the interval.

She was getting a drink at the bar when he finally found her – or at least trying to attract the attention of the barman who was rushed off his feet with orders.

'Tell you what,' he whispered in her ear, 'you go and grab a spot for us to sit, and I'll organise the drinks. What do you fancy?'

Annie smiled up at him gratefully. 'I seem to become the Invisible Woman whenever I'm standing at a bar. You're tall. You'll make an impression! Just a Coke for me, please, and Keith will have a lager.'

'Is he here? I didn't see him.'

'A bit of a surprise, isn't it? He hates being anywhere where there's a crowd these days, but he just couldn't resist this evening. He loves this kind of music.'

'So where is he?'

'Gone to the loo. He shouldn't be long. Look, there are some seats over there. I'll go and claim them.'

It was a good five minutes before he was able to weave his way over to her, balancing three glasses and a couple of bags of roasted nuts.

'I'm starving. Do you like these?'

'Love them. Sit down quickly. That woman in the blue dress is definitely eyeing up this seat.'

'No husband this evening?'

The shrug of her shoulders was barely noticeable as she struggled to open the packet of nuts. 'Not Derek's thing, really. He's always complaining when I have classical music on while

I'm working. I find it soothing, but if it hasn't got a beat, it's lost on him.' She took a mouthful of her drink before continuing. 'Tell me, how did you think Keith was yesterday? He seems a bit better to me.'

'These periods of remission are quite common. And actually, if he's lucky and doesn't pick up any bugs or viruses to lay him low, he might be quite well for fairly long periods.'

'He tells me you want him to come in for some tests.'

'I know he's not keen, but I really do need to see him in the surgery for the next appointment.'

'I'll see what I can do.'

'I'm going home. Now.'

They both looked up to see an ashen-faced Keith beside them. Annie leapt to her feet.

'What's the matter? Are you feeling bad?'

Keith shook his head, plainly ill-at-ease as he became aware of faces turning in his direction. 'I want to go. You stay. I'll make my own way back.'

'Something's happened,' said Simon. 'When you were in the toilet?'

Keith nodded dumbly, looking down at his shaking hands. 'I just came out the cubicle, and someone else started to go in after me, when another guy said to him in a very loud voice, "I wouldn't go in there, mate. Don't you know that's the bloke with AIDS? Want to catch it, do you?" I just wished the floor would swallow me up.'

'What did you do?'

'I scarpered. It was packed in there. What else could I do?'

'Oh Keith.' Tears shone in Annie's eyes.

'I tell you what,' said Simon, 'I'm not having much fun at this concert either. Annie, you stay and enjoy the second half . . .'

'But . . .'

'Don't worry, I'll take him home. He'll be fine.'

'Are you sure?'

'Absolutely.'

Simon put his hand on Keith's shoulder as he led him towards the door, when one person's voice was heard above the hum of conversation. 'Better move back a bit. He's that Ryder bloke, the one with AIDS.'

The crowd in the bar parted to let them through, curious eyes turning in their direction. Simon became aware of a face he knew – Sean Williams, the rugby player whose knee often needed attention.

'Hello Dr Gatward. Nice to see you out enjoying yourself. Interesting company you keep . . .'

Sean's face was perfectly innocent, but the innuendo was plain. Without a word Simon propelled Keith past him, keeping up the pace until they were out of the theatre, across the car park and into the safety of Simon's car, where Keith laid his head back against the rest and closed his eyes with relief.

'How often do things like that happen?'

'Feels as if it's whenever I go out these days.'

'They're just ignorant and insensitive.'

Keith sighed. 'This is a small, tight community. Everyone knows everyone else's business. Someone with AIDS is news. Bad news.'

'Well, there's been so much information about it in the media. Why don't they just *listen*? Why don't they get the facts right before they start shooting their mouths off?'

'It doesn't matter.'

'Yes it does. And you don't have to pretend otherwise, not with me.'

Keith turned to face Simon in the darkness.

'Thank you.'

'No thanks needed. It's my job.'

'This isn't your job. You're here with me now because you're my friend, perhaps my only friend. Thank you for that.'

For a moment, Simon seemed lost for words. Then he stretched out to turn on the ignition and pull away slowly in the direction of Berston.

★

Derek arrived at the reception desk promptly at ten o'clock, Martin Balcombe's plans for the extension of the practice premises firmly wedged under his arm. Gerald was just finishing surgery, so it was Patricia who greeted him and gave him an initial tour of the area scheduled for change. Finally they arrived back in her office where, minutes later, Gerald joined them. Detailed discussion followed about particular aspects of the development, and various options on finer points which were still open to consideration.

Eventually Patricia leaned forward at her desk, her hands clasped in front of her. 'We are getting other quotes, of course, but I have to say that Martin Balcombe highly recommended your work.'

Derek smiled in acknowledgement.

'So, assuming your price is right, when could you hope to start? And how long would the job take?'

'Bearing in mind, of course,' added Gerald, 'that this is a medical centre. Our service to patients must be interrupted as little as possible. Most important of all is the issue of hygiene. It will be essential to dust-proof with absolute security the area where you're working. Can you guarantee that?'

Derek's pen scribbled animatedly in his notebook. 'I'll give that some thought. I'm sure it can be arranged.'

'And the timing?'

'Would you like it done for mid-January?'

Gerald and Patricia exchanged enthusiastic glances. 'Is that possible?'

'It might be. I reckon there's about seven weeks' work here. We'll need about three weeks for the first fix, that's the initial foundations, framework and wires. The second fixers, the carpenters and electricians, come next to put in the wiring, sockets, lighting, door frames, lining, architrave and skirting boards; then last of all, the finals – that's the decorating and furnishing. It's the end of October now. If you give us the go-ahead immediately, I think there's every possibility it will be ready for use reasonably early in the New Year.'

'Well, that's most impressive, Mr Ryder.'

'Derek.'

'Derek. So, if you can let us have your detailed quotation as soon as possible, we may well be in business.'

'Fine. I'll be in touch within a couple of days.' Derek rose from his seat, gathering up papers to place them in his briefcase. 'Don't worry about seeing me out. I'd like to take just one more look at the back room and check those measurements. I know the way.'

Five minutes on, the measurements safely listed on his pad, Derek was making his way down the narrow corridor towards reception when he heard his name called.

'Mr Ryder, isn't it? Nice to see you.'

Derek's face registered no reaction to Simon's greeting.

'I was hoping to have a word with you some time. Have you got a moment?'

Derek looked pointedly at his watch. 'Not really.'

'This will only take a minute or two, and it is important.'

Reluctantly Derek allowed himself to be propelled into Simon's surgery, although he made it clear that he had no intention of staying long enough to take a seat.

'About your son,' began Simon, noting the shutter of disinterest that descended over Derek's face. 'Having someone in the family who is so seriously ill takes its toll on everyone in the home. I wondered if it would help for you to know more about Keith's condition, and how it might be expected to develop.'

'You'd better talk to my wife. She's the one who needs to know about that. Mind you, you already know her rather well, as I recall.'

'Hardly at all, Mr Ryder, and it's Keith who chiefly concerns me. He's reasonably stable at the moment, but his level of health could change dramatically at any time. He's refusing various medical options that are available to him, did you know that?'

'No.'

'There is a specialist centre for AIDS sufferers at the General Hospital, which Keith has decided not to visit. He insists that he wants to let the condition take its course, without allowing us to make any attempt to intervene, or prolong his life.'

Derek's eyes widened.

'Why?'

'He watched his companion die. He knows how intrusive the treatment can be, and he doesn't want to go through that.'

'You mean, he *wants* to die?'

'No – but under the circumstances, he wants to go with dignity.'

Derek snorted. 'Then he's even more of a silly bleeder than I thought he was.'

Simon sat back in his chair and eyed the other man with curiosity. 'Why the animosity towards him?'

'No animosity. I'm not interested enough for that.'

'But he's your son. He's dying. He's hurting and frightened. Surely you can see how much he needs your support?'

'I expect one of his boyfriends would be better at that than I am. And his daft mother is running round after him all the time. He's OK.'

'He's not OK. And my guess is, neither are you.'

Derek picked up his briefcase abruptly. 'I haven't got time for this psycho mumbo-jumbo. What you people can't accept is that I have no interest in my son. I used to love him, but he betrayed that love. He made his bed, he most definitely lay in it – and it's killing him. His choice. His problem. Goodbye doctor.'

He was through the door and slamming it behind him before Simon had time for another word. It wasn't until he'd left the building and was in the privacy of his own car that Derek realised he couldn't see for the mist in his eyes. Anger, of course. It couldn't be any other emotion.

Could it?

'Is that all right then? Lunch one Sunday just as soon as your mother feels up to it. Give her a month or so, and I think she'll be itching to get out again.'

Alistair grinned. His parents had always had an active and well-organised social life. His mother's recent illness with shingles had curtailed their outings somewhat, but he knew she must be feeling better if she was filling the diary once again.

'That should be fine. Just let me know when.'

'I was wondering about calling on Gerald and Patricia while we're in the area. It would be delightful to see them both after all this time. I'd appreciate the chance to look round the practice too.

'Checking up, are you? Making sure it's up to scratch for your darling son?'

'Not at all,' replied James gruffly, although both men knew Alistair had hit the nail neatly on the head.

'By the way,' Alistair continued, 'there's someone I'd like you to meet while you're here.'

'Oh?'

'A girl.'

'I hope you're not allowing yourself to be distracted from your work. This is an important year for you, your last in GP training.'

'Dad, I understand that.'

'And we need to talk about what should be the next step of your career. I've been talking to my old friend, Stephen Babcock. You know, he's a very senior man at Guy's these days. He says there may well be some interesting openings there for a young doctor who wants to get on . . .'

'I am getting on, Dad, and I'm perfectly happy where I am.'

'Yes, but after this year is up, you need to think where . . .'

'And I will. Look, I must go. I'm late for my house calls. Give Mum my love – and I'll look forward to seeing you both soon.'

Ivy loved shopping. Most of all, she loved the supermarket. She could happily while away the best part of a whole morning wandering round her local. It was where she met everyone she knew, where she picked up the latest gossip, and where very occasionally she even bought something. In fact, being a canny soul who made her pension stretch to the absolute limit, she did most of her purchasing at the market on a Friday morning, but that never stopped her enjoying her frequent visits to the supermarket. And it was there, in between the cat food and the washing powders that she bumped into Pauline Gregory.

'Pauline, my dear! How lovely to see you. And my, hasn't Naomi grown! How old is she now?'

'She'll have her first birthday in January,' beamed Pauline who never tired of admiration for her beautiful daughter. 'I can't believe how quickly this year has flown.'

'After all those years you waited for her too.' Ivy leaned down to stroke the bemused baby's cheek. 'And doesn't she look like Dave! The spitting image! Remarkable really, when you think how she came into the world.'

Pauline leaned down towards the pram too, tucking the fluffy pink cover more tightly around her daughter's chubby body.

'We're still her parents, Ivy. IVF treatment doesn't change that. Dave's her dad, so we're really pleased she takes after him. His looks, my brains.'

'And how are *you*, my dear?' clucked Ivy sympathetically. 'You look tired. Well, of course, it's so exhausting having a baby to look after, especially when you're such a *devoted* mother.'

'Actually, she's been sleeping quite well lately. I suppose

that's because she's more active now and wears herself out.'

'And she's fit and well, is she? Teething perhaps? Her cheeks look a bit red.'

'Do you think so?' Pauline's face creased with worry. 'I thought she was looking better.'

'Well,' said Ivy, setting into her role as knowledgeable adviser, 'I'd get those gums checked, if I were you. Her cheeks shouldn't be inflamed like that . . .'

'Inflamed!' Pauline peered at Naomi's face in alarm.

'Take her to the doctor, I should. I never took any chances with my two. Oh, I know my Fred thought I worried too much, but mothers are born to worry, aren't they?'

'Actually, I am seeing the doctor later this afternoon.'

'Oh? Something wrong?'

Pauline hesitated 'Probably not. Just a check-up.'

'For Naomi? Her gums?'

'No, nothing like that. She's had some hearing tests.'

Ivy's expression was one of dramatic concern. 'She's not deaf! Oh, the poor little mite!'

'They're just doing tests at the moment, Dr Gatward says there may be all sorts of explanations for her lack of reaction to some sounds . . .'

'Dr Gatward?'

'Lovely man. So caring.'

'So I understand.'

'Don't you go to him then? It's always difficult to get an appointment when you need it, because patients queue up to see him. He'll sort Naomi out, I'm sure he will.'

Ivy didn't answer, but her silence spoke volumes. Pauline stared at the older woman with curiosity. 'What's the matter?'

'Well, perhaps it's nothing – but I certainly wouldn't choose to see him, not after what I've heard.'

'Heard?'

Ivy appeared to think better of continuing, and gathered up her shopping bag and wire basket as if to continue on her way. 'I shouldn't say anything. I'm sorry I spoke.'

'Ivy, what are you talking about? What have you heard?'

Ivy sighed reluctantly as she edged in closer to where Pauline stood holding the handle of the buggy. 'Well, I've heard that he's gay.'

'Oh, don't be ridiculous. Of course he's not!'

'You know he's not married?'

'So?'

'So, why not?'

'He's never met the right woman.'

'Perhaps it wasn't a woman he was wanting to meet.'

'What do you mean?'

'Well, he seems to be spending a lot of time – *social* time, if you know what I mean – with that Ryder boy . . .'

'I don't know him.'

'*He's* gay.'

'Really?'

'And he's got AIDS. Looks dreadful. He'll probably die from it soon.'

'Well, he's ill then. That's why Dr Gatward is seeing a lot of him.'

'At the theatre? Fishing on the river bank together? Out in his car?'

Pauline's mouth dropped open with disbelief. 'No!'

'And you have to ask yourself why an unmarried middle-aged doctor should choose to keep company like that.'

Pauline had already asked herself that question, and thought about the possible answer.

'And you think they're . . .'

'I have no idea. It does seem odd though, doesn't it?'

'Then he could be . . .'

'. . . HIV positive himself.'

Pauline's face was ashen. 'I don't believe this. I simply don't believe it of him.'

'But you never know, do you? And where there's smoke, there's probably fire.'

Pauline bent down to tuck the baby's covers in even more tightly. 'Only I'm not prepared to take any risks with Naomi.'

'Of course not! How could you even think of such a thing?'

'And I'm supposed to be seeing him this afternoon . . .'

'Perhaps you could mention this to him then? He can probably explain.'

'I hardly think so.'

Ivy sighed. 'It's very difficult for you really.'

'I just don't fancy the idea of anyone prodding my baby around if there's even the smallest possibility that he's . . .'

'. . . contaminated?'

'Exactly.'

'So what will you do? Change your appointment?'

'More than that. I'm going to change my doctor!'

'Still working? I thought you'd be gone by now.'

Derek was surprised to see Julie at her desk later that evening when he finally got back from Acorn Grove. Her face lit up to see him, although he went straight through to his office and probably didn't notice.

'There have been a couple of complicated messages for you. I wanted to make sure you got them right away.'

'Thanks, Jules.' His reply was absent-minded as he scanned the pile of faxes on his desk. 'Any chance of a coffee?'

She put the cup she was carrying down on the desk in front of him. He glanced up and grinned before his expression changed. 'You look pale. You OK?'

'Just a bit tired, I suppose. And hungry. I didn't even stop for a sandwich today.'

To Derek, who loved his food, this was an appalling thought. 'Well, no wonder you're fading away. Come on, I'm taking you down to the Three Horseshoes for a bite to eat.'

'But what about you? Annie will have a meal waiting for you.'

'No she won't,' was the curt reply as he picked up the phone. It was some time before she answered, and even then, he didn't waste time on niceties.

'I'm eating out tonight. Got a meeting. Don't wait up.'

He listened for a while as Annie obviously passed on a message or two – then, 'Right! Got to go. See you later.'

He slammed the phone down and turned to Julie, whose face was gaining colour by the moment.

'Come on, before I change my mind. Get your coat!'

At half past eleven that night, when Julie finally arrived home, she wondered where the hours had gone. They'd found a quiet corner in the pub, chosen from the menu, then ordered a bottle of wine which disappeared before they knew it. By the second bottle, their conversation was not only more relaxed, but distinctly more personal. He asked her about her love life now that she was no longer married. She managed to sound suitably sought-after, although in reality she spent most evenings at home thinking about her day at work. She asked him about his family, and that led to him opening up about Annie, and the gulf in communication he felt was between them. As the wine flowed, he sounded lonely and wronged and misunderstood, so she took his hand and looked into his eyes as he poured out his heart. She was warm and caring and compassionate, until he began to feel the ice around his heart soften. For just a moment, he wondered about the wisdom of getting too close to someone he employed. Then he put it out of his mind. They were friends, and friends are meant to lean on each other. With that comforting thought, his arm slipped round her shoulders as their relationship slipped into a new and exciting realm of closeness.

★

Simon couldn't sleep. He heard the hall clock strike two. When he realised he was still wide awake as it struck an hour later, he threw back the bedclothes and padded down to the kitchen. He considered making a warm milky drink, but abandoned that thought as he reached instead for the whisky bottle and a large tumbler. Carrying both through to the lounge, he settled into the soft cushions of the settee and flicked through the television channels for several minutes before switching off again. There was nothing there to hold his interest. With a sigh, he closed his eyes, every now and then taking large gulps from the tumbler.

He was tired, but his mind was racing with images from the past. Disconnected thoughts, faces, names, places, feelings, all tumbled round his head, dancing in front of his tightly-closed eyes, filling his senses with daggers of pain and numbing melancholy. He rubbed his eyes hard with the tips of his fingers, but nothing could stop the anguish that jabbed, nagged and exposed gaping wounds in his raw emotions.

Suddenly he stood up. He moved over to the unit at the end of the room, and opened the drawer in the far left corner. It stuck a bit. It always did, but then, he hardly ever opened it – only on nights like this when the pain simply wouldn't go away. With shaking hands he drew out a long thin blue box, carrying it carefully back over to the settee where he sat down heavily, the box spread across his knees. Slowly he lifted off the lid, and putting the box to one side opened the photo album. For minutes he sat turning the pages one after one, covering his mouth with a hand to stop the racking sobs that threatened to choke him. Finally, when he came to the last picture, the one he loved best and dreaded most, he lay his head back against the cushion and with his face contorted in bleak despair, screamed until he felt his lungs would burst and his heart break.

Chapter Ten

There was a bite in the wind as it whistled around the circle of trees, catching the last remaining leaves, tossing them in swirling heaps on the wet grass. The rain had finally stopped and watery sunshine was struggling to make its way through the heavy November sky. Annie chose a bench which was almost hidden from the rest of the park by a circle of thick hedging. She didn't mind the cold, nor the bleak dampness of the late autumn land-scape. Bleakness matched her mood. A bleak present. An even bleaker future. A future alone.

The thought of being alone had never previously held any fear for her. In fact she was happy in her own company, especially when it was her choice. She worked alone, and preferred it that way. But the events of that morning had made her realise that in future the choice might not be hers. Keith would leave her. And now she knew that Derek would go too.

The day had started normally enough. As usual, he'd woken with the alarm at half past six. Keith had had a bad night, and consequently so had she – but if Derek noticed her red-rimmed eyes as he got out of their bed, he made no comment. She heard him in the bathroom, taking a shower and having a shave. Then the sound of the Radio 4 News drifted up from the kitchen, and she knew that within minutes she'd hear the bang of the front door. He wouldn't come up to say goodbye. He never did. These days there was nothing to say.

Suddenly that thought became unbearable. She wanted to matter to him. She longed for him to notice her, talk to her, to care enough to see how much she was hurting. She wanted arms around her and soothing words in her ear, someone to share the fear and pain. She wanted a partner, a husband. *Her* husband.

At once she was out of bed, padding down the stairs in her bare feet, arriving breathless in the kitchen to stand before him, his face a cautious mask of surprise and reserve.

'We need to talk.'

Slowly he took a sip of tea, a trace of suspicion in his eyes. 'Not now. I'm late.'

'When then?'

He sighed. 'Annie, what is there to talk about?'

'Exactly that. There is so much going on, so much we should share, and we never talk to each other. Derek, I can't go through this on my own. Keith is our only son − *your* son as much as mine. I know I've been so sick with worry that I've allowed things to drift between us, but I don't want that any more. I can't do this alone. I'm begging you, please don't turn your back on him. He needs you, and so do I. Oh, Derek, so do I . . .'

From his stunned silence, she knew he hadn't expected such an outburst. She waited for his expression to soften, for him to rise and put his arms round her, tell her it would be all right, they'd face this together. She watched the familiar face before her, this man she'd lived with for thirty years − and knew in an instant of blinding clarity that she didn't know him at all.

'Don't start on this, Annie. Not now.'

Her feet remained rooted to the floor, but she felt herself recede from him. At that moment, any last remnant of love she felt for him died within her.

'We'll talk tonight.' He rose from the stool, stepping round her en route to the door.

Too late, she thought. This was the moment, and the moment was gone.

Within seconds he was in the hallway pulling on his coat, slamming the front door behind him. Her shoulders slumped at the sound as she dropped heavily on to the stool where he'd been sitting. She wondered if she'd cry, but soon recognised the emotion choking her at that moment was not despair, but cold anger. No tears. Just rage.

There was only one thing for her to do. Taking the stairs two at a time, she grabbed her jeans and thick jersey from the bedroom, and hurriedly dressed, splashing her face with cold water and pinning her tousled hair back in the clip she found beside the bathroom mirror. Then she was downstairs again, unlocking the side door to the garage which had for many years been her studio. It was still dark outside, and the bare strip lights seemed harsh and relentless at such an early hour of the morning. But Annie didn't notice. Carefully taking down the piece she'd been working on so lovingly for days, she focused her eye and closed her mind to everything beyond that particular carving in walnut, the most important she'd ever made.

It was several hours before she emerged from her studio, her back stiff, and her throat aching for a cup of something hot. She made a pot of tea, then poured two cups, one for herself and one for Keith. When she tiptoed into his room he was still asleep, his face showing signs of exhaustion and weariness even in deep slumber. Silently, she placed the cup beside the bed, then quietly left the room again. It was as she returned downstairs that she noticed the light flashing on the answerphone.

'Annie,' said Derek's voice, 'Where are you? I thought you'd be there at this time in the morning. I must have left my Filofax on the study desk. Could you drop it into the office for me? Is it your art class today? You could call in on your way there.' *No, it's not my sculpture class. That's on Tuesday. I've been teaching that class on Tuesday for three years. How could you not know that?* 'Anyway, it's urgent. Please get it to me as soon as possible.'

Annie glanced at her watch. Half past eleven. So he needed his Filofax? Well, she needed a shower. And something to eat. Then there was the laundry to be done. Glancing through the study door to check that the diary was indeed on the desk, she made her way upstairs determined to take all the time she needed.

It was gone two o'clock before she had finally completed all her chores. By then, Keith was awake, and together they had shared a plate of scrambled egg, a reasonable portion for her, a mouthful for him. She had got beyond thinking he was deliberately starving himself. Food had become an agony for him, scratching at the sores in his mouth as he swallowed, then reappearing sometimes minutes later as his digestive system grumbled and rebelled.

The journey to Derek's office took little more than ten minutes, and as she parked she realised his car was not in its usual spot. Perhaps he was out. Good.

Brian Turner was alone at his desk as she walked in. No Julie, which was unusual. The office without her seemed strangely empty. Annie had always liked Derek's warm-hearted, efficient secretary. In fact a real closeness had developed between the two women when Julie's husband first left her, and she had leaned heavily on her friendship with Derek and Annie. That was some years back now, and although their paths crossed infrequently, the genuine liking remained.

'I can see I've missed him. Is he likely to be long?'

'He's gone out to lunch.' The phone rang, and Brian made hand signals to her that she shouldn't rush off as he'd enjoy a chat. The call went on for some minutes, while Annie absent-mindedly glanced at charts on the wall, plans on the desk and ornaments on the filing cabinet. It was as she picked up that day's newspaper from the windowsill that she saw them – Derek and Julie, close in more than just the way they walked together from his car. The affection between them was plain to see. They were a couple. And to Annie's surprise, that was no surprise at all.

Grabbing her bag and with the briefest of waves in Brian's direction, she slipped out of the door, heading in the opposite direction around the building so as not to meet them. She was in the car and heading for the park before she even realised where she was going.

So she sat on the park bench, glad of the privacy given by the circle of thick hedging around her. She stared ahead, the biting wind stinging her cheeks. She didn't cry. There was no more anger. Just sadness that in the end, she felt nothing. Nothing at all.

'Alistair, I couldn't. I'm not good with people I don't know, especially when I'm nervous – and I'm sick with nerves already at the whole idea of meeting your parents!'

'Look, you know Gerald and Patricia . . .'

'I know them as my employers. I don't know them socially.'

'Well, why shouldn't you? They're lovely people and they'll . . .'

'I'll be out of my depth, without a word to say . . .'

'But I'll be there right beside you!'

'I won't be able to eat a thing!'

'Christine, I know you are a lovely, interesting woman. They will think so too.'

'Even if I'm mumbling and dribbling?'

At that point, Alistair laughed. He couldn't help it – and in spite of herself, sitting beside him in the front seat of his car, Christine found herself laughing too.

'Was that a joke, Mum?' piped up from Robbie from the back seat. 'Daniel told me a joke, but I don't like Daniel so I can't remember it.'

'Hey look Robbie! The fireworks have started. Come on, we're late!'

Hurriedly, they parked on a muddy bank at the side of the road, and the three of them linked hands to join the crowd heading towards the field where the Bonfire Night display was taking place. Finally, they found a spot halfway up a grassy slope where Alistair could heave Robbie up on to his shoulders for a bird's-eye view. Christine watched her son clasp his small arms round Alistair's head. As Robbie's face glowed with wonder at the myriad of colours exploding and crackling in the sky above them, she marvelled at the very thought that she could be this happy.

Twenty minutes later, when a cascade of silver flames had spelled out GOOD NIGHT in giant letters, they joined the queue at the barbecue, then wandered over to munch hot dogs loaded with ketchup as they stood beside the bonfire, their faces warmed and reddened by the flickering flames. Suddenly Alistair delved into his inside coat pocket to draw out an interesting-looking package, his expression serious as he bent down towards Robbie. 'Now, you and I need a chat, man to man. In here are some sparklers, but they're giant coloured ones, and probably a bit dangerous for your mum. So she's in charge of the lighter, but you are in charge of choosing the sparklers. Right?'

'Right!' agreed Robbie, a grin stretching from ear to ear.

Before long, the excitement of the evening began to tell on the little boy who was usually tucked up in bed by half past seven at night. As the three of them made their way back towards the car Christine stopped to pick up the weary child, who immediately relaxed against her, snuggling into her shoulder. Alistair was some way ahead of her before she moved on again to catch up with him – then she stopped in her tracks. A slim, exceedingly attractive girl was making a beeline for him, calling his name, her arms outstretched to embrace him as she planted a loving kiss on his cheek. From the expression on his face, it was obvious that Alistair knew her well.

'Sorry I missed you when you rang earlier,' gushed the girl in what Christine could only describe as a sickeningly affected girly voice. 'Yes, I'm fine for tomorrow. Were you worried I wouldn't be?'

Alistair's face was a picture of pleasure as he smiled down at her. 'That's great. Shall I pick you up at your place as usual?'

Did she really have to have such enormous appealing eyes, thought Christine miserably. And those lashes at least an inch long?

'Quarter to seven,' replied the vision, eyelashes batting to full effect. 'I'll look forward to it. *Ciao!*' And with another kiss brushed across his lips, she disappeared into the crowd.

Christine's heart was thumping, the shock of what she'd seen rooting her to the ground. She had known all along that men were not to be trusted. So why on earth had she let down her defences, and allowed herself to believe a man just because he'd told her she could?

She could see Alistair looking for her, scouring the faces in the crowd. When he arrived at her side she made no mention of his companion, and neither did he as he chatted away brightly, apparently unaware of her lack of enthusiasm for conversation. At her house, he climbed out of the car ready to carry in the sleeping Robbie, but she stepped in first, clasping her son tightly to her.

'Let me take him,' he said. 'You put the kettle on.'

'Not tonight, Alistair. I'm very tired.'

Disappointment mingled with concern as he put his arms round her. 'Are you all right? This isn't like you.'

'Robbie's heavy. I'll drop him if I don't go quickly. Thank you for this evening. Good night.' Leaving a bemused Alistair staring after her, she walked quickly up the garden path and kicked the front door shut behind her.

Keith's arm shook as he tipped the contents of the bottle out into the palm of his hand. There was an assortment of pills there; some saved from Ian's supplies, some collected from his mum's bathroom cabinet, some prescribed for him but not taken. He had never been much of a pill-taker. Funny really, as things turned out.

He checked to make sure he'd remembered everything. The note for mum was the most important. This would be hard on her. Easier in the long run though.

He opened the beige cardboard folder and spread the contents out on the bed around him. The sight of that familiar handwriting stabbed like a knife as he read the loving lines Ian had written in cards and letters sent to him over the years. As he sifted through the photos – Ian smiling at the camera; Ian in an armchair with a glass of wine in his hand; Ian looking dear and wonderful at his design desk – Keith's eyes clouded over. Finally he picked up one large photo, a shot of the two of them on holiday, arms around each other, faces filled with happiness and love. He turned it over to read again the in-scription Ian had written on the back just a few days before he died.

Sometimes when we touch . . .
With all my love, until we meet again

Well, they would soon meet again, united in love for ever. No more pain. No more fear. No more ignorant people with their hurtful comments.

He stuffed the pills into his mouth in handfuls, washing them down with the glass of lager at his bedside. Then he lay back on to the pillow, a smile on his face, the photo clutched to his chest, and his mind full of Ian as he closed his eyes with a sigh of peaceful relief.

'The strangest thing!' Lynn Webster had just returned to the surgery at the end of her rounds to find Jill in the nurses' room about to start the Verucca and Wart Clinic.

'Pauline Gregory was due to see me earlier in the week,' continued Lynn, 'but she didn't turn up. She's become quite a good friend over the years, especially after all her IVF treatment and when she was pregnant, so I was a bit worried when I didn't see her as planned.'

Jill turned with a smile. 'I shall never forget when Naomi was born. Such wonderful news after all that family had been through.'

'Exactly, so I thought I'd pop in and see her when I was passing this afternoon.'

'And? Is the baby OK?'

'Well, you know about her possible deafness, don't you?'

'Has she been to the hospital for tests yet? I forgot to ask Simon.'

'That's just it. Pauline was really odd about Simon. I got the impression she wasn't planning to see him again.'

Jill stared at her. 'Surely not. Pauline's always adored him. He's looked after her for years.'

'Well, she definitely reacted very oddly when his name came up.'

'Whatever could she be thinking of? She must keep her appointments to make sure the baby gets proper treatment, especially with this possibility of deafness at the moment.'

'Perhaps we should ask Simon to have a word?'

'I suggested that, and she was very determined that she didn't want to talk to him.'

'Why not?'

'She said she'd been doing a lot of thinking, and decided she'd prefer to take the baby not just to another doctor, but to another practice from now on.'

'No! I don't believe it!'

'Something about the company Simon keeps, she said. When I asked her to explain, she simply wouldn't be drawn. It was really embarrassing. I didn't know what to say.'

A cold finger of premonition slid down Jill's back. Surely Pauline couldn't mean . . . ? No, of course not. Nevertheless, she thought, as she mechanically went on laying out the instruments and notes she needed for the clinic, she'd like to get to the bottom of this. And perhaps have a word with Simon?

Joan's voice buzzed through on the intercom to let her know her first patient was on his way.

Yes, she thought. Simon should know, and perhaps when she'd found out more, she'd talk it over with him. Perhaps.

Derek whistled softly to himself as he climbed into his car. One turn of the ignition key, and the engine started immediately. He glanced at the clock on the illuminated dashboard display as he steered away from the office and out on to the main road. Half past six. Quite early considering the time he usually got away; but then tonight was Club Night, and he always looked forward to a soak in the bath before he got changed for an evening out with the boys. The journey home took little more than ten minutes, which were filled usefully with calls on his mobile. In fact, having turned into his drive and parked, he remained in the car for several more minutes while he finished a particularly involved conversation.

He still hadn't got used to the dark evenings, and he cursed Annie for not switching on the porch light which made it easier to pick a path up to the front door. What was the point of having a light that she never bothered to use?

Once inside, he realised the house was in darkness too. She was probably working in her studio, forgetting the time as usual. The figures she sculpted seemed amusing enough. Some people even bought them, which he'd always found faintly curious. Perhaps he'd seen too many of them over the years for them to hold much interest for him now. It never seemed like *real* work to him – not that she'd ever needed to work anyway. She could make the choice to spend her days on a hobby like making models, because he had always provided comfortably for her. The occasional show of gratitude wouldn't go amiss.

Her studio was empty. Good, he'd have a bit of peace to relax in the bath. Taking off his jacket as he climbed the stairs,

Derek made his way into the bedroom to pick a suit for the evening. He flicked on the television, scanning through the channels without concentration before selecting the local news programme which he then ignored as he pulled off his clothes and climbed into his dressing gown. Padding on bare feet across the landing to the largest bathroom in the house, he opened the door.

Sprawled on the floor in front of him was Keith. He lay deathly white in a pool of vomit at one end and diarrhoea at the other.

Putting his hand to his mouth to stop the retching that instantly gripped his stomach and throat, Derek backed out of the door. He didn't feel his son's pulse. He didn't check to see if he was breathing. Instead he quietly shut the door behind him and walked to the phone.

Annie ran into the hospital, breathless and ashen-faced. She was directed to Intensive Care, where she found Derek perched on the front of an upright plastic chair, his hands clasped between his knees, head lowered.

'How is he? What's the news?'

He looked up slowly. 'Not much. He's alive, which seems to be a bit of a surprise.'

'What happened?'

'An overdose. There were pill bottles all over his bed. He must have taken a fistful.'

She sat down heavily beside him, her eyes dark with shock and dread.

'Have you seen him?'

'He's not conscious, and they've been fussing round him ever since we got here. No one's said anything about seeing him.'

She rose suddenly to her feet. 'Who can I talk to?'

'There's a doctor. He walked through just a moment ago. I expect he'll be back soon.'

'I need to be with him. Even if he doesn't know I'm there, I want to be with him. I'm going to find someone.'

The one member of staff at the nurses' station was on the phone, and made no sign of either recognising she was waiting, or of finishing the call. Finally Annie gave up, and started to make her way down the corridor, peering in first this door, then another. There was no sign of Keith.

She hurried back to the nurses' station. It was empty. Clenching her fists with despair and frustration, she scanned the deserted corridors wondering what to do next. In an instant, she knew. Running to the phone kiosk, she controlled the shaking of her hand just long enough to punch in Simon's number.

'Christine?'

There was a pause before she answered. 'Hello Alistair.'

'Are you all right? It's been so difficult to speak to you at the surgery, and whenever I've rung you at home, there's been no answer.'

'I'm fine.'

'You don't sound it.'

'Alistair, I'm in the middle of bathing Robbie. I need to go.'

'Hang on a minute! What's going on? Are you mad at me or something? Talk to me!'

'Look, I'm busy right now. Ring me later.'

'I've done that for the past three nights, when I knew you were there but you didn't pick up the phone.'

'I've had a fault on the line.'

'I think the fault is mine. I don't know how or why, but I know I'm in trouble for something.'

'Alistair, please . . .'

'I'm coming round!'

'I'd rather you didn't.'

'Well, I'm coming anyway, and I intend to keep my hand on the car horn outside your door until you let me in.'

'Robbie's calling me. I've got to go.' And the line went dead in his hand.

When she got back to the waiting area, Derek was gone.

'He's gone in to see your son,' said a nurse's voice at her elbow. 'Come through and join him – only for a minute, mind!'

Keith lay on a bed that was high and wide, surrounded by monitors and tubes. The nurse checked the readings and adjusted one of the drips before tiptoeing out of the room. As Derek stood to one side of the bed, Annie was struck by the likeness between father and son: the same sandy hair, the same shape to the chin and mouth, those matching blue-grey eyes. But would Keith ever open his eyes again?

She squatted on the chair beside her son, taking his hand, stroking the wispy blond hair that covered his forehead. 'Keith! Keith, darling, it's Mum. It's all right, you're going to be all right. Can you hear me, love? Try and open your eyes.'

'Why should he? He tried to kill himself. He won't be pleased to find he's still here.'

She turned on Derek then, her eyes blazing. 'Just clear off, would you, if that's all you have to say. We don't need you.'

'Well, it stands to reason, doesn't it? He tried to kill himself, and he even made a mess of that!'

She was on her feet, fists pummelling his chest. 'Get out! Just get out! Go back to your little secretary and tell her how no one understands you! Just get out of my sight.'

For one endless moment he stared down at her in shock at what he'd heard. Then his shoulders slumped and his expression softened. 'Annie, it's not that I don't care. I do. Of course I do. It's just that I can't fathom him. He's not someone I know any more.' He reached out clumsily to take her arms, to bring her closer to him, aware that every muscle in her body was stiff against him.

'Just leave, Derek,' she said quietly, avoiding his eyes. 'Please.'

Hardness crept into his face again as he dropped his hold on her and left the room. The shaking in her hands crept down her backbone, rooting her to the ground with anger and anguish. It wasn't until she sat down to steady herself, and draw the chair closer to the bed, that she noticed the tear that coursed its slow sad path down Keith's cheek. She leaned forward urgently towards him. His voice was hoarse, his words racked with pain and effort.

'He's right, you know. I wanted to stop living. I tried to kill myself. And I couldn't even do that right . . .'

When she didn't respond to the doorbell, Alistair was uncertain what to do. He felt like thumping on the door until she opened it, but knowing Robbie would be asleep he realised that such action would hardly endear him to her. Instead, he prised open the letter box and called her name urgently. It was while he was bending over with his lips to the box that the door suddenly opened.

'Christine! Thank God! Are you all right? What's going on?'

She didn't reply immediately, but handed him a small white envelope.

'I can't talk to you, Alistair. And I'm not much of a letter writer, but I'd like you to read this. Then, please leave us alone. It's kinder that way. Good night.'

And before he could speak, the door was shut firmly in his face.

By the light of the lamppost at the end of her road, he ripped open the envelope, then tilted the letter so that he could read the small neat handwriting in the yellow light.

Dear Alistair,

    You are the kindest, most wonderful man I have ever known. Then, when I saw you kissing that girl in the field on Bonfire Night, I realised that any real relationship between us would be quite wrong for you. You are a talented young doctor from a well-to-do medical family. I am an unmarried mother and part-time secretary. You deserve more — the very best — and I could never be what's best for you.

Thank you for the magic you brought into our lives. Thank you especially for Robbie, who in all his life has never known a man he could trust enough to want to sit on his shoulders at a bonfire display. And thank you from me — for letting me believe for just a little while that I was special. I'm not. We both know that. But I shall never forget the feeling, nor the pain of recognising the truth. And because of that pain, I ask you to care enough to leave us alone now.

With love
Christine

Alistair wiped his hand across his forehead in a familiar gesture of frustration and disbelief. Then, stuffing the letter into his pocket, he turned away, leaving the crumpled envelope discarded on the pavement in the pool of ochre lamplight until a slight gust of wind blew it away.

Simon came immediately. She felt the warm touch of his hands on her shoulders and his breath on her hair before he moved round to look closely at Keith. He was asleep, a troubled slumber in which his face twitched and contorted, perhaps with pain, perhaps with thoughts too painful to bear.

'I've had a word with the consultant. He thinks they caught him just in time, but what they don't know yet is exactly what he took. It seems it was a cocktail of anything he could lay his hands on, and that probably includes a measure of paracetamol and aspirin. Because of that, they're monitoring him for liver and kidney damage . . .'

He felt her shocked intake of breath, and covered her hand with his as he continued.

'Both are possible, but it's too soon to know just how much his long-term health will be affected by this.'

'But we're not talking about the long term, are we? The question now is not how long, but how little time does he have left?'

'His condition is serious, but stable at the moment. We'll know more when he's strong enough for further tests.'

Her head fell, shoulders slumped, as without thinking she leaned towards him. His arms went round her, rocking her gently, reassuringly. Her hair smelled faintly of lemons and white spirit. She felt slight and fragile and small against him. Needy. Nice.

'Come on,' he said at last, 'you look all in. Let's go and find a cup of coffee, and somewhere to talk properly.'

Reluctant to take her eyes off her sleeping son, she allowed Simon to pull her to her feet. Then after brushing the backs of her hands across her tear-stained cheeks, she unclipped her hair so that it fell in soft strands around her pale face, masking her gaunt expression. He led her along anonymous hospital corridors, guiding her to a quiet corner in the canteen where she sat expressionless until he returned with two lukewarm cups of coffee.

'He's going to die, isn't he.' A statement, not a question.

He stretched out to cover her hand. 'Yes. He's very poorly.'

'When? How much time do you think he has?'

'I'm not sure, Annie. He's survived this attempt to take his life, but in the end it will have brought the inevitable nearer.'

'How long? Days?'

'Oh, certainly.'

'Weeks?'

'Probably.'

'Months?'

'Perhaps. We'll have a better idea once he's through the next couple of days.'

'But he doesn't want to be here, does he? He thinks he's

failed. He wanted to die. And I want him to live so much . . .'
Tears spilled from her eyes, rolling down her cheeks, but she
ignored them. 'And what do I say to him now? That I'm relieved
beyond belief that he's alive, when we both know he wishes he
were dead? He's my son, my only child. He's killing himself,
and all I can do is sit and watch him.'

'Annie . . .'

'I feel so helpless. Powerless, hopeless and totally alone. I
want to scoop him into my arms, and give him *my* will to live.
I would gladly give him my life. I should die first. He should be
the one crying at my funeral. That's the natural way of things.
And yet, the day will soon come when I'll be walking behind
my own child's coffin – and there's nothing I can do to stop it,
nothing at all, is there?'

'We'll do all we can, all he will allow. We'll keep him
comfortable and . . .'

'Is there?' Her eyes blazed into his, challenging, demanding,
unspeakably sad.

He returned her gaze steadily. 'No, not if he won't work
with us.'

'And he won't. We both know that.'

He didn't reply. He didn't need to. She stood up abruptly,
her coffee untouched. 'I'm going back. I want to be with him.'

'It's nearly midnight. You're whacked, and it's unlikely he'll
wake tonight. Let me take you home.'

'I want to be with him.'

'Of course you do, and it's important you're here when he
wakes up. But that won't be until the morning. Believe me,
you're going to need all your energy for what lies ahead.'

'I won't be able to sleep. I might just as well be here.'

'And give the nurses two ill people to look after? Let them
do their job with Keith, and come back in the morning.'

'I'll just lie awake.'

'No you won't. I'm your doctor. I'll give you something to
help you rest.'

'I don't want to be tranquillised. I might miss a call.'

'Nothing's going to happen tonight, I promise you.'

She looked into his eyes, searching for signs of patronising insincerity, yet all she found was compassion and . . . something else? Friendship perhaps? A bond of trust and empathy that danced between them? But how could he possibly know what she was going through? He'd never been a parent. Nevertheless she felt his arm beneath her elbow, and together they walked back to Keith's room to find the nurse carefully checking the jumble of drips, gauges and monitors that surrounded him. She smiled at them as they entered.

'He's doing fine, much more settled and peaceful. He'll just sleep, I'm sure. You go off home, and I'll give you a call if there's anything you need to know.'

'I'll be back first thing. What time can I come?'

'Whenever you want to.' The nurse's voice was reassuring, kind enough to bring tears perilously near again to Annie's reddened eyes. A look of complete understanding passed between doctor and nurse before Simon gently led Annie away.

He drew the car right up to her front door. The house was in darkness.

'Derek will be in, won't he? I don't think you should be alone.'

'Of course. He's probably gone to bed.'

'You do the same then. Take a couple of those tablets.'

'They won't make me feel muggy in the morning? I want to be on the ball when Keith wakes up . . .'

'Annie, they'll be fine. Ring me if you hear or need anything. Just call me. OK?'

She nodded, then turned to open the car door. With her fingers on the handle she stopped, pale and lovely as she faced him in the darkness.

'You've been wonderful. I couldn't have got through tonight without you.'

'I'm your doctor.'

'You're my friend. When I'm angry and scared and un-reasonable, you take it all. You seem to understand that what I say isn't always what I mean. You make sense of what feels sense-less. Thank you.'

She climbed slowly from the car, walking up the path without a backward glance, as if it needed all her concentration to put one foot in front of the other.

Simon watched until the front door finally closed behind her, then wearily rested his head back against the seat. Of course he understood. Of course he knew what she was going through. Only too well . . .

Derek wasn't at home, at least not at his own home. When he'd left Keith and Annie earlier that evening he'd stood outside the hospital not knowing what to do, where to go. For him, that was a new experience. He always knew what his plans were, where he was heading – but for the first time in his life, his mind was a blank, his emotions in turmoil. And because he was unable to think of anything he'd rather do, he drove to Julie.

She was in her dressing gown, her face registering surprise and pleasure at the sight of him on her doorstep. Within seconds she realised something was wrong, dreadfully wrong. Leading him through to the living room, she sat him down and fixed him a neat whisky.

It was some time before he finally spoke. Then it all came tumbling out: about finding Keith, the shock and squalor of the sight of his son on the floor of the bathroom; the ambulance, the intensive care room, the consultant, the drips; Keith's face as he lay pallid and drained on the crisp white hospital sheet. And Annie.

'She knows.'

'What do you mean?'

'About us.'

'What about us?'

'That we're closer than we should be.'

'How does she know?'

'I'm not sure, but she was very specific.'

'What did she say?'

'Do you know, we stood beside that bed, with our son practically dead in front of us, and all we could do was argue?'

'Well, she must have been very upset about Keith.'

'More upset with me. She can't take the truth, that's her trouble. She can't see him as he is. He makes a hash of everything – even killing himself.'

Julie knelt down in front of him, so that her face was practically level with his. 'Don't try and pretend you don't care, Derek Ryder. I know you better. You're a tough man. You know your own mind, but you have no idea when it comes to emotions. You can't put into words what you feel, so you tell yourself that means you feel nothing. You care. I know you do.'

He held her gaze for seconds before leaning towards her, sighing deeply. 'I can't help myself, Jules. And I can't help him . . .'

To her surprise he crumpled before her, shoulders shuddering with sobs that came from the depths of his being. And she found herself crying with him as she cradled his head in her arms, and held him tightly to her.

Chapter Eleven

It began as just a whisper – a word in an ear here, a nod to the knowing there. Of course Pauline Gregory had to explain to her mum about her decision to take Naomi to another practice, especially when that meant a trip into Southampton, and because her mum simply couldn't believe anything but good of Dr Gatward, she felt she must chat it over with her friend, Betty. Betty happened to be a dinner lady at the local school, and somehow while dishing out the nutritionally-correct menu of quiche and stir-fry, she sought the advice of her friend, Barbara, who would definitely have a relevant opinion seeing as her daughter was a nurse. After chatting it over with her husband who announced that he had no intention of letting a gay doctor feel *his* bumps, Barbara felt duty-bound to mention it both to her daughter, and to her daughter-in-law, who was well known in Berston as a child minder. She discussed it over a cup of tea with a couple of mums who arrived at the same time one evening to collect their youngsters – and that was how it finally became the topic of conversation at the playgroup. The playgroup leader mentioned it to her fiancé who brought up the subject with his team mates after football practice – and one of them told his mum because he really thought she ought to know. As it happened, she worked at the surgery, and Joan was so aghast at the stupidity of the tale she heard from her son that she simply couldn't wait until she saw Moira at the surgery the next morning to talk about it. She rang her straight away that night, and the two worried receptionists were on the phone for almost an hour as they agreed the suggestion was quite ridiculous. Of course, Simon wasn't gay. They'd have known if he was.

Wouldn't they?

Alistair didn't feel like going to the gym any more. Oh, he liked the exercise well enough, and the crowd of lads he'd got to know there were a good bunch – but it was Wendy. He couldn't deny that he had been flattered from the start by the obvious attention of such an attractive young woman. She was fun and flirty, and he'd come to enjoy their après-exercise drinks in the bar. Why he'd started giving her a lift to the gym was a little vague to him now. He remembered how, on that first evening, she'd mentioned that she'd cycled in, then turned her amazing blue eyes towards the drops of rain that were dribbling steadily down the window pane. Without a moment's hesitation, he'd heard himself offering her, and her bike, a ride home. She'd needed help getting the bike out of his car and into her garage, which led on to a cup of coffee and a chat that lasted beyond midnight. Before he knew it, he was offering to pick her up en route the following week. Nothing in it, of course. He was too fond of Christine for that. Nevertheless, he found himself looking forward to the undoubted pleasure of Wendy's company on gym night.

Why he'd never mentioned the arrangement to Christine, he was unsure. Why he'd not put an immediate stop to the way in which Wendy kissed him to say hello, goodbye – and just about everything else – he was uncertain. And why he hadn't introduced the two women when he'd had the chance on Bonfire Night, he simply couldn't fathom. But the hurt in Christine's dignified expression as she handed him her letter had brought him down with a bump. For the sake of being flattered by a gorgeous but rather empty-headed companion, he had lost the woman he'd grown to love. He hadn't realised how much Christine meant to him until suddenly she was no longer there. She remained distant and self-contained. His phone calls were unanswered, his notes returned still sealed. Leave us alone, she had said. She'd meant it.

He missed her – her warmth and vulnerability and sense of humour. He missed her fry-up suppers, her frugal habit of never throwing anything away, and the darns in her old woolly socks. He missed the way she hiccoughed when she giggled, and smiled while she slept. He missed the smell of her, and the feel of her skin. He missed her arms around him and taste of her kisses. He missed the blush that crept across her cheeks when she looked at him, and the trust in her eyes.

But he had betrayed that trust – and now she was gone.

At the surgery, she spoke to him when work required it. She was pleasant and polite, but if he came too close she moved away. It was all very proper and civilised, and it was tearing him apart.

After days of this, he looked up to find Moira eyeing him sympathetically. Minutes later there was a quiet knock on his surgery door and she walked in carrying some notes. But it wasn't the notes she wanted to talk about. Ten minutes and a motherly chat later, she'd suggested a plan of action to which he'd found himself agreeing. It probably wouldn't work, but he was desperate enough to try anything.

But they didn't dwell on the subject of his love life for long. Moira had a much more pressing matter she needed to discuss with young Dr Norris.

Bert had always taken pride in being a greenhouse man. The fact that he'd persuaded Simon to invest in a new greenhouse that autumn was a source of great satisfaction to him. The doctor might only have succumbed to the idea as a sop to Bert for hurting his feelings earlier in the year, but that mattered not a jot. The splendid structure had arrived in September, since when he'd had hours of pleasure in it: planning, fitting, thinning, pruning, potting, mulching and sprinkling. Ivy had been anxious to take a peep, but he'd resisted all her pleadings until he was good and ready. Nonetheless he was touched by her interest and encouragement, especially as he'd never thought of her being that interested in gardening matters before. But then, being a simple soul, it wouldn't occur to him that Ivy's interest stemmed more from a chance to take a good look round the house both outside and hopefully inside too. With all the intriguing talk going round about Dr Gatward and his leanings, a visit to his home would make for a very pleasant and fascinating couple of hours. Very interesting indeed!

For the first half hour of her visit, during which Bert explained the layout of the greenhouse and his plans for the coming summer and all the summers beyond, she clucked and made encouraging sounds in what she hoped were the right places. Her eyes began to glaze over slightly as she wondered if he was ever going to suggest going inside the house. A cup of tea perhaps? A comfy seat to rest the poorly knee he knew caused her so much discomfort – not that she mentioned it, of course? Finally, desperate measures were called for. From the depths of her shopping bag she drew out her winning weapon – a packet of Jaffa Cakes. Bert stopped mid-sentence.

'I don't know about you,' she said, her eyes twinkling provocatively, 'but I'm parched. Where's the kettle? Do you keep one in the shed?'

Bert eyed the biscuits as he shook his head. 'The kitchen's the place. He'll have milk there too.'

'What a good idea. But should we, do you think?' Her face was a picture of innocent concern.

Without bothering to reply, he carefully put down the pelargonium cutting he'd been showing her and led the way out of the greenhouse. Digging under the usual flower pot for the door key, he let them both into the house. Bert made straight for the kitchen and kettle while Ivy took her time, peering at this painting and that photo, opening this cupboard and that door.

Her scream brought Bert hurrying through from the kitchen. He followed her horrified gaze to see Keith stretched out on the living room settee, quite at home in his dressing gown and pyjamas. He was awake. No chance of sleep once Ivy had let out her banshee-like cry – but he looked as surprised as they were to find he had company.

'Did you ring? I'm sorry, I didn't hear you.'

'No need,' replied Bert, who was first to recover his composure, 'Always let myself in. There shouldn't be anyone here.'

'Only me. Didn't Simon tell you I'm staying?'

'Can't say he did.' Bert's voice was gruff as he stuffed his hands deep into his pockets, unsure how he felt at this unexpected intrusion.

But Ivy's mind was already in overdrive. Dr Gatward might not have told anyone about his live-in companion – but *she* most certainly would!

News travels fast in a small community. Scandal travels faster. At seven o'clock the next evening, just as Simon closed the surgery door on his last patient, it opened again and Jill stepped inside. He was pleased to see her. Their paths had crossed very little over the past couple of weeks. She'd been tied up with clinics, trying to keep everything running smoothly in spite of the building work that had just started. He'd had his surgeries, of course, and house calls – and beyond that he'd just not been there much. She'd wondered if he was avoiding her. Or, in view of the rumours flying around, was it just their builder he was trying to avoid?

'Time for a chat?'

'With you, always.'

'Are you OK?'

'Of course. I'm fine. You?'

She ignored the question. 'Nothing worrying you?'

'Should there be?'

'That depends.'

'On what?'

'On whether the stories circulating about you at the moment are true.'

He looked at her coolly, then walked back to sit down behind the desk. 'Am I supposed to know what you mean by that?'

'Is Keith Ryder living with you?'

'Yes.'

It was her turn to sit down heavily. 'Why?'

'Why should it matter to anyone at all who lives at my house, *my* house?'

'Come on, Simon, you're not a fool. Figure it out for yourself.'

'Oh, I can figure out what mean-minded, malicious people with nothing better to do with their time might make of it. But you? What do you think?'

'I think . . .' She paused to consider for a moment. 'I think I don't know you any more.'

'I can't believe I'm hearing this. Of course you do! And you should know better!'

'So tell me why? Why is Keith with you, and not at his own home?'

'Because he didn't want to go back there.'

'That's up to him. What's it got to do with you?'

'Because he asked if he could stay with me. He's not getting on with his father. He knows how upset his mother is, and was concerned about being a burden on her. He wanted to stay with me – and because he's dying, and because at my house he can get the peace and quiet he needs where I can keep a convenient eye on him, I agreed. Why not? It seemed a very small favour to me.'

'What about professional detachment? What about the accepted line between doctor and patient? What about your reputation? Have you thought of that?'

'I see no dilemma at all.'

'Simon, do you know what they're saying? That you're emotionally, and therefore probably physically, involved with this man? That you could be HIV positive too? That you could be putting our patients at risk?'

His expression darkened. 'That's complete rubbish. I can't even be bothered to answer accusations like that.'

'But you must face them. Patients are leaving because of this!'

'They're not that stupid.'

'Not stupid, just confused and frightened. They're terrified at the very thought of AIDS. They've never been this close to a sufferer before. You can tell them till you're blue in the face that they are in no danger, and in their heads they'll believe you, while in their hearts they're in a state of panic.'

'What do you mean, they're leaving?'

'Pauline Gregory. Did you wonder why she didn't bring Naomi to see you again? And Janet Wharton, who's worried about that lump in her breast, but obviously even more worried about you, so she's joined another practice? They are just the tip of the iceberg. We've had notification from other surgeries that several of our long-term patients have asked to transfer to them, and many more patients who've insisted on seeing you for years have rung up this week asking to see Gerald or Alistair, even when you're free.'

In the harsh light of the surgery Jill saw the blood drain from Simon's face. 'This is unbelievable, just unbelievable.'

'What is it with this boy, Simon? Why have you got so involved?'

He didn't answer, except to shake his head and stare down at the papers before him. There was an awkward silence while she decided how to ask her next question.

'Simon, have you ever been involved with a woman?'

He looked up at her sharply. 'Jill, how can you of all people ask that?'

'Why didn't you sleep with me the other night? I made my feelings quite plain. I know you feel something for me. Why didn't we make love?'

'Because you're married.'

'Unhappily. You know that. And I love you. You know that too. So, why didn't you sleep with me?'

He looked at her for seconds before he spoke again. 'Because I love you too, and I don't want to hurt you.'

'Why should you hurt me?'

'Because I think I might.'

'Because you don't find me attractive? Or because you don't want to make love to any woman?'

He stared at her before a grimace of disbelief crossed his face. He bent his head, wearily running the fingers of both hands through his hair.

'Is that what you think? That I'm gay? Because I respect you, and care for you, and want to be sure of my feelings before I do anything that may hurt you, something that may break up your marriage and your family, and possibly break your heart? If I take time to consider all of that, the only explanation is that I must be gay?'

'Are you?'

'You've known me for years. You know I've always loved the company of women.'

'But I have no idea what your relationship has been with them. All I know is that from the very start I made it clear that I would enjoy a physical relationship with you, and you held back. You pushed me away. And you've just done it again. Is it simply that you don't fancy me? I could understand and accept that. I would be embarrassed and humiliated − but I would understand.'

He reached out a hand towards her. 'You're a beautiful, wonderful woman, probably the most attractive I've ever known . . .'

'But?'

'But I'm confused about exactly what I feel for you.'

'And your feelings for Keith are less confusing?'

'In some ways, yes. In others I completely agree with you. I can't explain why I invited him to stay, except that I *like* him. I like his intelligence, his sense of humour, his talent, his personality. I ache at the sadness of his situation. He's so young, yet so tragically determined to die.'

'But you come into contact all the time with dear people who are facing their own death. Why should this one touch you so much?'

To her surprise his eyes became glassy as he answered bleakly, 'I can't explain.'

'Can't or won't?'

He thought for a moment before replying. 'I can't.'

'Why not?'

'It's too complicated.'

'We've been friends for a long time, Simon. Try me.'

He looked straight at her. 'I'm sorry, Jill. I just can't.'

She came round to stand beside him, kneeling down until her face was level with his. 'OK, but you must ask him to leave. He must go to his own home, or you can arrange residential care for him. He must leave your house for the sake of the practice and your reputation.'

He pulled back from her. 'I'll do what I feel is right for my patient, a tragic young man who has no more than a few weeks to live. Beyond that I promise nothing.'

'Please, Simon, think this through. I'm serious.'

He covered her hand with one of his own. 'I appreciate your concern. You had no choice but to mention it, no more than I have any choice except to do what I instinctively feel is right.'

He got up quickly, and while she returned to her seat deep

in thought he gathered papers into his briefcase and glanced at his watch.

'I've got to go. Will you be all right?'

She smiled weakly back at him. 'Of course.'

He leaned down, and lifting her chin with one hand, gently kissed her lips.

'There was someone, you know.'

She stared at him, uncertain that she'd heard correctly.

'For six years. Her name was Alison.'

'When? How come you never told me?'

'While I was in Cardiff. While you and Michael were setting up the Home Beautiful with the two lovely children and the two new cars in the drive.'

'Were you married?'

'She didn't want that. I did ask her.'

'And were you happy together?'

'Yes, I certainly was, for some of the time anyway.'

'So what happened?'

A shadow crossed his face as he pulled back abruptly. 'She left.'

'Why?'

'Things happened. Her feelings for me changed.'

'What things?'

His hand was on the door handle. 'It would take too long to explain.'

'Why have you never mentioned this before?'

'It was a long time ago.'

'It lasted six years – and you forgot to mention it?'

He pulled the door open.

'The trouble is I can never forget. I wish to God I could.'

Shocked by the bleakness of his expression, Jill stared help-lessly after him as he left the room.

It was late when Derek got back to the office. He knew Julie would wait. After all, as she'd told him only the evening before, what was an hour or two considering how long she'd waited for him already? What she'd gone on to say – and do – after that brought a secret smile to his face as he took the stairs two at a time. She heard him coming and had a coffee ready, along with a kiss, the moment he was inside the door.

'Interesting phone call this afternoon. Martin Balcombe was very anxious to get hold of you. Something about the contract for the school being decided this week.'

'Is it now?' He looked at his watch. 'Too late to ring him tonight, but that will be a phone call I'll look forward to in the morning. I'll need to sort our schedules out and ring round some of the extra men I'll have to take on. I want to be completely ready when Gareth offers me the contract.'

'Will he? Are you that sure?'

Derek's smile was slow and confident. 'Absolutely. He owes me one. Two thousand "ones", in fact.'

She pulled back to peer closely at him.

'You look tired. How's it going at the surgery?'

'It's the mucky part at the moment, digging out the foundations, knocking walls down, and this weather doesn't help. It's going OK though. We're on time so far.'

'What about Dr Gatward? Have you seen him?'

'As little as possible. I heard his appointments over the tannoy when I called in this morning, so he must have been there, but I stayed out of his way. I've got nothing to say to him.'

'How's Keith? Has Annie seen him?'

'She's there most days. It's all very cosy, this arrangement.'

'Well, have you spoken to Keith about it? Couldn't you persuade him to come home?'

He looked at her levelly. 'I have no intention of begging him. Apparently he no longer wants to live in his own home, and that's my fault – so Annie tells me anyway.'

'Oh, Derek.'

'She said something about him wanting to rebuild his

relationship with me. How does he expect to do that if he's living somewhere else?'

'But if you wouldn't talk to him when he was living there, the atmosphere at home must have been unbearable for all of you. And after what's happened, it's not surprising that Keith felt he couldn't cope with your disapproval when he's feeling so ill.'

'Look, don't you start.'

She laid her hand gently on his arm. 'Sometimes you need a good friend to tell you what's obvious to everyone else. If Keith dies before you get round to repairing the rift between you, you will regret it for the rest of your life.'

This stopped him in his tracks. He looked at her wordlessly.

'I love you, Derek, but you're all bluster. You're hurting about this, so you know very well what you have to do. Make your peace with Keith. Go and see him. Bring him home.'

'He won't come.'

'How do you know if you don't try?'

He sighed. 'It's all too late now.'

'It can never be too late. This matters, Derek.'

'I'm blowed if I'm going to go crawling round to that doctor's place to speak to my own son . . .'

'But he's too ill to come to you, so that's where you must go.'

He broke away from her, walking over to his usual seat behind his desk. He sat there for a while, elbows on the table in front of him.

'Talk to Annie.' Her voice was quietly persistent. 'She'll help you.'

His laugh was hollow. 'We don't talk. We haven't spoken for days.'

'How do you feel about that?'

When he didn't answer, she waited a while before continuing. 'Do you still love her?'

'We've been together a long time. Thirty years.'

'Do you love her?'

'I care about her.'

'Could you live without her?'

'Perhaps.'

'Could she live without you?'

'I'm not sure. She probably doesn't realise how much I provide for her, how much she needs me.'

'Women are very resourceful, you know. They manage when they have to, when they *want* to.'

'She'd never want me to leave her.'

'Are you sure about that?'

'Of course I'm sure. She's my wife.'

'Your wife, but not your possession. She's a person in her own right. She has a career of her own, things that she cares about that hold no interest for you.'

He shrugged his shoulders, looking through papers on his desk, seeing none of them.

'Why should she want to stay with someone who's no longer interested in her?'

'I've always looked after her. I'm not sure she'd cope . . .'

'Oh, she'd be fine. But you? Could you really bear not to have her in your life?'

He considered for a moment before answering. 'She's always been there. Even in the last few years through all this business with Keith, she's always been there.'

'And you'd miss her?'

'I suppose I would.'

'Enough to make you want to stay?'

'I couldn't live alone. I could never sleep by myself night after night.'

'Ah, but you wouldn't be by yourself.' She was beside him now, her voice softly seductive. 'And what makes you think you'd want to spend your nights sleeping?'

★

She turned at the sound of his key in the door, then sat back on her heels, rubbing her aching shoulders. She heard him drop his keys in the hall before the lounge door opened and Simon was beside her.

'How is he?'

'Asleep. He's been very peaceful for an hour or so, much more settled than he's been for the past few days.'

Simon bent over the makeshift bed that had been brought downstairs, peering at the sleeping form as he checked Keith's pulse, colour, temperature and breathing.

'Those pills are obviously doing the trick. What he needs most of all is rest. He should be out for the count until the morning.' He glanced at her pale face. 'You look out for the count yourself. I'll take over now. Why don't you go home and get a good night's sleep?'

She nodded dumbly as he gently pulled her to her feet before settling her on the nearby settee where she sank down with her head back, eyes closed. He poured them both a glass of wine, then came over to sit beside her.

'Have you eaten? I made a casserole.' She spoke without opening her eyes, her voice toneless with fatigue.

'Did you have some yourself?'

'I made it for Keith, and for you.'

'Annie, you must eat. You need your strength too.'

She turned her head towards him, her smile almost reaching her eyes. 'You sound like a wife, nag, nag, nag. Besides, if I'd not made that casserole, would you have cooked this evening? What have you eaten today?'

It was his turn to smile, their faces almost touching as they laughed together. 'I'd go and dish up for both of us if I had the energy to get off this settee.'

'It'll keep. This wine won't.' She took a deep gulp from her glass and leaned back with a sigh. 'I like this room. It's very peaceful, especially in the evening as the sun goes down.'

'That's my favourite time too. Sometimes I sit here with

music on, just looking out over the trees as the sky changes colour. I've always loved huge skies. Must be my East Anglian upbringing . . .'

'Really? Where did you live?'

'Suffolk. My dad was a farmer, one of a long family line. It was quite a shock when his first-born son chose to become a doctor rather than take over the farm as he expected me to.'

'Was he disappointed?'

'Probably, but he never put it into words. My mum was as pleased as punch to have a son with a "profession". Given a different upbringing I think she would have enjoyed an academic life herself, but an education was considered unnecessary for a farmer's daughter in her day.'

'Shame. Did your dad realise how she felt?'

'Yes, but he never really understood it. He needed a wife who would cook, clean, organise and tackle any job that no one else was available for on the farm, and she did all of that without a word of complaint. But what I remember most about her was how she loved to read with me. When I was small, of course, she would do the reading, and I still recall the way she used to make the story come alive, full of drama and pathos. Then later we'd pore over books together. I'd bring something home, or she would take a trip to the library. It kept us very close.'

'Still?'

'She died about twelve years ago, and even now not a day goes by when I don't think about her. I owe her so much.'

'And your dad?'

'He's in his seventies now, still farming, but in a different way.'

'What happened to the farm?'

'My sister made up for everything. She married an ox of a man who's not just a gentle giant but has the knack for farming running in his blood. They took over the family house and Dad's farm, and brought up four sons of their own there. Dad just has a small flock of rare-species sheep he calls his own, but really it's

David's farm now. And it's a relief for me to know that he's well looked after.'

'A farmer's son. I'd never have imagined you as that.'

'Well, I still grab every opportunity to get out where there's fresh air and no people.'

'Hence the fishing . . .'

'Hence the fishing. I've always loved it.' He took another mouthful of wine before turning again to look at her. 'What about you? Do you come from this area?'

'No, it was Derek's work that brought me here. My family lived on the south coast. My father was an engineer working as a civilian mostly in Portsmouth Dockyard.'

'So you grew up with the sea lapping your toes. Do you miss that?'

'Very much. Every now and then, when I need to get away for a while, I head for the little bay where I played as a child which I've always thought of as my own.'

'Any fish there?'

'I think so. I'll never forget my dad took me fishing there once years ago, and it was a complete disaster. I did absolutely everything wrong. I talked too loud, I used the wrong bait, I reeled in too soon – and then I caught more than he did!'

Simon laughed out loud – and perhaps because of the tension surrounding Keith, perhaps because they were both laid low with exhaustion – for whatever reason, she burst out laughing too. The pair of them felt it bubble up inside them like steam escaping from a pressure cooker. How good it felt to throw their heads back and giggle like children! At last, as the laughter finally subsided, they sat together, faces and fingers almost touching. She looked down at their hands and sighed.

'I haven't laughed for so long.'

'It's good for you. Doctor's orders.'

'Not a lot to laugh about these days.'

'How are things at home?'

'I'm not there much.'

'I've seen Derek around the surgery, even tried to speak to him a couple of times. He makes a point of avoiding me.'

'He probably is. He blames you for Keith's decision not to go home when the hospital discharged him. Being at logger-heads with his father was wearing him down, but Derek can't see that. I can never thank you enough for making him so welcome here.'

'His wellbeing matters to me. I can keep an eye on him under my own roof.'

'That's part of the explanation. But there's more to it, I know.'

He didn't answer.

'Is there any problem about him being here?' she continued. 'What about the practice? Have they made any comment?'

'It's no one's business but my own.'

'Don't make any trouble for yourself, Simon, not on our account. I couldn't bear that after all your kindness.'

'He's here because I want him to be.'

'Just because he's your patient?'

In the half-light, he looked over towards Keith.

'Doctors are trained to detach themselves from their patients. They have to, if they're to keep their own sanity. But from the first moment I met Keith, something about him touched me deeply . . .'

He stopped for a moment, feeling her fingers touch his.

'His dignity, the trust in his eyes as he looked at me – they stirred something inside, a feeling I thought I'd forgotten.'

'Forgotten?'

'And then I saw the way people reacted to him, their prejudice and fear about a condition they didn't understand, and . . .'

'. . . you wanted to protect him.'

'Yes.'

'Fight the battles he wasn't strong enough to fight himself?'

'Exactly that. To put my arm around his shoulder and . . .'

'. . . love him?'

His gaze was direct and slightly questioning. 'Yes. *Love* him. That was the feeling I thought I'd forgotten, the emotion I was no longer capable of experiencing.'

'Because loving in the past has brought you pain?'

He nodded. 'And for some reason Keith brought all that back to me. Don't ask me why, because I can't explain, not now. But yes, I find myself loving him, in the purest sense of the word. I'm not talking about anything physical. I could never feel physical attraction for another man. I'm talking about quite a different love.'

'Like a father for a son?'

If he heard her, he chose not to respond to her question, his mind clearly set on his own train of thought. 'Men aren't supposed to love each other, are they? It would be misunderstood. To show such emotion would be a display of weakness.'

'There's nothing weak about you. It takes great courage to follow your heart rather than your head in a situation like this. I can imagine the gossip . . .'

'There's plenty of that!'

'Could that damage you? Have implications for your job and career?'

'It might.'

'Then, Simon, Keith must leave.'

'No! Until he's too ill to be anywhere but in hospital, he's better off here. We both know that.'

'You,' she said gently, cupping his hand in both of her own, 'are the most remarkable man I've ever met.'

'No.'

'No words are enough to thank you for your skill, your care – and your love.' Leaning towards him, she gently laid her lips against his cheek for some seconds, until she felt him relax against her and his head drop to rest on the soft gold of her hair.

★

Later that night, three miles as the crow flies from Simon's house, Jill was sitting up in bed reading when she finally heard Michael's car in the drive. She listened as he pottered around for several minutes before coming upstairs. She heard him drop his briefcase in his study before tearing open his mail, then opening the fridge door to get himself his customary orange juice before bed. He was taking gulps of it as he came into their bedroom.

'Good meeting?' she asked without taking her eyes off her book.

'Nothing resolved. You know what these committees are like. Need a rocket under them before they achieve anything worthwhile.'

He dropped his watch, gold fountain pen and money into a dish on his bedside cabinet and headed towards the bathroom leaving the door slightly ajar as he went. Jill sighed. There had been an uneasy truce between them since the episode at the charity music night. With unspoken agreement, the matter had not been mentioned since. In fact, conversation between them had been polite and only when strictly necessary. Jill had been grateful for that. Her emotions were too confused to be sure either of her feelings or reactions.

The shower ran for several minutes before he eventually emerged, smelling of expensive body spray and toothpaste. He was rubbing his wet hair with a deep blue towel which he discarded beside the bed before climbing in. Then he leaned down to pick up a letter he must have placed on the floor when he first came into the room.

'I need to talk to you.'

She laid down her book and turned to face him.

'This is the confirmation letter of my post in London. Take a look.'

She did. The wording was effusive and complimentary, leaving no doubt that the company felt privileged to have Michael join their team. When she got to the terms of employ-ment – the pension, private health care package, bonus company shares and top-of-the-range car, coupled with a salary that seemed to have too many noughts on it to be anything other than a typing error – the truth hit her. Michael was leaving Berston. Now she had to decide. Was she going with him?

'When do you start?'

'The beginning of February.'

'Have you handed in your notice yet?'

'First thing tomorrow, but I already mentioned informally that my resignation was imminent.'

'How did they react?'

'What do you expect? They were devastated.'

'They would be.' The wryness of her reply was lost on Michael.

'However, my darling, it's *your* reaction that interests me most. I'm not the only one who has to hand in my notice. This place must go on the market, although I'm assured by Denis Garside – you know, the estate agent – that it will be snapped up in no time. More important is the issue of finding the right house for us to move on to. Somewhere spacious with a bit of land attached, perhaps with a tennis court, I'd especially like that, and of course, in the right social area. That's what Denis is putting out feelers to find for us.'

'You've spoken to an estate agent without talking to me first?'

'We've hardly been speaking. Remember?'

'Did you remember, Michael, that you are not a single man who only has his own commitments and wishes to take into account? I may be your wife, but I am not just an appendage, dragged around without my opinion mattering at all. How dare you organise all this without discussing it properly with me?'

Surprisingly, the arrogance left his face as he squared his body to face her. 'To be honest, Jill, I haven't dared to bring it up. You've been so quiet and distant. Whatever I said, it would be wrong.'

The honesty of this disarmed her. 'I hate living like this, in stony silence.'

'So do I.' He reached out to squeeze her hand. 'You mean the world to me, you know that, don't you?'

'No, I'm not sure I do. I know that as your wife I'm part of your grand scheme of things. I know I'm supposed to live up to your image of us, whatever that is. And I know I'm not performing up to scratch at the moment. But I can't, Michael, I just can't.'

'Why not? What's different now?'

'I love this village. I love my friends and neighbours here. And I love my job . . .'

'You love Simon Gatward, you mean. You always have. I've known that since I first met you.'

She gazed directly into his eyes. There seemed little point in answering.

'What I never understood before is why he didn't claim you. His fondness for you is obvious. But why did he never make a move? Why did he let me steal you from under his nose?'

She shrugged, still saying nothing.

'Of course, it's all become plain now. He's showing his true colours at last, inviting that homosexual boy to share his home. It's his lack of common sense which really amazes me. He must know the consequences of such an action, the ethical dilemma it places on his partners, not to mention the Local Medical Committee, who will undoubtedly have views on the matter. How fortunate that I am currently the chairman! It will give me a great deal of pleasure to take Dr High and Mighty Gatward down a peg or two . . .'

Jill snatched away her hand, shocked at the vindictive tone of his voice. 'You wouldn't . . . ?'

'Without a moment's hesitation, my darling. His behaviour is highly questionable at the very least. That young man is dying of AIDS, for which excellent treatment is now available. Has any of that treatment been given to him? No. Has Dr Gatward involved himself on a personal level with his patient? Without question. Has his medical judgement been impaired by his personal feelings? Undoubtedly. Has the dear doctor acted unethically, and contrary to the interests of his patients and his practice? Yes, yes, yes!'

'You don't understand him. You've never understood . . .'

'And you do? So how do you explain this recent turn of events? How can you feel anything but contempt for him now?' Jill recoiled from the look of pure triumph in his eyes. 'After all, my dear, he's hardly going to want you, is he, seeing as he's a poof?'

Chapter Twelve

The weather was unseasonably mild as December arrived. It seemed odd to have the shops full of Christmas decorations and present suggestions when the sun was shining as it should have been in October. Along the covered walkway to the Berston surgery, Moira had even managed to keep a few geraniums in flower much longer than usual.

'What's the use of me buying all these poinsettias cheap at the market if I can't plant them out because the summer bedding plants are still there?' she grumbled to Joan.

'It's a bad sign, mild weather at this time of year,' agreed Joan. 'We're in for a vicious cold snap in the New Year, you mark my words!'

'I'm not complaining about being warm, you understand, but it's no good for the flu patients. Nothing to kill off the bugs. Thank goodness Gerald insisted we all have flu jabs this year. We're going to need them to deal with the crowds of people coming in here with one virus or another.'

'Mind you,' chuckled Joan, 'it will be the plaster dust that kills us instead. How much longer is this building work going to take? I'm getting really fed up with the debris everywhere. This is supposed to be a sterile, hygienic area, for heaven's sake!'

Just at that moment Christine walked past with an armful of files. 'Just the girl I need to see!' announced Moira, grabbing the

most precariously balanced folders off the top of the pile and
following Christine to her desk.

'Good news and bad news! You know how I never win
anything?'

'No,' grinned Christine, 'but go on.'

'Well, my luck changed. I went in for that caption competition in the local paper the other week, and I won! I got the
prize through this morning – dinner for four in that lovely new
Italian place in the market square!'

'Moira, that's wonderful. Congratulations! When are you
going?'

'That's just it. The prize has to be taken on the restaurant's
opening night, and that's next Friday.'

'So? Friday's all right, isn't it?'

'Well, for me, it's fine. For Joan and Sandy who are coming with us, it's OK too. But for my John, it's a complete disaster!
He's away in Manchester with the bowls team that weekend.'

'Well, can't your daughter come instead?'

'I've asked her. She's on a diet for the next four weeks, so
that she can pig out at Christmas.'

'That means,' added Joan, joining the conversation, 'you'll
have to come!'

'Really? Are you sure?'

'Absolutely! You could do with a square meal.'

'But what about Robbie?'

'Ah well, providing you promise to have nothing fattening
in the house, my daughter will be happy to babysit. No payment
necessary, or anything daft like that. She likes to get away from
that hubby of hers once in a while anyway.'

'Moira, that's terrific! What do we wear?'

'It's a dressy do, so you'll need something slinky – you know,
a cocktail dress, a little off-the-shoulder number perhaps?'

Christine's face fell.

'And that's all organised too. I've had a word with Lynn
Webster and she says she has just the thing in her wardrobe.

She's bringing it in for you to try tomorrow.'

Christine, plainly speechless with delight, simply threw her arms around Moira's neck and hugged her.

'Thank you, that's wonderful! I could do with a bit of cheering up.'

Moira clucked sympathetically. 'I know, love. We'll have a great night.' Alistair's flashing call button caught her eye. 'Hang on, the next patient's needed.' She ran her finger expertly down the list of names, then spoke clearly into the tannoy. 'Ms Barbara Gordon please, to Dr Norris, surgery three.'

Alistair looked up from his notes to take in the vision of womanhood that entered his surgery. He had heard her name mentioned, of course, by the reception staff who giggled about the divorcee's tight skirt, lowcut top and roving eye whenever Simon was about. Strange that she should be visiting him, when Simon was in business just across the corridor.

'What can I do for you?'

'It's my chest.'

'Yes?'

'It hurts.'

'What sort of pain?'

'Achy.'

'Do you smoke?'

'Of course.'

'Any problems with shortage of breath?'

'Only after extreme exertion.' Her eyes twinkled at him.

'Such as?'

'Making love – or playing tennis.'

'Well, if you'd just like to pull up the back of your top, I'll have a listen to your chest.'

He looked down to scribble a line on her notes, only to find her sitting in just her minuscule bra when he looked up again. Without comment, he plugged the stethoscope into his ears and began the examination, aware that her eyes never left his face the whole time.

'That all sounds fine. Could it be muscle strain, do you think?'

'Probably. Too much exercise.'

'Well, get as much rest as possible – and stay off the, uh, exertion for a while, until it feels fully recovered. If you see no improvement in three or four days come back and see me.'

'Oh, I will,' she replied, as she sinuously slid back into her top, smoothing the thin material over her ample breasts. 'Tell me, doctor, are you a man who likes sport?'

Alistair swallowed. 'Rugby at medical school, regular visits to the gym, the odd game of badminton.'

'So, you must be very fit.' The word took on new meaning when she said it. 'Badminton? That probably means you'd be good at tennis. Perhaps you'd fancy coming along to the club some time?'

'Well, I'm kept very busy . . .'

'All work, doctor? I simply won't take "no" for an answer. You'd make the perfect tennis partner.'

'Really, Ms Gordon, I haven't got the time to . . .'

'And it would be such a good way for you to meet the right people, considering you're new to the area.'

'That's most kind of you, but . . .'

'And I *did* ask Dr Gatward to join me at one point. I thought it odd that he didn't take up my offer, but I realise why now. Correct me if I'm wrong, doctor, but I've heard he's only into Men's Doubles, isn't that right?'

'Gareth, at last! You're a very difficult man to get hold of!'

'Derek, good to hear from you. Yes, I'm sorry but with Mandy's wedding coming up at the weekend, it's been chaos at home.'

Derek settled back in his chair as he spoke into the receiver. 'The women get so keyed up about these things, don't they?'

'Carole has been wittering on about what she's going to wear for weeks. And now we've got through the battle about which of the aged relatives we're going to invite and which we're hoping don't hear about it, we're on to arguments about who's going to pick up who, when and from where. It's a nightmare! I'll be glad when the whole thing's over.'

'And where's the wedding to be? Somewhere local?'

'No, in the Brighton area where they're both living. They were both at college down that way, so most of their friends are in that neck of the woods.'

'I'm sure it will be a grand day, Gareth. Let's hope the weather holds.'

'Thanks, Derek – but it wasn't the weather you rang up to talk about. I'm sorry that the decision on the school contract is taking so long. The committee didn't get round to talking about it last week – too many other projects on the go. But as Chairman, I can assure you a final selection will be made next Wednesday evening.'

'I'd appreciate a straight answer, Gareth. What chance do you think we have?'

'Well, of course the decision isn't mine alone, as you well understand, but I see no reason why you shouldn't be in with an excellent chance.'

'Much competition?'

'It would be unethical for me to say, of course – but although I think you'll have a run for your money, things look very optimistic for you, especially with my endorsement.'

'And speaking of your endorsement, you'll be having a run on *your* money at the moment, Gareth, with everything that's going on.'

'How very right you are.'

'Tell me, are you taking your usual table at the club dinner on Thursday?'

'Will you be there too? How pleasant. I'll look forward to buying you a drink.'

'Until Thursday then. 'Bye, Gareth.'

Derek looked up towards Julie, who was listening to his end of the conversation as she perched on the side of his desk.

'Yes!' He shouted, punching the air with his fist. 'That contract is as good as ours!'

'Bless you!'

As Bert wiped his sleeve across his nose for the umpteenth time that morning, he became aware of the small, white-haired lady in her neat pink overall whose head had now appeared over the garden fence.

'Bad cold you've got.'

'A cold never hurt no one. I'm not complaining.'

'A lot of it around. My daughter told me there's practically no teachers left at the school. It's a killer flu this time, you know. Said so on TV.'

Without reply, Bert carried on shaking dirt from the roots of the lavender clump he was in the process of splitting.

'How's Ivy?'

'She's all right,' he replied, not bothering to look up from his chore.

'Still go to the Eventide Club on Tuesdays, does she? Only I've not been since my leg's been bad.'

'Reckon so.'

'Saw her with you over the fence the other week, but you'd gone by the time I got out here to say hello. Go in the house, did you?'

'I reckon.'

'We were at school together, you know, Ivy and me. Knew her husband, I did. Nice man, but funny eyes. Never trust a man with funny eyes.'

There was another explosion as Bert straightened his back painfully to sneeze again.

'Have you tried balsam? Two spoonfuls in a bowl of boiling water. Always does the trick for me. Mind you, if it's that flu, you need to be careful. The crematoriums can't cope, the TV said.'

That was enough for Bert. He threw down his fork and turned to head for the kitchen door.

'Going in, are you? Best thing probably. Got some medicine?'

Without looking back, he rummaged in his pocket to find a sachet of hot lemon cold remedy which he waved at her.

'That's right, you go and get warm. Just the ticket . . .' And her voice faded from him as he put the key in the lock, and stepped inside. His relief was short-lived though. Standing by the kettle, looking gaunt and pale, was Keith Ryder.

'Catch you, did she?' smiled the younger man. 'That old biddy doesn't miss a thing.'

Almost without thinking, Bert took a step back towards the door.

'The kettle's just boiled. Do you want me to make up that sachet for you?'

'No, it's all right. I think I'll just head off home . . .'

Another sneeze racked Bert's body, propelling the sachet out of his hand to land neatly at Keith's feet. He picked it up, and tipped the contents into a cup with 'HEAD GARDENER' engraved on the side. Eyeing Bert thoughtfully, he handed back the steaming concoction. 'You should be home in bed.'

'Don't you start. There's naught wrong with me.'

'I'm not sure Simon would agree with that. Anyway, it's started to rain. Can't do much in the garden now.'

'A little bit of rain never hurt . . .' Another sneeze had Bert painfully clutching his back, his eyes glassy and bloodshot.

'You've cut yourself.'

Bert looked down at his index finger dismissively. 'Just a scratch.'

'Let me put a plaster on it for you.'

'Don't bother . . .'

'Look, they're only in the cupboard here. It's no bother at all.'

'No!' Bert snatched his hand away with real fear in his eyes. Without bothering to take even one mouthful from the steaming lemon drink, he turned to open the kitchen door.

'Tell Simon I'll be back – some time, not sure when . . .'

For a second, a blast of wind blew a flurry of rain into the kitchen – then he was gone.

'Derek, just the man I was hoping to see.'

He turned to find Michael, looking suave yet relaxed in a smart dark suit, standing at his elbow.

'Good to see you again.' Derek stretched out to shake hands. 'Good turn-out for the club tonight, isn't it? A chance for the fellas to get away from the girls for a few hours. I hear they've got an interesting cabaret lined up for later.'

To his surprise, Derek felt Michael's hand firmly under his arm as he was propelled to a quiet corner of the bar.

'I've been meaning to ring you. How's your son?'

'Not good.'

'So I've heard. A suicide attempt. Most distressing for you and your family, on top of everything else. How's your wife taking it?'

'As badly as you'd expect. She's his mother, after all.'

'Forgive me, Derek, if I've been wrongly informed, but I thought someone told me that Keith was discharged from hospital.'

'That's right.'

'So he's at home now, is he?'

Derek stiffened. 'No, he's not, actually.'

'A special nursing home then? That's probably best, under the circumstances.'

'No.'

'Oh?' Michael's face was a picture of studied innocence. 'With a relative perhaps?'

'He's staying with Dr Gatward.'

'No! What, in his *home*, do you mean?'

'That's right.'

'And you're happy about that?'

'I most certainly am not. Personally I think hospital is the right place for him in his condition . . .'

'I'm inclined to agree with you.'

'. . . but there's nothing wrong with our house, if he needs somewhere to stay.'

'So why isn't he at home with you?'

'That, Michael, is a very good question.'

'Do you mean that Dr Gatward has not taken your concerns into account in this matter?'

'Dr Gatward seems to be a law unto himself, if you ask me.'

'And your wife? How does she feel about all this?'

'Women can be easily led, as I'm sure you well know.'

'And Keith?'

'Well, to be fair, I think the idea has come from him.'

'But why?'

'I'm not a man to hide my opinions, doctor. I consider the sexual leanings of my son to be totally unnatural, and I've made no secret of that – not to him, not to anyone. Perhaps he expected my attitude to change because those "leanings" have now brought him close to death, but I'm afraid he's wrong. Perhaps Dr Gatward is more lenient in these matters, and therefore more comfortable company than I am. But I must say I consider Dr Gatward's intervention to be an intrusion into our family life.'

'So do I, Derek, and I speak – unofficially at present, of course – in my role as Chairman of the Local Medical Committee. The question of Dr Gatward's "leanings" plainly needs to be carefully considered in the light of recent events.'

'I'm very relieved to hear it.'

'Would you consider making an official complaint?'

Derek eyed him thoughtfully. 'Depends. I might do.'

In a confiding gesture, Michael placed an arm around his

shoulders. 'Leave this to me, Derek, and thank you for drawing this disturbing situation to my attention.'

Derek found himself turning that conversation over in his mind for some minutes after Michael had drifted away into the crowd. However, the sight of Gareth Walters arriving at the other end of the bar cut across his thoughts. In fact it was almost an hour later before he managed to catch Gareth on his own, as he made his way out into the hall, presumably on the way to the Gents.

'Gareth, good to see you. What do you think of tonight's little get-together?'

Gareth was grinning broadly as he turned to greet Derek like an old friend. The free-flowing wine and 'boys will be boys' atmosphere of the evening had brought a flush to his cheeks and a sparkle to his eye.

'Derek, dear boy. Fingers crossed for you next week, eh?'

'So firmly crossed,' agreed Derek fishing into his inside pocket, 'that I must make sure I don't drop your Christmas card. And may I be the first to wish you and yours a wonderful day on Saturday! This,' he added quietly, tapping the envelope as he spoke, 'should stop the wine from running out . . .'

With a conspiratorial smile, Gareth quickly put the envelope straight into his back pocket. 'And a merry Christmas to you too! I'll be in touch – Thursday morning at the latest.'

Few would have noticed the look of quiet satisfaction which crossed Derek's face as he turned away. No doubt one thousand pounds would make Mandy's wedding go with a swing; but that was nothing to the Christmas he and his team would have when they were told officially that the lucrative Farthing Corner job was theirs!

Christine was awake long before the alarm clock on Friday morning, but allowed herself the luxury of lying snugly in bed, savouring the prospect of the evening ahead. Tonight she'd be having a glamorous meal at the lovely new Italian restaurant in the market square. With Robbie still so young, evening outings were few and far between for her. In fact she'd not been out for weeks, not since Bonfire Night to be precise. The memory of the events of that night clouded her thoughts for just a moment before she swung her legs out of bed, deliberately shutting the vision of Alistair's face out of her mind. But as she ran the bath and watched the bubbles swirl around the tub, she found herself thinking of him again. It still hurt. The memories of him in her home, her life, her arms were too recent and poignant to be laid aside that easily.

Robbie was still asleep. She had at least twenty minutes before she needed to rouse him for school, twenty minutes in which to wash her hair, give herself a face-pack, and shave those important little places which might show under the low-cut stylish cocktail dress that Lynn had so kindly lent her.

Her shoulders slipped under the water as Alistair slipped once more into her mind's eye. She loved his face: the way he frowned when he was concentrating, the lock of hair that fell across his forehead, those grey-blue eyes . . .

But he didn't love her. It had all been a dream, and she was far too much of a realist to believe that such dreams could come true. He was a good-looking man who would always have attractive girls around him. Not her though. She was neither attractive enough, nor willing to join a queue for any man. He wasn't to know that she'd never forget a moment of knowing him. It was past and gone. Best if she kept her distance, however much he tried to change her mind. He meant to be kind, she recognised that, but his kindness was almost more than she could bear.

A glance at the small clock on the windowsill galvanised her into action. She submerged her hair beneath the warm, caressing bubbles, sinking all treacherous thoughts of Alistair Norris in the process.

Well, almost.

★

'Oh, you poor man! Bed's the right place for you, no arguments now! My Fred always used to say "a bad fever needs good food". You get yourself upstairs, and I'll be back in an hour or two with a bit of my special beef broth, the one you liked so much last time.'

When Bert had not appeared at her house as usual at lunchtime, Ivy knew she'd been right again. Bert had flu. Oh, he'd been trying to fight it, soldiered on gallantly when she'd told him he should take her advice to look after himself, but would he? Of course not. But then, Bert was the sort who knew his own mind, and she rather liked that in a man. *Her* man. Not that perhaps he realised it yet . . .

As Bert delicately negotiated his aching back into a comfortable position in bed, he sighed with relief to hear the door close behind her. Her beef broth was fine. Her dumplings were first rate. But the rantings of a bossy woman were more than a chap could honestly bear, especially when his head thumped and his throat felt as dry as a sandpit.

Annie was surprised by the darkness of the house as she emerged from her garage studio dusty and thirsty, her mind preoccupied with the intricacies of the piece she'd been working on. It was important to get it just right. This had to be her very best work. She'd be reassured to know that over the long years ahead.

'Oh, so you're in then. I wasn't sure you still lived here.'

Derek was sitting on a stool beside the breakfast bar, the evening paper spread out before him, a half-finished cup of coffee in his hand. Ignoring his comment, she bent down to open the fridge door.

'Have you eaten? I've got quiche and salad, if you'd like some.'

'I'm not staying. I'm meeting Brian Turner down the pub in an hour.'

'I didn't ask you that. Are you hungry or not?'

'What flavour quiche?'

'Salmon and dill.'

'All right then, if it's quick.'

Annie took a deep breath to control the rising anger which nowadays threatened to engulf her whenever she was in his company. She put the quiche in the oven and carried the salad drawer over to the work surface, working in silence for some minutes, while he returned to scanning the newspaper.

'Aren't you even going to ask how your son is?'

'How is he?'

'Much better, but still very weak, mostly because of the damage done to his kidneys by the concoction of pills he took.'

'Can they do anything about that?'

'Simon's talking about dialysis as a possibility.'

'Oh, it's first-name terms, is it? He's just a doctor, Annie, not a social friend.'

'Actually, he's the best possible friend we could have right now.'

'That's a matter of opinion.'

'It's my opinion. And your opinion matters very little to me as your own son's health plainly matters so little to you.'

'I'm not alone in thinking that the good Dr Gatward has overstepped the mark. There are others, people with influence, who feel exactly as I do.'

'If you cause trouble for Simon I will never ever forgive you.'

'Let's face it, Annie, you already think I'm unforgivable. If you think I'm nothing more than an uncaring, selfish pig, I might just as well *be* one, mightn't I?'

'Right, well, as you've brought up the subject of how unforgivably selfish you are, let's talk about Julie.'

For a moment, raw vulnerability flashed into his eyes before his expression became guarded and defensive, but that split second of revelation was enough to shock Annie, who would never associate vulnerability of any kind with the husband she knew. Carefully, she laid down the kitchen knife and drew up a stool to sit beside him.

'Do you love her?'

'I don't know.'

'Do you see a future together?'

'I might.'

'Is that what you want?'

'All I know is that I don't want to go on like this. What we have is no life at all. We share a house, a bed, a name – but we live in separate worlds. What I want is a friend, a partner, someone who's interested in what interests me, who wants my company and time. And I want to be fancied and cherished by someone who laughs at my jokes and sees the same future as me. Someone who *likes* me. Is that so unreasonable, Annie?'

Her voice was low as she stretched out to place her hand on his knee. 'No, not at all.'

'Isn't that what we all want?'

'Of course'

'And you're not happy, are you? We lost our way years ago, and we've both been trapped in this marriage ever since.'

'But we have a son . . .'

'And it's because of him I stayed – until recently, that is. But all this business with Keith has surely made us both realise how different we are. He doesn't hold us together. His condition has simply thrown in our faces how little we have in common.'

'Yes.'

'You do understand, Annie? It's not you, not your fault at all. But it's not all mine either.'

She took his big hand in hers, staring at it as she answered. 'I know.'

'I can't pretend to be something I'm not. I can't hide my disappointment in him.'

'That, I suppose, I can understand – but you act as if you no longer feel any love for him.'

'Of course I do. He's my son.'

'It's love he craves from you. Please, Derek, show him you care in the time you have with him, before he leaves you with nothing but a life of regret.'

'And what about the two of us? Are we destined for a life of regret?'

'Honestly, I feel so punch-drunk with worry for Keith that I don't seem to feel much about anything right now.'

'Do you mind about Julie?'

'If you're asking me if I'm outraged and jealous, the answer is no. Is it a surprise? Not really. Do I care? Well, I'm not sure. I don't want it thrust down my throat, and I especially don't want your relationship to become an embarrassment for us as a family, at a time when Keith is our main concern.'

He nodded in agreement.

'As for Julie – I can no longer think of her as my friend. But,' she added, leaning against him, 'I think she's what you need. This is probably the very best thing that could happen for you.'

'Oh, Annie . . .' His voice broke as he drew her to him to cling together as they hadn't done for years.

Moira had insisted on organising a taxi to collect Christine for the restaurant. 'None of us will want to drive home after all that Italian wine. Taxis all round, that's the best idea!' And so at twenty-five past seven, when the cab drew up at the gate, Christine caught her breath as she took a last look at herself in the hall mirror. What she saw was a slim, stylish young woman with a bob of shining dark auburn hair. The little black dress she'd borrowed from Lynn, with its plunging neckline and expert cut, accentuated her trim figure and shapely legs. She hardly recognised herself, and the thought brought a smile to her face as she slipped on the matching bolero jacket.

'Crumbs!' piped up Robbie at her elbow. 'You look like Cinderella.'

'Thanks, Robbie. I feel like just like that.'

'I like this.' The small boy fingered the sleeves of her jacket, savouring the feel and texture. 'And I like these buttons at the bottom. Are they to stop you wiping your nose on your sleeve?'

Moira's daughter, Jean, on babysitting duty that night, guffawed with laughter from the door of the living room. Laughing too, Christine bent down to give her son a huge hug.

'Look!' She pulled out a delicate lace hankie from her impossibly small handbag which could not have contained much more than her keys. 'I won't let you down, honest! And now, young man, it's past your bed time. Wave to me at the window, and then straight to bed!'

In the cab she turned round to watch the small face in the window for as long as possible before settling back into her seat, relishing the evening before her. And the moment she was out of sight, Jean picked up the phone to ring her mother's number.

Simon realised the moment he arrived home that Keith was very unwell. His temperature was up, face flushed, lips cracked with sores, and his breathing laboured.

'How long have you been like this?' he asked as he reached into his bag for a stethoscope.

'I've caught a cold, I think – probably from Bert when he was here the other morning.'

Simon's brow furrowed as he continued his examination. He'd been to see Bert a few hours before, laid low in bed with full-blown flu, suffering as so many of his patients were from the epidemic that seemed to have gripped the country. But none of his other patients had AIDS, which undermined their ability to fight even minor infection. For Keith a simple dose of flu could be a death sentence.

He smiled encouragingly down at him as he put his instruments away. 'I think you need to be in hospital, for a while at least. Is that OK?'

Keith nodded, his eyes meeting Simon's in total under-standing.

'I'll go and ring now. And then I'll phone your mum.'

'Hello Christine.'

As she stepped into the reception area of the restaurant he was there, looking unspeakably handsome in a dinner jacket and bow tie. Too surprised to remember she'd been avoiding him for days, she peered through the glass door to see if she could spy Moira and Joan inside.

Alistair took a step towards her, his hands on her shoulders. 'They're not here.'

'You mean, they're not here yet. It's still a few minutes to eight.'

'Chris, they're not coming at all. It's just us. That was all it was ever meant to be.'

She looked at him blankly, her mind racing as she tried to catch up with this unexpected turn of events.

'Was this your idea?'

'No, Moira and Joan's. But I have to say I was delighted to go along with it.'

'Why?'

'Because they know how unhappy both of us have been. Because they're kind and intuitive and caring . . .'

'. . . not to mention conniving . . .'

'. . . and they think we need a chance to talk. You've been so distant, Chris, and I've missed you more than words can say. Forgive the intrigue and give me this chance. Please stay.'

She didn't reply, but then neither did she resist as he gently propelled her through the restaurant door towards a corner table which was discreetly private. She looked around her with curiosity as she sat down.

'Is this the opening night?'

'Last Saturday, I think.'

'And was there a competition?'

'Only to win you, and I've no idea yet whether I'm in with a chance.'

'Alistair, I . . .'

His finger touched her mouth. 'Don't say it. Let's forget all that's happened, the mistakes I've made. We've just met. This is our first evening together – and we're faced with the exciting prospect of getting to know each other, really know each other. You look absolutely beautiful, and I've hired this suit in an effort to look my best! They tell me the food here is terrific, and there's a bottle of cold white wine waiting. Would madam care for a glass?'

She meant to be angry. She fully intended to remain aloof, keep her heart safely protected from the effects of his warm re-assuring smile, the feel of his fingers laced between hers. But somewhere between the pouring of that first sparkling glass and the serving of the tiramisu, her heart apparently made up its own mind, recognising what she was trying to deny. There was nowhere else she'd rather be, no one she'd sooner be with. Even if this evening was all she had, she would treasure the memory of it for a lifetime. Not that it changed anything. Their lives were too different, destined to take separate paths.

'Christine.' As if reading her thoughts, he reached out to hold her hand across the table. 'I know I've hurt you, and I can't begin to tell you how sorry I am. I was thoughtless and insensitive, and you deserve much better than an oaf like me.'

'It doesn't matter. Just forget it. It was probably for the best anyway.'

'How can you say that? Didn't you enjoy the time we spent together?'

'Of course, probably more than I should have, but . . .'

'. . . but then it doesn't have to be the end. I've missed you and Robbie so very much.'

'And in a few months' time, you'll be gone. Just as Robbie gets used to having you around and I find myself growing far too fond of you, you'll be heading off to a new job and an exciting social life.'

'That's not what I want, Chris.'

'Look, the world is at your feet. You're a wonderful doctor. There will be so many great opportunities and relationships coming your way, and you deserve them all.'

'They're worth nothing without you by my side.'

'Alistair, you can't mean that. You must see that we don't have a future together . . .'

'But I do.' He bent down to pick up something concealed beneath the table. 'Darling Christine, I most certainly do.'

The single diamond gleaming in the ring he revealed as he opened the small velvet box was reflected in the soft green of her eyes.

'I love you, and you would make me the happiest man on earth if you'd agree to become my wife. Will you, Chris? Marry me?'

Chapter Thirteen

Gerald carefully picked his way over the construction site at the back of the surgery building. It was coming on. Derek Ryder's men had worked round the clock, so that the walls were now erect, the roof on, and the interior definitely taking shape. On reflection, none of the surgery team had really anticipated just how intrusive the dust and noise would be, although the worst was now over. For weeks Patricia had been happily engrossed in the task of choosing and ordering the furnishings and equipment needed to fit out the additional areas so that, all being well, the surgery with its new-look facilities would be opening soon after the New Year.

Gerald sighed. If only all the practice problems could be sorted out so easily! Funny really, but he'd never imagined Simon becoming a 'problem' for the practice to which for years he'd been devoted. He glanced at his watch. Morning surgery should be over within half an hour or so. He'd take the chance to have a quiet talk with Simon then. Not a pleasant prospect, but it had to be done.

Nodding goodbye to the three workmen there that morning, he shut the door as tightly as possible behind him.

★

'I just don't understand why he's not called. He said he'd ring by Thursday afternoon at the latest, and it's Friday morning now.'

'Do we definitely know they made a decision?'

Across his desk Derek faced his foreman, Brian Turner. 'Martin Balcombe reckons so, but he says he's heard nothing.'

'Can you trust him?'

'What do you think?'

'I think that if he'd heard the contract had gone to someone else, he might not feel like being the bearer of bad news.'

'So I ought to ring Gareth, didn't I? I don't want to look too keen . . .'

'Listen, we have our schedules to sort out. With Christmas just a couple of weeks away, we need to know about the work-load ahead.'

'You're right!' Derek didn't need to look up the number as he dialled through to Gareth's office.

'Mr Walters' office,' announced a sing-song voice at the other end of the line.

'I'd like to talk to him. Is he there?'

There was a moment's hesitation. 'Who's calling please?'

'Derek Ryder.'

'Hold on, Mr Ryder, I'll just check.'

Derek held the phone away as half a chorus of 'Bobby Shaftoe' was played in his ear over and over again. It must have been a full minute later before Miss Sing-Song reconnected the line.

'I'm sorry, Mr Ryder. Mr Walters is not available today.'

'Is that so? Well, will you get him to ring me as soon as he's free?

'I'll ask him.'

'Make sure you do. It's important.'

'I can't do more than pass on the message, sir. Goodbye.' And the phone clicked dead.

'He's fobbing me off!'

'Look, there may be a good explanation for the delay. Maybe they're sorting out the letter of terms, or tweaking the budget after their meeting . . .'

'Brian, I know when I'm being played for a fool. I'm going to get to the bottom of this and I'm going to do it right now!'

Jill caught up with Simon as he walked towards the reception area. 'Can I have a word? A quiet word?'

Curiosity written across his face, he allowed himself to be pushed back in the direction of his surgery, where she shut the door firmly behind them.

'Gerald's gunning for you. Did you know?'

He sighed. 'I suppose it was inevitable, but no, I wasn't aware it was imminent.'

'I overheard him talking to Patricia earlier this morning. I'm sorry to say that I think Michael's been in touch.'

His smile was grim. 'Well, of course he'd want to put in his tuppence-worth. Any idea exactly what he's been saying?'

'He's heard about Keith staying at your house – not from me, although I'm sure I don't need to tell you that. I think he's been talking to Derek, but I'm not certain.'

Simon sat down heavily. 'Well, they can say what they like. My conscience is completely clear. If to respond to a dying young man with compassion is a cardinal sin in the medical profession today, it's time I got out.'

Jill came to stand close to him. 'Just be careful, please. Think about not just how things are, but how they look. I'm worried for you, Simon, I really am.'

He smiled fondly at her, taking her hand. 'And you? How are things at home?'

'Michael's new job is confirmed. He tells me he'll be starting in London at the beginning of February.'

'Are you going with him?'

'Do you think I should?'

'No. That's the very last thing I'd like to see, but my sentiments may not be entirely altruistic when I say that.'

'I need to see you. There's so much to talk about . . .'

'Of course, anytime, but I'm at the hospital quite a bit at the moment. Mind you, it wouldn't be so bad if you met me there. Then you can start spreading a few truthful whispers about my behaviour in the company of Keith Ryder.'

There was a sharp knock at the door before it opened to reveal Gerald. 'Can you spare me a moment, Simon? In the office?'

Simon looked at his watch. 'I'm running a bit late on my house calls . . .'

'This won't take long,' said Gerald firmly, 'and it's important. In the office before you leave please!'

Derek didn't take 'no' for an answer when he arrived at Robbins Design. Martin's estate was in the car park. He was in all right. Ignoring the protests of the bespectacled receptionist on the desk, he took the familiar stairs two at a time and within seconds was standing inside Martin's office in front of his desk. The architect, phone to his ear, stopped mid-sentence as his jaw dropped in surprise to see Derek planted squarely in front of him.

'Can I ring you back, Rosie? Something's just come up.' Deep apprehension registered momentarily on his face as he replaced the receiver, then turned to Derek with a smile.

'This is a nice surprise. Passing, were you?'

'Nope. You know why I am here. Something's going on, and I want to know what.'

'I really don't know what you're talking about . . .'

'Oh yes, you do. Gareth Walters is suddenly "not available" to take my calls. You're vague to the point of disbelief. What do you know? Tell me, or that spanking new estate car of yours may not be so pristine by the time my old crate leaves the car park.'

'Look, Derek, Gareth is the one you need to speak to. Go and smash up *his* car, not mine. I just come up with the plans. I don't decide who works on them.'

'Who's got that contract?' His voice was just threatening enough to bring a nervous flush to Martin's cheeks, and the tone of their discussion caught the attention of a couple of people in the outer area beyond his office, who began to crane their necks with interest to peer through the glass panelling towards Martin's desk.

'Let's go out on to the back landing. It's quieter there.'

Under the curious stare of Martin's colleagues, the two men walked as casually as possible to the back of the office and out of the door.

'Well?'

'I know nothing official, you understand.'

'But?'

'But I've heard a rumour that it's gone to Baskins.'

'Baskins!' The name exploded from Derek's lips. 'They can't cope with a contract that big.'

'Well, it's just a whisper, but that's what I heard.'

'But it doesn't make sense. There's got to be more to this. George Baskin's getting ready to retire. If anything, he's been running down his operation lately.'

'I believe he is retiring, yes.'

'So how can the council possibly give him a major contract like Farthing Corner?' Derek's brow creased with concentration. 'Unless, of course, he's grooming someone else to take over. But his crowd are all past it – none of them under fifty, and not an ounce of brains between them.'

Martin, plainly uncomfortable, stared down at his shoes.

'Come on, out with it! What's going on?'

'I've got to get back, Derek. I've told you all I know.'

'You never were a good liar, Martin. You go red. Now, tell me before I *really* get angry.'

'I've heard that his godson is taking over.'

'Godson? What godson?'

'He comes from a building family, somewhere down Brighton way.'

'Brighton?' Tiny bells of recognition were beginning to jangle in Derek's head. 'What's his name?'

'Mark, I think.'

'Not, by any chance, the "Mark" who married Gareth Walters' daughter in Brighton last Saturday?'

Martin didn't reply. He didn't need to when his squirming expression said it all. Derek turned away, breathing heavily, plainly beside himself with rage.

'Three thousand pounds!' A chunk of plaster by the window frame shot off as he thumped his fist against the wall. 'I gave that son of a bitch *three thousand pounds* towards the cost of that wedding!'

From a safe distance Martin watched nervously, wondering how soon he could make his escape. He needn't have worried. Without another word, Derek turned on his heel and headed down the stairs towards the back entrance.

'Oh, you poor dear man, you do still look peaky!'

Ivy bustled straight into Bert's bedroom without waiting for an invitation. From the depths of his pillows he groaned silently and sank deeper beneath the blankets. Suddenly his covers were whisked off him.

'What the blazes are you doing, woman?' he wailed, trying in vain to wrestle his eiderdown from her vice-like grip.

'Those sheets need a wash. With that high fever you've had, they must be soaked. You climb out for a minute, and I'll have that bed freshened up in no time.'

'I've got no sheets. Haven't done the washing.'

'Now, don't you worry about a thing. I've come prepared, and brought a set of my own. I've noticed you've not got much that's decent when it comes to linen. Come on now, out with you!'

With a determined tug Bert snatched the covers away from her, pulling them up tight round his neck.

'Then I'd like some privacy please.'

With a kittenish twinkle of her eye, she giggled. 'You silly man. I'm sure you've got nothing I haven't seen before . . .'

Bert shot a withering look in her direction to send her scuttling out of the door. 'I'll pop the kettle on then. I've brought the milk – and the Hobnobs!'

Patricia was in her usual seat behind her efficiently neat desk. Gerald chose not to sit down, standing behind his wife with arms folded. The whole scene reminded Simon of being carpeted by his headmaster years ago.

'Twenty patients this week alone . . .' Patricia ran her finger smartly down the list before her. 'Most have asked to transfer to the Turpin Way surgery, and let's face it, that's three miles from here. These patients are going to considerable trouble to leave our practice.'

'People have cars and free choice. There are fashions in everything, even GPs.'

'Well,' said Patricia firmly, 'we'd prefer to be in fashion. With all the expense of extending the building, we can't afford to lose any of our patients at present.'

'They aren't leaving because of a fashion whim,' interrupted Gerald, 'and you know that, Simon. They're leaving because they think there's a risk of infection if they come here.'

'That's ridiculous!'

'Of course it is, but when rumour is rife and panic sets in, people are like lemmings. These are mostly men, or families with young children whose health is paramount to them.'

'They're ignorant and bigoted.'

'Don't patronise them, Simon. That's not like you.'

'And,' added Patricia, clasping her hands on top of the papers in front of her, 'your behaviour recently has not been like you at all. At best, you've been insular and prickly, at worst self-righteous and secretive . . .'

'I've made a secret of nothing!'

'Then why haven't you spoken openly about Keith Ryder's treatment? Why have you been so reluctant to discuss it at team meetings? You've become possessive and defensive beyond belief! This is a partnership, Simon, in case you've forgotten. You lose us business, and it affects us all!'

'Personally, as a patient, I'd rather attend a practice where you're not just treated as a good financial prospect. Is that what it's come to? Do our patients mean nothing more than balancing figures in the accounts ledger these days? Yes, I've taken a personal interest in a young man whose condition worries me! Yes, the attitude towards him from small-minded people in this intolerant, prejudiced community has shocked and moved me. He's got AIDS. He's not a leper. He's not a fool. He's not planning to pass it on. How could he when people back away from him whenever he steps outside? He's been so lonely and tired of living that he tried to commit suicide. What does that tell you about a lad who's only twenty-eight years old, who's bright and articulate and who should have his whole life ahead of him? He didn't plan this! He simply fell in love with the wrong person – but love it most certainly was! You might not agree with men loving other men, but why shouldn't they? Are you saying that you have the monopoly on love – you, and all the other smug, respectable heterosexuals around you? That makes you as bigoted and frightened as the rest of them!'

'You have allowed your personal feelings to get in the way of your professional judgement. That is unethical and not in the patient's best interest . . .'

'Unethical? To treat him as a human being, not just a dying

body with intriguing medical problems? Is that the sin I've committed? To care for the person rather the patient? Is that financially unviable? Is it damaging to this practice? Does it undermine my worth as a doctor?'

'It makes your judgement suspect. Your lack of concern for the consequences of your actions on the practice is shocking. We have a right to question your loyalty towards the responsibilities you hold here.' Gerald's voice shook with cold fury.

'You're right!' A few quick paces and Simon's hand was on the door. 'We *should* question the responsibilities I hold here. And believe me, Gerald, in view of your attitude, I have a great many questions about the wisdom of my staying in this practice!'

He slammed the door shut behind him.

'Simon, just the man!' Moira's voice hailed him as he marched through reception. His pace didn't slacken.

'Just wanted to remind you about the practice Christmas party on Saturday. It's all booked and I just need to collect in the money from everyone now. You are coming, aren't you?'

But he was gone, leaving Moira staring open-mouthed after him.

Derek glanced at his watch. Quarter to one. Gareth had to have lunch some time, and although the pub known to be his most frequent watering hole was only five minutes' walk away, Derek knew he always chose to take the car. Drawing his works' estate car into line a couple of spaces away from the familiar Volvo, he switched off the engine, settled back in his seat, and waited.

Simon's fuming anger continued as he drove grim-faced towards his first house call. His fists gripped the steering wheel as memories of the conversation with Gerald and Patricia churned over in his mind. He had always considered Gerald a real friend, as well as a totally professional colleague whose opinion he sought and respected. The gulf between them now had shocked him to the core, and while he recognised the situation he faced was largely of his own making, he had expected more loyalty and understanding from someone whose support he'd always believed he could rely upon.

His mood wasn't lifted by the names at the top of his home visit list. Hetty Brown was the last person he felt like seeing, although Harry's deteriorating Parkinson's Disease was now cause for real concern. But the thought of her martyred self-pity was suddenly more than he could face. Without further thought he took the next turning off the main road and headed towards more familiar territory.

Bert's back door was never locked. Even at night, he considered the turn of a key to be an unnecessary chore when he had nothing worth stealing. Perhaps it wasn't strictly necessary to make a home visit to see if those antibiotics had done the trick in clearing up the old gardener's thick chest, but Bert was infinitely better company than Hetty Brown.

Simon was up the stairs in no time, opening the bedroom door to be greeted by a most unexpected sight. Bert was sitting up in bed, surrounded by frilly pillowcases in a delicate shade of lilac and an eiderdown which was mostly cerise pink with a mass of dark mauve flowers. Beside his bed a square box of pastel-coloured paper hankies nestled beneath a satin and lace box cover, and within reach of his hand stood a wicker waste-paper basket with an artistically-arranged ring of dried flowers around its rim. And the crowning glory, splendid in its neat knitted suit and clutching a ribbon attached to a silver balloon emblazoned with 'Get Well Soon' in huge red letters, was a teddy bear, sitting in the middle of an exotically embroidered throw which covered the foot of the bed.

'Bloomin' woman!' grumbled Bert. 'She's made me look like a flippin' girlie!'

In spite of everything, Simon couldn't help himself. He sat

down on a chair at the end of the room, threw his head back and roared with uncontrollable laughter.

It wasn't until the key was actually in the door of his car that Gareth became aware of someone behind him. He spun round with a smile which immediately disappeared when he saw Derek Ryder's expression.

'On your way to Baskins, by any chance?'

Regaining his composure with admirable speed, Gareth looked at his watch. 'No, but I am late. Can't stop. Give me a ring, Derek. We need to talk.'

Derek jammed his body against the car door. 'We most certainly do. About nepotism, perhaps? About giving the new son-in-law a leg-up by handing him the lucrative contract you promised me?'

Gareth's eyebrows shot up. 'Promised? I remember no such thing.'

'And I don't suppose you remember the backhanders either! Have a good party on Saturday, did you? At my expense!'

'Really, Derek, I have no idea what you're talking about. Now kindly let me get on. We'll speak later.'

'I wonder what the Chairman of the Opposition would make of your behaviour, Gareth? Quite a friend of mine is Bernie Smith . . .'

'Really? I'm glad because he's an old friend of mine too. I'll give him your regards, shall I?'

'Or shall I just make it a letter to the press? They're always interested in corrupt council members.'

'Try it if you like, but you'll never work for this council again.'

Derek's huge hand grabbed his collar as he pinned Gareth to the car door. 'You took my money! We had a gentlemen's agreement!'

Gareth disentangled himself, coolly brushing down his crumpled shirt and tie.

'No one would ever mistake you for a gentleman, Derek Ryder, and as for your money? I have absolutely no idea what you're talking about!'

And with a sinuous crab-like movement, he slipped inside his car and roared off, while Derek watched after him consumed by impotent fury.

'Thanks Mum.' Annie's heart lurched at the weakness of Keith's smile. She laid the sweet green grapes on the fruit bowl beside him, removing the older bunch to make room. He didn't eat them, but she brought them anyway. She felt better for it, even if he didn't.

'How are you today? Any improvement?'

'I think so.' He was lying, and they both knew it.

'Had your lunch yet? How was that?'

'Nice.' Another lie.

'Seen the consultant?'

'Not for long. He's given up on me, I think.'

'Don't say that . . .'

'It's true, Mum – and it's all right.'

'Oh, I almost forgot!' She dug down into her bag and drew out a small sketch pad and pencils. 'I thought you might like these.'

As he softly fingered the pad, she looked at his thin wrist and wondered if he'd have the strength to lift the pencil.

'You look tired. Why don't you have a sleep? I'll still be here when you wake up.'

'Thanks . . .' His eyelids closed as if they were too heavy for him to keep open. Annie sat still, looking at the slumbering figure beside her; pale, gaunt and almost unrecognisable as her son. It was as if the life had been sucked out of him; his blond hair thin and lank, lips swollen, skin dry and blotchy. All that remained was the striking blue of his eyes. Those same eyes which had charmed and amused in the boy, and spoke of gentle sensitivity in the man, now stared from a face that was drained and expressionless.

Suddenly she felt very alone. She glanced about her, wondering whether a nurse was available while she went to get a cup of tea, but there was no one in sight. Better to stay, she decided. He might wake and need her. She looked up at the clock in the hallway just outside the door. It was only three minutes later than the last time she'd looked.

It was the waiting that was hardest of all. And waiting for what? Not a recovery, for she was too realistic to expect that. She was waiting for him to die, for her own dear son to leave her. Bowing her head to hide her distress, loneliness over-whelmed her.

Minutes later she became dimly aware of voices in the hall, two women having a discussion just beyond the door of the room. When she heard Simon's name mentioned she let go of Keith's hand and moved across to the door where she could hear more clearly.

'This Sunday? That will be just wonderful!'

Alistair's father wasn't quite sure what to make of his son's enthusiasm to see him and his mother. Something was wrong. He must be unhappy at Berston. It had definitely been too long since they'd seen him, for him to react in such a manner.

'Alistair, are you feeling quite well?'

'Perfectly, thanks.'

'And work's going smoothly? No problems?'

'Fine.'

Alistair heard another voice in the background.

'Your mother says are you warm enough? Your room's not damp, is it? Are you eating properly?'

He could hear the delighted amusement in Alistair's voice as he replied. 'Dad, I couldn't be better – and I have some wonderful news for you both.'

'You've got a new post!'

'No! Much better than that! Look, we'll see you on Sunday, in the bar at the Country Park Hotel.'

'We?'

'There are some people I'd like you to meet.'

'Oh? From the practice?'

'Yes and no! All will be revealed on Sunday. 'Bye till then!'

Alistair's father replaced the receiver thoughtfully. It sounded as if a visit to Berston was well overdue.

Simon found Annie in exactly the same place that he'd left her the previous evening, in a seat beside Keith's bed. He walked over to squeeze her shoulder and look down intently at the sleeping figure, then moved to the end of the bed to peer at the medical notes. His face was sombre as he pulled up a chair alongside her.

'I spoke to the consultant.'

'Have you? What did he say?'

'It's not good, Annie. That flu really laid him low, on top of all the problems caused by the overdose. His immune system just can't cope. The medication they're giving him doesn't seem to be helping much yet – but who knows? He may turn a corner – if he chooses to.'

She looked down at her son sadly. 'Not much chance of that.'

Simon didn't feel the need to answer.

'Have you eaten?'

'I'll get something later.'

'I knew you'd say that, so I picked this up for you at that lovely baker's in the square.'

Annie wasn't hungry, or at least she thought she wasn't until she stuck her nose in the bag he handed her. The look of the flaky pastry, and the smell of its cheese and onion filling, made her realise with a jolt that it had been breakfast time when she'd forced down a slice of toast. Now it was nearly seven o'clock in the evening.

'There's a cup of tea too. Hope it's not cold.'

Her eyes shone with gratitude. 'Thanks.'

'How long has he been asleep?'

'A couple of hours.'

'Then he'll probably sleep for the next ten minutes too. Come and have a more comfortable seat to eat that.' Stiffly getting to her feet, she allowed him to lead the way through to the relatives' room.

'I heard your name mentioned today.'

'Oh?'

'I'm not sure whose conversation it was – one of the nurses, I think, and perhaps a visitor – but it was all I could do to stop myself from slapping them both very hard. I'm beginning to realise just how vicious gossip can be. I'm so sorry, Simon. I had no idea how badly your involvement with us might affect your work and reputation.'

He shrugged. 'Ignorance. Prejudice. I take no notice.'

'How can you? They were talking about people leaving the practice, about thinking you might contaminate them with the AIDS virus if you as much as look at them! How can they be so stupid?'

'Some people know no better, and that's understandable. Some simply want to think the worst of every situation. They thrive on scandal and tittle-tattle. I have no time for them. If they want to leave the practice, let them. I wish them well.'

'But you're obviously not gay!'

'They apparently think that's not obvious at all!'

'Of course it is – to me, anyway.'

'Why?'

There was affection in her eyes as she looked at him. 'I just know you. Don't ask me why. I feel as if I've always known you.'

It looked as if he was going to speak, but thought better of it, taking a deep calming breath instead.

'I know there's a raw hurt inside you, something that's drawing you to Keith, and driving you on in the face of such opposition, putting your job and reputation at risk.'

Still he didn't answer.

'And I know that one day, when you're ready, you'll tell me about it.'

He turned to her then, his eyes darkened by shafts of pain, breathing deeply, as if every breath hurt. 'You know, Annie, if I ever find the courage to face my demons, it will be to you that I turn. But some experiences can be so shocking, so destructive, that it's easier to shut down the memory and block it out. That's what I've done for years.'

'And something about Keith opened up old wounds?'

'The date.'

'Sorry?'

'It was the date. Keith's birthday, the twenty-fourth of May. That was what started it all.'

'Someone else has that birthday?'

Simon nodded before lowering his head as Annie reached out to take his shaking hands.

'Someone you love very much.'

'Loved.'

'Oh Simon . . .'

'My son.'

She waited quietly for him to continue. Then he stiffened, as if pulling himself together.

'I'm sorry. I can't do this . . .'

She released his hands as he rose and disappeared quickly down the corridor.

Chapter Fourteen

An uneasy truce had been accepted without discussion between Simon and the other members of the practice, although he was very aware of the conversations that stopped when he walked into the reception area, and of Patricia and Gerald avoiding his eye. Only Alistair seemed blissfully unaware of the turmoil going on around him. He never complained once about the mess and disruption caused by the building works, and he certainly never caught any of the gossip. He was on a higher plane, a level of bubbling happiness that assumed there could only be blissful harmony in others. It was on that cloud of rapturous contentment that he and Christine floated in late to join the others at the bar of the restaurant which had been chosen for the practice Christmas party. They were quite a crowd when they and their partners all assembled under one roof, and the whole of the upstairs area had been allocated to them, with a disco ready to get them dancing when dinner was over and the mood right.

A round of applause went up as the newly-engaged couple arrived. Christine was pink with pleasure as she was drawn into a bearhug first from Joan, and then from her equally well-upholstered husband, John. Lynn Webster joked that it was her little black number that had really done the trick, and Moira said that was nonsense when it was obviously *her* matchmaking that clinched it! Best of all, once everyone had taken their places around the huge table, Gerald got to his feet.

'Before we start eating, drinking and making merry, I know you'll join me in wishing Christine and Alistair many congratulations on the excellent news of their engagement. In fact we can't help thinking that young Alistair has shown uncommonly good sense and taste in snapping up our Christine, because in the time she's been with us, we have all come to value her warmth, intelligence and compassion when dealing with the bemused and bewildered. Of course, I'm talking about members of our medical team here! So impressed are we with his good judgement that we're delighted this evening to be able to make a very special announcement. With both our premises and our potential patient list expanding, we recognise that Alistair's medical skill – not to mention his bedside manner – is an invaluable asset to us all. And so today we offered Alistair a full partnership in our practice, to follow on next spring at the end of his training year.'

Delighted applause spontaneously broke out around the table.

'It took him a long time to make a decision – at least three seconds – and I know you'll be pleased to hear that he accepted our offer. But the best part of this of course, is not that we keep Alistair, but that we won't be losing our wonderful practice secretary!'

More applause, as Alistair hugged Christine to him.

Now please raise your glasses with me to toast the happy couple – Alistair and Christine!'

That was the start of many glasses raised that night. Wine flowed freely to wash down course upon course of delicious food. As the night wore on and the dancing began, it was only Jill who noticed when Simon quietly rose from his seat and slipped away.

★

'I've arranged to meet Denis Garside here this morning,' Michael announced at breakfast the next morning. 'He'll have the house on the market by Monday.'

'You're going ahead with this, knowing how I feel about this move? I don't want to leave Berston. We've lived in so many different houses over the years, and I'm tired of the constant upheaval. At last, I'm settled here. This is my home.'

'Well, it will no longer be mine. I'm leaving to take up that post in London at the beginning of February. I very much hope that you'll come with me. If you choose not to, you must decide what alternative arrangements you wish to make.'

She laid down the plate she was loading in the dishwasher, and turned to him. 'And that's it? A simple parting of the ways? You realise that we're talking about the break-up of our marriage here! Can't you even pretend to show some emotion about it?'

'My emotions have never been in question. It's where your affection lies that really needs to be answered. You've made no secret of the fact that you're in love with another man, and I refuse to let my decision to leave depend on his decision to ask you to stay.'

'Michael, you are simply irresistible! You certainly know how to charm a woman! You make it quite clear that it makes no difference whatsoever to you whether we remain a couple, or go our separate ways. No emotion. No pleading. No promises. Nothing! But then, what would I expect from a man who in more than twenty-five years has never once mentioned the word "love"? It's not in your vocabulary, just as it's not in your heart!'

She had reached the kitchen door on her way out as he spoke again, more quietly this time.

'But what would be the point of making emotional declarations to a woman who, ever since I've known her, has been in love with someone else? You never really wanted love from me. A marriage between compatible partners, that's what you settled for, and that's what we've always had. And somewhere over the years, love has crept in, for me anyway. I'm too proud to beg you, Jill, and too scared to declare my feelings when I feel an emotional outburst would be inconvenient and unwelcome for you. There's so much I could say – but not until you've decided what you really want, and who you love.

Alistair's parents' sleek Saab arrived at the Country Park Hotel at two minutes to one. One thing on which his father always prided himself was punctuality. Unfortunately it was not a quality which he'd managed to pass on to his son, who had been reliably late from the day of his birth, two weeks overdue.

'Relax, James,' said his wife soothingly, as she made herself comfortable in a plump armchair next to a bay window. 'He's a GP, you know. Perhaps he's been called out to a patient.'

'Iris, we've driven for an hour and a half, and still managed to get here on time. He lives two minutes away, and he's late!'

'Just time for you to get us both a glass of sherry then,' she replied with a twinkle in her eye. By five past one, having returned with their drinks, he'd just sat down to look at his watch again when he heard someone call his name. Alistair was framed in the doorway where to his father's astonishment he had one arm along the shoulders of a young red-haired woman and the other around an immaculately-dressed little boy who was grinning in their direction with a gappy lopsided smile.

'Dad! Mother! Great to see you! You made it down in good time . . .'

His mother was the first to regain her composure at the sight of the three of them as she got up from her comfortable chair to grasp her son in a fond hug. Father and son did not embrace. They never did. His father would have been appalled by such a flamboyant gesture, when a respectful handshake was perfectly adequate. Then both parents looked curiously at Alistair's companions.

'Christine, I'd like you to meet my parents. This is Christine Warburton and her son, Robbie.'

Before anyone else could say a word Robbie stepped forward, shyly holding out his hand to Alistair's mother.

'How do you do, Mrs Norris? How do you do, sir?'

Alistair's mother smiled warmly as she shook his small hand in her own. 'I can see you have impeccable manners, young man! How old are you? Are you at school yet?'

'Of course. I'm five now, and I won't be in Mrs Whiteley's class after Christmas. That's only for the babies, you see. I'm going to be in Class Three. They read real books there.'

'How very nice for you. And is this your mother?'

'She's wearing a suit she bought specially for today, but it's too expensive, so she hasn't cut the labels out, so that if she doesn't spill anything down it, she can take it back on Monday.'

The blood drained from Christine's face for two whole seconds before Alistair's mother burst into delighted laughter. 'How very sensible! I've done exactly the same thing before now! I'm delighted to meet you, my dear.'

James Norris nodded stiffly in Christine's direction, noticing the look of panic that flashed across her face as Alistair took Robbie with him to organise the table, leaving her alone with the two of them. It was Iris who broke the awkward silence.

'Have you lived in this area long, Christine?'

'For the past five years. My family were in Southampton, although I'm sad to say that I've lost both of my parents now. My dad died when I was quite young, and my mum developed cancer when I was fifteen. For her, the condition was brutally aggressive, but mercifully quick. I still miss her very much.'

'Oh, I'm sure you do, my dear. How tragic for you. Do you have other brothers and sisters?'

'One brother, who lives with his wife and family just outside Birmingham, so we're not able to see so much of each other these days.'

'How nice that you have Robbie then. What does his father do?'

Christine looked at her levelly. 'I have no idea, Mrs Norris. He disappeared once he realised Robbie was on the way.'

James Norris bristled, but didn't comment.

'That's a story we hear too often these days. So you've had to bring up young Robbie on your own then? Not an easy task, I'm sure.'

Christine's face broke into an affectionate smile. 'No task at all. Being Robbie's mum has brought me tremendous pleasure and fulfilment. I don't regret a moment of it. He's a very special boy.'

'I can see that,' replied Iris softly as Alistair and Robbie made their way back to join them.

Minutes later they were all seated round a table in the restaurant, and conversation was halted for a while as menus were scanned and decisions made.

'I'll have egg, bacon, sausage and chips please,' announced Robbie, 'but with no beans, and definitely none of those green pea things 'cos they make me feel sick – and will you tell them, Mum, I'd rather have an extra piece of bacon instead of a sausage? Oh, and red ketchup – and a big Coke.' Then as an afterthought when he realised all eyes were on him, he added, 'Please!'

'Nice to meet a chap with a good appetite!' said Iris, making her selection of roast beef and Yorkshire pudding.

Alistair laughed, ruffling Robbie's hair. 'No trouble getting him to eat. He never stops!'

'How are things going at the practice, son?' asked James. 'Have you come to any conclusions about where you'll go next?'

Alistair glanced at Christine, reaching out to take her hand. 'Yes, and yes. Gerald and Simon have asked me to stay on here, as a partner.'

Before James could open his mouth to object, Iris smoothly intervened. 'Well, you must have made a great impression – and dear Gerald always was very intuitive about other people's ability, if I remember rightly.'

Alistair beamed back at her. 'I have to say, Mother, I was surprised and delighted yesterday when they asked me.'

'Only yesterday? What prompted them to do that?'

'Well, our engagement, I suppose.'

His father's chin dropped with shock. 'Engaged! Whatever for? At this stage of your career, what a preposterous idea!'

Christine squirmed uncomfortably in her seat, as Alistair drew her proudly towards him.

'Actually, it's probably the most sensible decision I ever will make. I love Christine and Robbie very much indeed, and being able to share my life with them means more to me than the kind of high-flying career *you* have always had in mind for me. But you know, Dad, I'm not you, and I don't want to follow the same medical career that you would have chosen for yourself in my position. I want to be a GP. Since I first began my medical training, I've wanted to be a GP. I love being at the heart of this community, getting to know the people I treat, coming to care deeply about them. In every way, I feel that I've come home here. I have the woman I love by my side, and a job I want to excel at more than anything else in the world. I'm sorry if my choice is not the same as yours – but I am nearly twenty-five years old and quite capable of knowing my own mind.'

'Well said!' Iris radiated pleasure and pride in her expression as she reached over to hug Alistair. 'You're absolutely right. I always knew this was the life for you, and your father will realise it too in time. And he seems to have forgotten he was only twenty-three when he whisked me up the aisle! Now come along, James, take that scowl off your face, and let's welcome Christine and this delightful young man to our family. Tell me, Robbie, are you any good with computers? We've got one at home that really foxes me. Perhaps you'll be able to give me a bit of help when you come up to see us . . .'

★

Annie knew he was at Julie's house, but that didn't stop her ringing Derek on his mobile. She had to swallow the humiliation of having to beg for a word with her husband while he was at the home of his mistress, but this was an emergency.

'They've just rung me from the hospital, Derek. Keith's taken a turn for the worse. Pneumonia has set in. I thought you should know.'

'Are you there now?'

'On my way.'

'Will Simon Gatward be there too?'

'Possibly. I don't know.'

There was silence at the other end of the line.

'Derek? Are you there?'

'Thanks for letting me know. Try not to worry, Annie. You knew this could happen any time.'

'Will you come?'

'Later.'

She cut off the line in frustration. The deteriorating health of his only son plainly didn't matter enough for him to leave his lover before he was good and ready.

Damn him! Damn him because this hurts so much!

It was much later, as the last light of the winter's afternoon began to fade, that Iris sat comfortably across from Patricia in her elegant sitting room. The women supped their cups of Earl Grey and chatted amiably in spite of the snatches of conversation between James and Gerald which occasionally drifted through from the study.

'He's not very pleased, you know. James had such high hopes for Alistair.'

Patricia smiled. 'I get the feeling that Alistair has very definite hopes of his own.'

'I can't tell you how glad I am to know that. James has always been a bully. At last Alistair has climbed out from under his shadow.'

'He's happy at the practice. That's quite clear to all of us. He has a delightful way with the patients, and our old ladies absolutely adore him!'

His mother laughed. 'Oh, Alistair was always a charmer, with that cherubic face of his!'

'Well, he's certainly worked his magic on all of us.'

Iris' attention strayed towards the garden, where Alistair and Christine were pushing Robbie on the old swing that had been put there for a previous generation of children.

'Mind you, I'm not sure just who's worked the magic and who's been charmed between those two.'

'She's a lovely girl. We've both become extremely fond of her. She was very badly hurt when Robbie's dad let them down so badly. Apparently they had been talking about getting married, until news of her pregnancy sent him scuttling away. But she's become a wonderful mother, completely devoted to her little boy. She's most efficient at her job, but then we soon realised that she's an intelligent girl who deserves more academic qualifications than she's ever had the chance to achieve. She's loyal, hardworking, and very good with the patients. But do you know, in all the years I've known her, she has never allowed any man to get close to her? She was like a frightened little rabbit if anyone as much as said boo to her – until Alistair came along. They love each other, Iris, have no doubt about that. I've watched him mature and glow with pleasure in her company, as he's drawn her out of the shell she's been hiding in for too long.'

Iris watched as Alistair chased the small excited boy around the garden, until Robbie took a tumble over a stepping stone that was almost hidden by long grass. Quick as a flash Christine was beside him, picking him up with a warm smile, an even warmer hug, and a kiss on his sore knee. Then Alistair scooped him up on to his shoulders, reaching out to bring Chris into the circle of his arm where she rested her head against his shoulder.

'Who can tell what the future will bring?' Patricia's voice was soft as the two women watched the closeness of the trio before them. 'But I think this is the right thing for them.'

Iris didn't take her eyes off the tableau in the garden as she gently nodded agreement. 'Oh, I think so too. I really do.'

She'd needed a change of scenery. The four walls of his hospital room were closing in on her as she listened to every painful breath he took. An hour or so before, he'd opened his eyes and tried to smile through his cracked, ulcerated lips. She had held his head tenderly while he took small gulps of water, then helped him back onto the pillow where he lay, spent and exhausted.

'Mum?'

She moved nearer to hear him clearly.

'Can you put on that CD?'

She smiled. 'I don't need to ask what track, do I?'

Within seconds, the soaring sounds of the New York City Gay Men's Choir and Orchestra were filling the room, and as the track reached the lines Keith loved best of all, Annie found her eyes filling with tears to match his own.

> *I want to hold you till I die,*
> *Till we both break down and cry,*
> *I want to hold you till the fear in me subsides . . .*

By the end of the album, he was asleep. It was then that she knew she had to get out of that room, away from the smell, the sound, the feel of impending death.

She sat in a corner of the hospital canteen, her face streaked with tears. She felt completely alone and abandoned. No one to care, no one to tell as her only son slipped from her. Her tea went cold as she pushed an uninspiring sandwich around the plate for half an hour before she realised it was dark, and she should go back.

She stopped short at the door as she saw a figure crouched beside Keith. It was Derek. Anxious not to intrude, she stepped back into the shadows, watching from a distance, straining to hear the conversation between them.

'. . . just so good to see you here.' Keith grasped his father's hand as he spoke, each word filled with pain and emotion.

'Are they looking after you well? Got everything you need?'

'Too much really. There's nothing I need.'

'Because if you'd like me to bring in something you're not allowed but fancy anyway – a tot of the hard stuff, perhaps, or a Chinese takeaway – just you let me know.'

In his grey gaunt face, Keith's eyes lit up with pleasure at the suggestion. 'I'd only bring it back up again, but it's a lovely thought. Thank you.'

'And how are you? Feeling any better?'

'Not really – but I won't.'

Annie watched as Derek's shoulders visibly slumped.

'It's all right, Dad. I'm OK about this.'

'I just wish I could . . . you know . . .'

Keith nodded, too weary to say any more.

'Right, well, I'll leave you to rest now. Make sure they take care of you!'

Another nod, then Keith's noisy breathing settled into a regular pattern as sleep overwhelmed him. Derek sat beside him for some minutes, unwilling to leave. Finally he got to his feet and looked at the slumbering figure, stretching out to brush a stray hair from the lined forehead.

'Good night, son.' His voice was barely more than a whisper. 'I love you.' Then, with infinite tenderness, he bent down to kiss Keith's cheek, his lips soft against the dry skin for some seconds before he pulled away. As he turned towards the door, Annie left the shadows to meet him in the doorway as if she'd just arrived. She knew he'd hate the thought that she'd observed him being emotional.

'Oh, you've seen him. Did you manage to have a chat?'

'No, he didn't wake up.'

'I'm so glad you came, Derek.'

There was an awkward silence before, with a nod, they crossed each other's path, she towards the bed, and he down the long corridor towards the end of the ward. Like strangers, she thought, as she resumed her vigil at the bedside. And she ached with relief that Keith was indeed loved by his father – but saddened to the core to see that Derek was still unable to admit that love, even to her.

With little over a week to go before Christmas Berston took on a festive air, with strings of lights laced around the Market Square, and happily harassed shoppers scurrying along the streets loaded down with carrier bags full of mysterious bulky shapes. Father Christmas took up residence in his specially painted grotto at the local church hall on the next to last Saturday before the big day, and queues quickly formed of mothers either threatening their over-excited offspring, or cajoling along the youngsters who were frankly appalled at the prospect of sitting on the lap of a red-suited, whiskery stranger, even if there was a present in it. The church Ladies Circle were in charge of refreshments, which meant that Ivy Gibson was in her element, dispensing tea, collecting money and recommending her cakes above any of the others so ably baked by the pastry queens of the parish. In spite of his still delicate state of health Bert had been dragooned into action, partly because he'd been too weak to argue when Ivy told him he was desperately needed for raffle ticket duty. By the time Simon arrived to check that the PA system he'd dropped in the night before was working properly, Bert looked bored, hen-pecked and thoroughly fed up. It took Simon a moment to control the grin that quivered on his lips.

If he laughed, Bert would be mortified, and that wouldn't help his health at all. Instead he grabbed a couple of cups of tea and a jam doughnut for each of them, then ushered Bert off to a quiet spot behind the stage, with Ivy's loud warnings of, 'Don't you disappear, Bert! Your job's raffle tickets! If we don't sell enough, it'll be your fault!' ringing in their ears.

Bert sat silently munching his doughnut, his face a picture of woe and misery.

'Trouble with the ladies, eh?' enquired Simon gently.

'Never could understand them. Can't bear their nagging.'

His expression tragic, he took another sugar-laden bite. 'Trouble is, I do like her cooking. Never had nosh like it. Makes up for a lot really.'

'But are you happy, Bert? You've really not been yourself lately.'

Bert's shoulders shrugged as he licked a dollop of jam off his fingers. 'I'm not much good at cooking, see?'

'I certainly do. But what about the company? Isn't it nice having someone to talk to?'

Bert's eyes widened. 'I don't talk. I don't need to. She does enough for both of us.'

'And you're not getting any younger. It must be reassuring to know there's someone there to take care of you when you're ill?'

Bert snorted. 'There's a difference between taking care and smothering to death!'

'Couldn't you just have a chat with her, tell her honestly how you feel? Perhaps if she understands that a more relaxed friendship would suit you better, then . . .'

'She's after a husband, and she's set her sights on me.'

'Well, that's very flattering, isn't it?'

There was another snort of exasperation before Bert leaned back in his seat. 'I tried marriage once. Never again!'

'Then you must tell her. Explain how you feel.'

Bert looked at him coolly. 'Can you imagine trying to

explain anything to that woman, when her mind's already made up?'

Simon glanced across to the far end of the hall, from where Ivy's voice rang out above everyone else's as she issued orders to all around her. He sighed with understanding. 'Hmm, I can see you have a problem.'

Bert nodded in sad agreement, and the two men sat pondering the dilemma for a while. Finally Simon's face brightened.

'Are you saying that if you could get nice dinners some other way, you'd find the strength to get yourself out of this situation?'

'Suppose so.'

'Right, Bert! I've got an idea. You just leave it to me!'

At the surgery, glistening chains of tinsel and cards hanging around the waiting room soon took on the coat of plaster-dust that seemed to have settled on every nook and cranny of the building since the extension work got underway.

'They're bang on schedule though,' said Patricia when Moira came to complain that there was even a layer of dust on the gingernuts in the biscuit box. 'We'll just have to grin and bear it, knowing that it will be so much easier for us all to work when we can spread out a bit. Four more weeks – that's all Mr Ryder says it needs.'

In fact Derek only visited the surgery when it was absolutely necessary. His workmen commented that the boss, known for continually breathing down their necks, had left them to it on this job, which they all agreed was quite out of character for him. There had been rumours that his time was occupied with a certain lady who worked at his office. Someone even said they'd been seen kissing in the corridor one evening. Then, of course, there were all the tales surrounding his son. They said he had AIDS, and was close to death. There was even a whisper that Keith had been having an affair with a doctor before he was taken into hospital, and had probably passed the virus on. No wonder the boss had a lot on his mind, poor bloke!

In fact, it was neither Julie nor Keith who influenced Derek's decision to visit the surgery as little as possible. It was because of Simon Gatward. It wasn't that Simon had really done anything wrong. It wasn't that he really believed there was something unsavoury going on between Simon and his son. And it never seriously occurred to him that Simon was interested in Annie, because she was too much of a married woman, in spite of everything, to look seriously in the direction of any other man.

He was just angry. Anger constantly bubbled inside him, gnawing away at his heart and soul. Derek was angry with everyone and everything. As he couldn't help himself feeling that way, then surely his anger could not be his fault. He had to blame someone – so he blamed Simon Gatward.

Because there was always the possibility their paths might cross at the surgery, Derek avoided going there. Fortunately, when he'd made a formal complaint to the local medical committee about the doctor's behaviour, he'd simply had to go along to Michael Dunbar's office. That complaint committed to paper, it would be better now not to meet Simon in a narrow surgery corridor. The good doctor would know soon enough how dangerous it was to get on the wrong side of a man like Derek Ryder!

Keith went downhill fast. Once the pneumonia had taken grip, his periods of sleeping grew longer as his strength visibly ebbed away. Nurses who hovered around him also watched Annie anxiously, noting her red-rimmed eyes and pale complexion. They were reassured that Dr Gatward was plainly keeping an eye on her too, bringing her intriguing bags of tasty snacks, and leading her down every now and then for a cup of soup and a bread roll in the canteen.

In the small hours of the night before Christmas Eve Simon

and Annie sat side by side at the far end of Keith's room. Sometimes they chatted, their voices muffled so as not to disturb the patient. Sometimes they just sat in companionable silence.

'You know,' said Simon at last, 'you are a very easy person to be with. You don't mind silence, don't feel the need to fill every moment with chatter.'

She smiled. 'That's probably because I spend so much time on my own. Sometimes I speak to no one from one end of the day to the next.'

'Do you get lonely?'

'Once in a while, yes. In recent years, as Derek and I have drifted so far apart, I've felt desperately lonely.'

'What will happen between the two of you? Will you stay together?'

She shook her head. 'Not much point. We're such different people now. I can never forgive him for not being around for Keith, let alone for me. Besides, he's in love with someone else.'

'Are you sure about that?'

'Quite, and it doesn't matter. I feel nothing. Perhaps I will never be capable of feeling anything again after this. It's as if every emotion has been drained out of me. I feel nothing. I am nothing.'

He took her hand. 'Don't ask too much of yourself, Annie. You're doing brilliantly. Perhaps right now you think you'll never feel a moment's happiness again – but you will. Believe me, however dreadful things are, life turns such unexpected corners, and you never know what lies ahead. There'll be happiness for you, I know it.'

She turned bright disbelieving eyes towards him. 'How can you say that? How do you know?'

He fixed his gaze on the circle of light around the bed, seeing not Keith, but a picture in his own memory. His voice low and trembling, he began to speak.

'Soon after I qualified, I got a job in Cardiff, in the Accident and Emergency Department of one of the hospitals there. It was a new beginning for me, after all the friendship and gregariousness of being a medical student in London. Suddenly there I was, in a new city, even a different country. In London most of the people I worked with were single, so we were inclined to socialise a lot in whatever spare time we had. Once I got out into the real world, I discovered that people prefer to go home. They'd got partners and children, dogs to walk and gardens to tend, so for the first time ever I was alone.

'All that changed the day a new social worker arrived to take up a post on the hospital team. She specialised in supporting victims of child abuse, and we called her in if we ever felt there was the possibility that a young patient had been injured or hurt in an inappropriate way. Her name was Alison. She was pretty and bright, and brilliant at her job. I liked her straight away. I first saw her talking to a young boy who had taken a beating from his stepfather. The lad was defeated and resigned, torn between fear of his stepdad and love for his mum and sister. Alison was gentle with him, so skilful in the way she won his confidence. I remember watching her hands as she listened and spoke, and I thought how wonderful it would be to have those gentle hands stroke my face . . .

'The friendship between us was instant and powerful. I've never known a feeling like it. I felt as if I was out of control and tumbling in my love for her, head over heels in ecstasy, wonder and blissful pleasure.'

'And she felt the same?'

'She said she did. We spent every spare moment in each other's company. There was never any question from the second we met that the future was ours to share. We ate, slept, dreamed and worked together. We set up house in a leafy suburb on the edge of the city, and I found myself wanting all the trappings of commitment and domesticity that I'd never understood in other people before. I wanted a home with HP on the carpets, a freezer in the utility room, an estate car in the garage, a well-stocked wine-rack and a cat on the hearth.'

'Marriage and children too?'

'Marriage and children most of all! I wanted the lot!'

'And Alison? What did she want?'

'The same as me, or so I thought. I realise now that we never really got round to talking about getting married and having children before we moved in together. At the time, I didn't notice because I was so convinced our hopes and dreams were the same.'

'But she didn't want to marry?'

'Not only that, but she had no wish to have children either, and I shall never forget the moment when I realised that to be the truth of the matter. She was an ambitious girl – with reason, because she was good at the job and keen to go far. It was when she was promoted to a management post within the social services team for the hospital about two years after we'd first got together that I began to notice a change in her. Looking back, perhaps it wasn't that she changed at all, but I suddenly began to notice how her reactions and comments about our future were not quite in line with mine. Marriage was a perfect example of that. I had always assumed we'd get round to marrying some time. Certainly before we had children, I thought we'd tie the knot.

'Then she got pregnant. Don't ask me how it happened. I'm a doctor. I should know better. But when it happened I was over the moon!'

'And she wasn't?'

He turned to Annie, his eyes puzzled as he spoke. 'I couldn't believe it. Not only did she not want to be pregnant, but she was talking about an abortion! It was almost as if my opinion was of no value or interest at all. A baby would get in the way at this particular point in her career. She had no intention of getting married just because she was pregnant, especially as she didn't plan to stay pregnant for long.'

'So what happened?'

'We argued. We argued for hours and days and weeks. I felt

so strongly that this baby was a real person, *my* son or daughter, and even if I had to bring that child up on my own, I wanted to give it a chance for life. In the end she relented. Reluctantly and with great resentment, she agreed to have the baby as long as I became the main carer from the moment it was born. And that was exactly what happened. Daniel Simon was born on the twenty-fourth of May at three o'clock in the morning. I remember when we took them both up to the ward. Alison was exhausted and asleep in no time, so I sat with Daniel in my arms, his huge blue eyes studying me with curiosity and interest. Most of all I remember how the room was pink from the early morning sun streaming through the hospital window. I have never had a single moment in my life which was happier than that one.'

'And did you take over caring for him? How did you manage that when you were working all the time?'

'I'd become a GP by then, and tried to juggle my hours as much as I could to spend every possible minute with him. Otherwise he was with a child minder, a cuddly granny a few doors down whom he adored on sight.'

'And how did Alison react to him?'

'She liked him. Perhaps in her own way she even loved him. She just couldn't show it.'

'And was she better at showing her love for you? How were you getting along as a couple by then?'

'The magic was gone. I had become a boring, domestic house-husband and father, talking about little else but our wonderful son. And she was flying high, with promotion after promotion coming her way. I was glad for her. She was obviously very capable, and I knew she would be unhappy if she weren't able to achieve her potential in the work field.'

Looking down with mild surprise to see he was still holding Annie's hand, he kept his head down as he went on. 'Apart from the void between the two of us which was a great sadness for me, I remember those years as being completely happy. I adored

Daniel. He was bright like his mother, but cheeky and charming too. He was into everything, always curious, asking questions until I thought I would despair of his constant "why, why, why?". We spent hours together, just happy in our own company – playing, exploring, singing, walking with Rusty.'

'Rusty?'

'A dopey golden retriever who somehow became part of the family. Daniel loved him with a passion. The two of them were inseparable.'

'So what happened?'

His face clouded as he swallowed hard, unsure if he could go on.

'It's OK, Simon. You need to talk about this. I'm here. It's OK.'

'It was the week before his fourth birthday, and on the big day the plan was that he should have a party in the garden to let his friends see the special treat I was building for him. He had always been such an adventurous little boy, shinning up trees, sliding down banks – so when I took a close look at the huge hawthorn in our back garden, I came up with the idea of building him a tree house. He was thrilled at the idea, and couldn't wait for it to be finished. We worked on it during every spare minute, him down below with his own plank of wood and toy carpentry set, and me clearing room in the middle of the tree and building a platform up on the strongest branches. I'll never forget how the tree was just coming into blossom that day, so that I felt as if my head was in a sweet red cloud as I worked. He used to love it when I climbed up and down the tree on an old rope ladder I'd found in the garage when we moved in. He couldn't manage it, of course, and he was strictly forbidden to go anywhere near until I'd had time to build a proper safe ladder for him.'

His hands were shaking now, and she could feel his palms were hot and clammy. He seemed no longer aware that she was there as the images of that afternoon filled his mind.

'It was a lovely spring day, with real warmth in the sunshine for the first time that year. We'd been out in the garden for an hour or so. He was wearing a little blue overall which he was really proud of. He called it his "digger suit" because he thought it made him look like a real builder, and that's what he planned to be when he grew up. I remember him looking at me as he stood there with his plastic hammer in his hand, fair hair flopping over his forehead, his face animated and excited as he spoke. He was dying to be up on the platform with me, and I knew that. He'd been talking about it for days, but I'd told him it wasn't safe yet. He was just so curious. Children never understand when they have to wait for anything, do they? Daniel never did anyway.'

Simon's hand went to his mouth and he breathed deeply, gulping back the gagging sobs that threatened to choke him. For some time he sat in the darkness trying to compose his thoughts, before hesitantly, wretchedly, he went on.

'The phone rang. I could hear it through the French windows. The first time I just ignored it because I didn't want to stop what I was doing, and I thought the answerphone was on. Finally it rang off – but started again immediately. Obviously someone was very anxious to get hold of me. I told Daniel I'd only be a minute and not to do anything he shouldn't, and I left him with Rusty. I left him . . .'

Annie watched appalled as his face contorted with pain at the memory. 'I took the call in the kitchen. It was the surgery, a query about a patient who was causing some concern that week. They needed an answer and my briefcase was up in the study, so I put the call on hold and went upstairs to take it. That meant I was right up at the front of the house away from the back garden, so I couldn't see him, couldn't hear him . . .'

Another pause while he smeared away with the back of his hand the tears which were now flowing freely down his face. 'It must have been five minutes or more before I got back to the garden. I could hear the dog barking. He never barked, not much anyway, and I felt the first shiver of fear trickle down my backbone. Something was wrong, dreadfully wrong.'

'Oh, Simon.'

'I called, Daniel, and ran round the corner on to the lawn. There was no reply. I couldn't see him. He wasn't there! Daniel, Daniel! Where are you?'

Simon's eyes stared blankly ahead of him, seeing nothing, seeing too much.

'Then I saw Rusty. He had got his leg tangled up in the bottom of the rope ladder and in his panic had dragged the rope round and round the tree trunk trying to release himself. I went over to free him – and that's when I saw Daniel. He was hanging upside down from the ladder, with a sandal caught in the top rung. He must have been climbing up when Rusty tried to join him. The dog probably made the ladder unstable. Perhaps Daniel simply turned round too quickly to try and stop Rusty tugging at the rope below him. Whatever happened, he had toppled backwards with his foot held fast in the top of the ladder. His head probably hit the base of the trunk on the way down, because his neck was contorted at a terrible angle. His eyes were open, staring in fright and pain – but he was dead. I could see that straight away . . .'

Annie's hands shot to her mouth as nausea overcame her.

'I'm a doctor. I save people's lives. I make people better. And I did nothing to save my darling boy but fall to my knees and wail. I remember the sound of my own scream coming back to me from far away. I remember cradling his broken neck in my arms, knowing there must be something I could do to make the nightmare stop, but having no strength or skill or presence of mind to do anything at all. I don't remember how long I sat there, or how people arrived around me. I don't recall seeing them take Daniel down. I don't remember anything except his poor dear face which haunts me even now every time I close my eyes.'

Grabbing his hand tightly and pulling herself closer to him

to give him strength and comfort, Annie was unable to say a word. It didn't matter. There were no words worth saying.

'Daniel's funeral was on the day that should have been his fourth birthday, the twenty-fourth of May. I haven't been able to face a funeral since. His coffin was so small and white, surrounded by piles of sweet flowers that would soon be as dead as he was. Alison and I stood together, but worlds apart. She was sad, I could see that. She grieved in her own way. But for me the grief was like a raw, open, nagging wound. I was responsible. I was responsible that afternoon when he was alive. And I was responsible for his death.'

'No, you mustn't think that. It was just an accident, a terrible accident that you couldn't have foreseen or prevented.'

'I'll never believe that.'

'It was Daniel's time, Simon, just as it's Keith's now.'

He turned his brimming eyes towards her then. 'Keith brought it all back. It wasn't just the date, but the look of him too – something in his eyes, something about the way his hair fell over his face. And in you I glimpsed myself: my grief reflected in yours.'

Her arms went around him, holding him close, tears wet on his cheek. She felt his lips against her neck, a hand cupping the back of her head, breath on her face. Then he drew back, looking into her eyes, an intensity in his gaze that spoke words he couldn't mouth himself. She thought he was going to kiss her, and she longed for it – but instead he pulled her gently towards his shoulder.

'Annie, I'm tumbling again. That was the start of it all last time. I can't feel like this. I've not allowed myself to feel anything since . . .'

'Sshh . . .'

'I've just buried it all, told no one.'

'How did you manage that? Surely you must have had friends who were close to you then? What about Jill? You've known her for years, haven't you?'

'We lost touch for quite a while until they moved here. By that time, Alison and I had gone our separate ways, and I'd cut all links with Cardiff. I didn't talk about it, because I simply couldn't. It was easier that way. Out of sight, but never ever out of mind.'

She took his face in both her hands. 'Then it's time you faced your demons, Simon, and you can do that by helping me face mine. You know what I'm going through. Somehow I recognised from the start that you understood my guilt and fear and pain. And I need you now, so very much. Be with me, please. And perhaps by helping me through my grief, you'll be able to fathom your own.'

Chapter Fifteen

The phone rang early the next day, Christmas Eve. At least it seemed early to Simon, having been at the hospital until the early hours of the morning. It was Jill.

Simon groped out towards the alarm clock. 'What time is it?'

'Ten o'clock. I didn't wake you, did I?'

'Doesn't matter. It's good to hear from you. We never did have that chat, did we?'

'You've been at the hospital a lot, I know. How is he?'

'Very poorly, and fading fast.'

'I'm sorry. How are his parents taking it?'

'I've not seen his dad, although I have tried to catch him at the surgery once or twice. I think he's avoiding me.'

'And his mum?'

'Well, you can imagine . . .'

'Good job you're there for her then.'

'Yes, Jill, it probably is.'

There was an awkward silence before she spoke again.

'I'm worried about you, Simon. I heard about your conversation with Gerald the other day, and I know the time you're spending at the hospital is regularly noted.'

'The time I spend there is my own, nothing to do with them.'

'Come on, you know how they'll view it.'

'How Michael will view it, you mean. How is your delightful husband?'

'In the bath.'

'What's happening with you two? Are you going to
London?'

'Look, Simon, are you busy this morning? Can I come over
and see you?'

'Of course. That would be great. I've just got a couple of
house calls this afternoon, and a rather special delivery to make.'

'Oh?'

'Nothing urgent. Yes, I'd love to see you. How long will
you be?'

'Is half an hour too soon?'

'Give me time to have a shower and shave, then we can have
breakfast together.'

She took him at his word, because half an hour later she was
at the door with a bag of crisp warm croissants and some fresh
ground beans from the coffee importers in the marketplace. He
noticed how pale she looked the moment she stepped inside the
door, but left mentioning that fact until the croissants were eaten
and they were both on their second cup of coffee. They were
sitting on his settee, which was flooded in wintry sunshine from
the huge windows in his lounge, when she leaned her head back
against the cushions, closing her eyes against the glare of the sun.

'You look bushed.'

'Hmm.'

'Can I help?'

'Yes. You can be honest with me.'

He didn't answer, waiting for her to go on.

'Michael has given me a choice. I can go with him to
London, or I can stay here – with you.'

She avoided his eyes as she continued. 'He says that he's
always known of my feelings for you, that I married him
although I was in love with you even then.'

'And what of his feelings? Has he got any?'

'In all the years we've been married, he's never told me that he loves me until now, when he thinks he may be losing me. He says that he has always held back from declaring his love for me, because he felt it was pointless when it was you I wanted all along.'

'Do you trust him? Or is he just saying what he thinks you want to hear?'

'Honestly, I don't know. All I am sure of is that I can't make a decision about my future unless you make a decision about yours too. I could make you happy, Simon, I know I could. We're a team. We always have been. I know there's been great sadness in your past, and I want to take the burden of hurt away from you and fill your life with affection, laughter, happy memories and a future built on trust and love.'

'Jill . . .'

She covered his lips with her finger. 'Don't. Don't say anything just now. Think about it. I know I have no pride to face you with this, but I've wasted a lifetime by not being honest with you years ago. I love you, Simon, and if you'll have me, I promise I'll never let you down.'

'You'll be all right then, will you?'

'For heaven's sake, woman, stop fussing!'

'But you've been so peaky. I do worry about you.'

'I've got a visitor coming later. I need to get sorted.'

'Visitor?' Ivy's antennae quivered with curiosity.

'That's right.'

'Anyone I know?'

'An old friend.'

'Yes?'

'Yes.'

'Not that Dr Gatward!'

'Why not *that* Dr Gatward?'

She sniffed daintily. 'Well, just don't let him give you an

injection or anything like that – and wash your hands before you eat anything!'

Bert almost pushed her towards the front door.

'It's toad in the hole tonight, your favourite. I'll come and collect you in the car about five.'

'I can walk.'

'Not in your delicate state, you can't. Five it is!'

And in a flurry of Lily of the Valley perfume, she finally disappeared down the garden path.

'Simon?'

Annie's call came on his mobile phone as he headed towards his second house call that afternoon. He could hear the fear in her voice.

'Keith's going downhill fast. They've told me to prepare for the worst.'

'Is Derek there? You're not alone, are you?'

'He says he's coming. He should be here soon.'

'I don't want to get in the way. This is something the two of you should share without intrusion.'

'You don't intrude . . .'

'Look, I've got a couple of calls to make, then I'll come over. If Derek's there, I'll make myself scarce. But Annie, I'm not far away, and all you have to do is call.'

The line was abruptly cut off as the coins ran out on the payphone she was using, but the sorrowful catch in her voice haunted him as he went through the motions of visiting his patient that afternoon. He was still thinking about her as later he walked up the path to Bert's door. Bert's eyes widened to find him on the doorstep, almost hidden behind a huge cardboard box.

'Christmas delivery!' announced Simon, flattening Bert against the wall as he squeezed himself and the parcel down the hallway to the kitchen. 'There's another box in my boot, Bert, but don't you dare touch it with your back! It needs to go in the garage, so meet me there!'

At five o'clock that afternoon, just as Simon was turning into the hospital car park, Ivy took only three attempts to manoeuvre her white Metro into the spot outside Bert's house. To her surprise, the gentleman in question was waiting at the door to greet her.

'My, my!' she commented, 'You look better!'

'I feel it.'

'Ready for toad in the hole?'

'I'm afraid not. I have other plans.'

Her smile dropped and her expression darkened. 'Plans?'

'I plan to cook for myself this evening.'

'You! Cook?'

'Certainly. I've got a Lancashire hotpot in the oven right now.'

'Let me see!'

'Certainly.' He stood back to allow her to march through to the kitchen. Sure enough, the meaty aroma of something delicious in the oven tickled her flaring nostrils.

'OK, Bert Davies, out with it! What floozie's been cooking for you?'

'No one. I've done it myself – well, with *that* Dr Gatward's help, of course.'

Eyes blazing, she folded her arms across her pink crocheted jumper and glared at him. 'I'm waiting. You have just five seconds to explain yourself before I walk out of this house for ever!'

'It's my Christmas present – my freezer out in the garage packed to the roof with homemade meals for one, made for me by Simon's devoted patient Doris Donaghue, who's as good at cooking dinners as she is at baking cakes – and a new microwave to defrost them. Simple, eh?'

'How can you treat me like this,' spluttered Ivy, groping in her sleeve for her lace handkerchief, 'after all I've done for you?'

'And I appreciate every cup of tea, crumble and Garibaldi, truly I do. But I'm not so keen on the idea of being Fred Mark Two. You've got designs on me, Ivy Gibson, and I'm flattered you should think of me that way – but I'm not the marrying kind, and that's that. Best to tell you now. I believe in being honest.'

'Oh, Bert,' she sobbed, wiping her eyes delicately with her hankie.

The oven timer pinged behind her head.

'Dinner's ready. You always tell me I shouldn't let it get cold.'

'But the toad in the hole . . . ?'

'. . . will taste lovely when you get home. Now, I've got all your sheets and stuff ready for you on the hall-stand here. Thank you so much, Ivy – and Merry Christmas!'

When Simon peered through the glass panel of Keith's door and saw two figures crouched beside the bed, he tiptoed away. It was only right that Derek and Annie should share this special time together – but as he walked down the corridor alone, he couldn't shake off the feeling that a door had been firmly shut in his face.

Robbie needed no persuasion at all to go to bed on Christmas Eve. Unless he was tucked up and asleep Father Christmas wouldn't come, and Robbie wanted Santa to come more than anything in the world. Christine smiled as she sat on his bed, listening with affection as he bubbled with anticipation at the day ahead.

'Do you think he'll bring me that remote control car? My friend Martin says he's getting one, so I'd really like a car too, then we can race them together. Do you think Santa got my note, Mum?'

Christine nodded as she gently brushed the hair out of his eyes. 'Definitely, but don't forget he's got a lot of little boys and girls to think about, so he may not be able to find everything on your list.'

Robbie's eyes were thoughtful as he picked at the corner of his duvet. 'Well, I hope he manages the car. And the yo-yo. And the ant farm . . .'

'Ant farm?' Standing further down the bed, Alistair laughed out loud at the thought. 'What happens if they get out?'

'They don't,' was Robbie's serious reply, 'but they're really brill 'cos you can see them tunnelling and carrying food about on their backs.'

'Sounds like something your mum will really love!' Alistair placed an arm around Christine's shoulder as she bent down to kiss the excited youngster.

''Night then, Robbie. Sleep tight.'

When his mother rose to leave the room Alistair took her place, sitting beside Robbie for a moment before switching out the light.

'Don't forget about Mum's present, will you? Where did you hide it?'

The little boy beckoned for Alistair to come closer so that he could whisper his answer. 'It's in my shoe box, hidden in the toe of my wellie boot. She'll never think to look there.'

'Good man!' Planting a kiss on Robbie's forehead, and ruffling his shiny brown mop of hair, Alistair got up and switched off the main light, leaving a small night light to throw a soft glow into the darkness of the room.

''Night Robbie!'

''Night Dad!'

At those words Alistair leaned against the wall outside the door and closed his eyes as warm pleasure seeped through him. He was a dad – and what could possibly be a more wonderful Christmas present than that?

Keith's breathing was laboured and guttural, with such irregular spaces between each painfilled gasp that Annie sometimes wondered if he'd ever breathe again. He had been in a deep sleep for most of the day, rarely stirring or giving any sign of knowing she was there

She glanced at Derek sitting beside her, his face ashen as he gazed at his son. For all his bluster, the sight of Keith like this had visibly shaken him. No parent could ever truly come to terms with the loss of their own child, the next generation whose turn in the queue for healthy life had been so cruelly usurped. Without thinking she stretched over to take Derek's hand in hers, and when he turned she saw his eyes were welling with tears.

'Do you remember that holiday down in Cornwall? How old was he then? Four?'

Annie smiled at the memory. 'And you fell off the sea wall? Good job the tide was only just coming in.'

'Remember how scared he was, his little face when I climbed back up again? We were laughing, weren't we – but he was really frightened for me.' He looked down at Keith, so pale against the starched white pillow. 'I'll never forget the look on his face. He did love me then, didn't he – and God, how I loved him . . .'

'You never stopped, not really. I know that.'

'Does he?'

'I think he realised you hid your shock and confusion about his sexuality by anger. You turned away from him because you couldn't cope with the complexity of your own feelings. He was used to people reacting with confusion and fear around him. He's had a barrage of that since he came home to Berston. He's intelligent and generous enough to understand, but he felt it very deeply.'

'I hurt him, didn't I? I hurt that little boy who loved me so much.' Tears were flowing freely down his face as he spoke. 'I let him down, when I should have been there for him.'

'You're here for him now.'

'I took my time though, didn't I?'

Keith's face was impassive as they both looked at him. Derek got unsteadily to his feet, stretching over to bring himself close to the sleeping figure. Tears still sliding down his cheeks, he gently bent forward until his lips were on Keith's cheek.

'I love you, son. I always have, and I am so sorry I wasn't able to show how much. I may have been the worst possible father – but you are a wonderful son. I'm proud of you, proud of what you've achieved, what you've faced and how you've come through. And I love you so much. It's important to me that you know that . . .'

He slid back into his seat, distressed and broken. Annie's arm went round his shoulders, heads touching, sorrow shared, estranged as husband and wife, together at last as grieving parents.

It was Annie who noticed first – an almost imperceptible movement in Keith's hand, the flicker of a thumb which at first she thought she'd imagined. Derek followed her gaze as slowly, so slowly, their son's fingers stretched out until they touched his father's sleeve. His eyes didn't open. His face was still, yet they both sensed the slightest change in his expression – from lifeless to almost aware as the shadow of a smile reached his swollen lips. A second later it was gone. His fingers had recoiled, and his expression returned to the blank mask which had become so familiar in recent days.

But they both saw it, and turning to each other in relief and disbelief Derek clutched the thin hand and lowered his head to rest softly on Keith's shoulder.

The bells had just rung to herald in Christmas Day when Keith gasped his last rattling breath. Numb and grieving, Annie and

Derek clung together beside him until at last the nurse gently suggested that they should come away. As they emerged, blinking, into the brightness and reality of the hospital corridor, Simon stepped forward. For a moment Derek's eyes blazed with anger to see him – until he became aware of Julie, standing uncertainly by the doorway.

'I wondered if either of you need anything,' she said hesitantly. 'Can I drive you home?'

Annie looked beyond her into Simon's eyes. 'My husband and I don't live together any more. It's you he needs, Julie. And I see I already have a lift home.'

The steady drenching drizzle matched the mood of the day. It had been almost a week before the cremation could be arranged, and even then the number of people attending was scant. As Annie followed the coffin down the aisle she saw a few distant relatives, a couple of neighbours, one of the nurses from the hospital – but no young people, no friends to wish her bright young son a fond farewell. She took her place in the front pew beside Derek and they stood with their heads bowed, hands almost touching, not hearing the words nor singing the hymns. Then the minister turned towards Derek. 'A few words from Keith's father,' he said, and Annie gazed reassuringly at her husband as he moved unsteadily up to the pulpit.

'My son's illness has split not just my family, but this community. AIDS is something that happens to other people, not us, not me. But I was as guilty as anyone of looking at Keith and condemning him for his condition, rather than supporting him for the wonderful, brave individual he actually was. I overlooked his need for love and compassion because I was frightened for myself rather than for him, and I will live with the knowledge of that for the rest of my life. Keith's life was short, tragically short, but he left us a legacy from which we must all learn. The son taught the father – and what a sad and painful lesson that's turned out to be.' He turned towards the flower-covered coffin. 'I love you, son. God bless you, wherever you are.' And head down, his steps slow and careful, he returned to Annie's side.

There wasn't much more. A few prayers, another hymn. Jill sat beside Simon, her fingers resting on his thigh as she glanced up at his white face. She recognised that Keith's death had stirred deep, painful memories in him, and although he'd not yet opened up to her, she hoped he would. For the time being his grief and sadness were more than she could bear, and she didn't care who saw her, or what people said, as she willed him her strength and comfort through the warmth of her body beside him.

The strains of Keith's favourite track filled the chapel as the coffin began its relentless journey out of sight behind the blue velvet curtains.

I want to hold you till I die,
Till we both break down and cry,
I want to hold you till the fear in me subsides . . .

And one by one they watched, each wondering if there'd be anyone to hold them when their fear just wouldn't go away.

They hadn't organised anything for after the service. No one had the heart for it. Instead they stood in straggling groups around the few wreaths and flowers, reading cards, uncertain what to say. When at last they emerged into the drizzle from the cover of the Garden of Remembrance, Jill saw that Michael was standing by his car, staring at her from some yards away. If Simon saw him he made no sign of it. Instead, for just a moment, his eyes met Annie's across the top of his car as Derek took her arm to help her into his estate. No words. No need. Ignoring Michael as if she hadn't seen him, Jill slipped into Simon's passenger seat and kept her eyes down as they swept out through the gates.

'Michael Dunbar's here!' hissed Moira in his ear as he arrived at the practice the next morning. Simon's eyes closed wearily at the news, but he continued on without comment to his own surgery. His phone buzzed within minutes. It was Patricia.

'Could you come into my office for a chat before you start, Simon?'

'I've got a queue of people waiting outside.'

'This is important. As soon as you can please!'

The three of them were arranged like magistrates behind Patricia's desk, she sitting, Gerald perched on the desk beside her, and Michael standing back towards the window. It was Gerald who spoke first.

'Now this whole business of Keith Ryder is over, we feel the need to clear the air somewhat. Frankly, Simon, your behaviour throughout this affair has been puzzling to say the very least. In all the years you've been in practice here, I've never known you react so personally towards someone who was, after all, simply a patient. Not a friend, not a relative – just a patient.'

Patricia began as her husband finished. 'As you know, your unusual relationship with Mr Ryder attracted a great deal of concern and criticism among our patients, some of whom chose to leave our lists rather than let you remain as their doctor. So we are not alone in being disappointed by your blank refusal to either explain yourself, or remedy your behaviour to a level which could be considered correct and professional.'

'As a result of rumours which have reached us,' continued Michael, 'and the formal complaint about your conduct made by Keith Ryder's father, the Local Medical Committee is bound to consider your position as a GP in this area.'

'Oh really?' asked Simon wryly.

'Really – and I have to say that there has been a great deal of discussion both among my committee members and your colleagues here. Considerable thought was given to your position, and whether it was in the interest both of the practice and the patients that you should continue your duties in Berston.'

Gerald's voice softened as he moved round the desk to stand beside his partner. 'Simon, you're a good doctor, the very best, we all know that. God knows what's been going on with you over the past few months, but you've not been yourself. We think you should go away for a bit, take a holiday maybe? And perhaps when the gossip's died down and people have something new to whisper about, this unfortunate episode will simply be forgotten.'

Simon took his time looking at each of the speakers in turn. Then he put his hand inside his jacket pocket and drew out a long white envelope. 'I will never forget, and I regret nothing. I'm glad Dr Norris is already lined up to join you, because as of this moment I resign. Thank you, all of you, for the hard consideration you've put in on my behalf – but you can stuff your bloody job!'

It took him just a few minutes to gather together the only possessions he wanted to take with him from the years he'd spent at the practice. He wasn't seeing or thinking clearly. He simply wanted to get this over, and leave the building. Suddenly the door burst open and Jill was there, one glance at the emptied room telling her all she needed to know.

'If you go, I'm going too.'

He laid down the papers he was stacking on the desk and came over to take her gently by the shoulders.

'No Jill.'

'I can't stay, Simon. I'll leave anyway. Let me be with you.'

'That wouldn't be right, not for either of us.'

Her eyes were huge and glassy as she stared up at him. 'You

don't want me, do you? After all we've been through, all I've offered you, you don't want me.'

'I love you very dearly, you know I do, but . . .'

'But you're in love with Annie Ryder.'

In the agonised silence that followed Michael stepped into the doorway, his face dark as he watched their embrace.

'I will say this only once, Jill. That man is not worthy of you. He is not capable of loving you as you deserve to be loved. He won't support you. He won't stand by you. And he has no intention of taking you with him.'

She turned to face her husband as he continued. 'I have always known you thought of me as second-best, but I have provided for you and tried to make your life comfortable in every way I know how. I may be clumsy at times. I may get carried away with my own enthusiasm, and overlook your wishes and needs. I know I've never been good at revealing my true feelings for you – but having you beside me as my wife has been the greatest gift of my life. Without you, I have nothing. Nothing at all.'

He took a step towards her. 'Waste your life waiting for him, if you want, but haven't you had enough of that? Come with me to London and let's make a new start, put all this behind us. Because, my darling, if what you want is true love, you have it in me – endless, devoted love from a man who needs you more than you could ever have known. Stay my wife, Jill, I beg of you. Please.'

Simon didn't wait to hear her answer. Gathering up the last remaining papers, he quietly left his surgery without a backward glance.

Surprised looks followed him as he walked through the reception area in front of patients who were waiting for their call into his surgery. He kept his head down, avoiding all eyes, until he quite literally walked into an immovable object. It was Dolly.

'Dr Simon!' she squealed, opening her huge embrace and

drawing him close to her enormous bosom until the life was almost squeezed out of him. 'Oh, Dr Simon, I do love you!'

And as he disappeared down into the folds of her, his last grateful thought was that at least somebody did.

She found his car boot wide open and his front door ajar when she arrived at the house. He was leaving, that was clear. She followed the rustling noises coming from the back of the house and finally came across him in the living room. He was turning out the unit at the far end of the room, and sat on his knees surrounded by boxes, cuttings, letters and books. His face registered no surprise to see her, just simple pleasure. He held out his hand to her and she fell to her knees to join him, carefully laying down a package of her own on the floor beside her.

'I have something to show you,' he said, 'something I've never shared with anyone.' He leaned over to tug the top left-hand drawer, which stuck awkwardly for a while until at last he was able to open it enough to pull out a long thin blue box. Almost with reverence, he laid the box on his knees, and carefully took off the lid to reveal a photo album inside.

'Daniel,' she said softly.

There he was – Daniel's lifetime told in faded, curling photos: first the newborn baby, then a six-month-old eating his first chocolate button; Daniel in the bathtub, angelically sleeping in his cot, and later his buggy. And there was Simon – younger, fairer, happier – face unmistakably full of pride as he held two chubby little hands when his son took his very first steps. Daniel preoccupied with a toy tractor, running in the park, splashing happily in the paddling pool – memory followed memory, laugh followed smile, as Simon retold the stories and relived the precious moments of Daniel's life. Annie's curiosity was drawn to Alison who appeared almost in passing in one or two of the pictures. She was small and pretty, with neat glasses and a halo of shiny dark curls.

'Do you miss her?' she asked.

'Not any more. With Daniel gone, the void between us became a chasm. We grieved in different ways, and couldn't help each other through it.'

'Like Derek and me.'

'Yes.'

'Do you know where she is now?'

'No. It's better that way — and it's a long time ago.'

'Does time heal?'

'No, it simply deadens the pain. It was always there, festering away, and I realise now that I've never dealt with it at all. Until Keith, until you . . .'

She leaned towards him until their heads touched. She watched him turn the pages, then stop, drawing back his shaking hand as if he could go no further. Covering his fingers with her own, she stretched out to turn the page for him. It was a picture which filled the whole sheet, a full-length shot of Daniel in a smoky blue overall suit, with a bright red zip up the middle. Round his waist was a belt carrying an impressive array of toy tools — a screwdriver, hammer, some brightly coloured nails — and in his small hands a saw and plane, held out with pride towards the camera. Behind him was the trunk of a tree, deep red blossom heads drooping down into the top of the picture, still in tight bud.

'I took it that afternoon. I thought he looked wonderful, so happy and healthy . . .'

'And so he was,' said Annie gently. 'His short life was very happy indeed. He was adored and cherished, and brought great joy to those who loved him. Allow yourself to be grateful for his life, Simon. Let go of the grief. It's time.'

'Can you let go of Keith?'

'I'll never forget, never stop loving him — but I had a lot of time to prepare for losing him. I didn't have to deal with shock, the way you did. Keith and I were able to reminisce together, and talk about the future too. He believed he would be joining

Ian, you see, so he wasn't sad to leave a life that had become unbearably painful for him. Perhaps you think I'm unnatural, but I was *glad* when he died. It was such a relief that his suffering was over. He was free – and in a way, so am I.'

'Free of Derek too?'

'Yes, I think I am. For years we've stayed together because we haven't had the courage to face the fact that we've grown apart. There was no joy between us.'

'Do you still love him?'

'A few weeks ago I'd have said no, but we've learned a lot about each other over the past few days. In coming together over the loss of Keith, we've recognised our need to be apart. No animosity, no recriminations. He's the man who's been the centre of my world for so long. Yes, I do wish him love, plenty of it, from someone else if not from me.'

'And what about you, Annie? What do you need?'

She lifted her head to look directly at him. 'What I need, what I've come to realise I've been searching for all my life, is you.'

Neither was sure who made the first move but in an instant his arms were around her, holding her close as if he'd never let her go, lips on hair and cheek and hungry mouth. She thought she heard him call her name, their bodies clinging and entwined, as the past slipped away with the promise of love and belonging ahead. They were together at last, soul on soul, heart on broken heart.

Alistair was the last to leave the surgery that evening, or at least he thought he was until, making his way out of the back of the building, he came across Derek Ryder in the new extension.

'Oh, I'm sorry, I didn't realise you were here. I was just about to lock up – or do you need more time?'

'No, it's all right, I've finished now. Just checking on progress.'

Alistair looked around admiringly. 'Nearly done, isn't it? How much longer do you think you'll be?'

'I promised Gerald we'd try to get it finished early in the New Year, and we will. Should be ready to start laying flooring by the end of next week.'

'That's a credit to you, Mr Ryder, knowing what you and your family have been through recently. I was really sorry to hear about the death of your son.'

'Thank you,' replied Derek stiffly.

'If there's anything I can do to help, you will let me know, won't you? We all feel you and your lads have become good friends during your time here.'

'It's fine, really – but thanks.'

Unsure what to say next, Alistair continued to make his way to the door.

'I hear you're getting married.'

The young doctor turned. 'That's right. We've set a date, the week before Easter. It will be just a small affair. That's how we want it.'

'Did someone say you're taking on a ready-made family?'

'That's the best bit of all. I had no idea how entertaining five-year-olds could be until I met Robbie. He's just terrific. Being a dad is a truly wonderful thing!'

Derek hesitated for a moment before following Alistair through the door.

'Yes, lad,' he agreed sadly, 'I know.'

They sat for hours in the lengthening shadows. There was so much to say, hopes to share, skin to touch, plans to make, secrets to whisper. Then she remembered the package she'd brought. She handed it to him with infinite care, being the precious gift it was.

'This was always for you. Open it. You'll see what I mean.'

Curiosity etched across his face, he pulled back the top of

the box, revealing layers of tissue paper underneath. She held the box firmly while he gently lifted out the package inside. Placing it on the low table in front of them, he peeled back the soft tissue paper until the figure was fully revealed. Simon gasped as he saw it, standing about ten inches high, in polished honey-coloured walnut with dark copper veins coursing through it. Its base was a pair of hands, fingers outspread, releasing a small bird from their grasp. It spoke of hope and joy.

'Annie, it's beautiful, just lovely.'

'He's free.' Her voice was no more than a whisper as she spoke. 'Keith's free, isn't he? And because of him, dearest Simon, at last so are we.'